CAMP ZERO

Book I

Books by Sean Ellis

Coming Soon
In the Camp Zero *series*
Ice Fall– Book II

CAMP ZERO series is based on characters created by Jerry Ahern, Sharon Ahern and Bob Anderson in *The Survivalist* series.

Books in *The Survivalist* series by Jerry Ahern

#1: Total War
#2: The Nightmare Begins
#3: The Quest
#4: The Doomsayer
#5: The Web
#6: The Savage Horde
#7: The Prophet
#8: The End is Coming
#9: Earth Fire
#10: The Awakening
#11: The Reprisal
#12: The Rebellion
#13: Pursuit
#14: The Terror
#15: Overlord

Mid-Wake
#16: The Arsenal
#17: The Ordeal
#18: The Struggle
#19: Final Rain
#20: Firestorm
#21: To End All War
The Legend
#22: Brutal Conquest
#23: Call To Battle
#24: Blood Assassins
#25: War Mountain
#26: Countdown
#27: Death Watch

Books in *The Survivalist* series by
Jerry Ahern, Sharon Ahern and Bob Anderson
#30: The Inheritors of Earth
#31: Earth Shine
#32: The Quisling Covenant
#33: Deep Star

Coming Soon
In The Survivalist *series*
#34: Lodestar

CAMP ZERO

BOOK I

Sean Ellis

CAMP ZERO is based on characters created by Jerry Ahern, Sharon Ahern and Bob Anderson.

SPEAKING VOLUMES, LLC
NAPLES, FLORIDA
2016

CAMP ZERO
Book I

ISBN 978-1-62815-481-8

Prologue - **Paula**

I should have seen it coming. My instincts should have been screaming from the moment he limped up to our table with his sob story about falling in a hole and that bullshit about being an archaeologist. But I didn't. I bought it hook, line, and sinker.

Why? How could I have been so naïve?

Paula tested her bonds as C.J.—that was the name he had given them. Probably a lie like everything else that had come out of his mouth—stalked toward her and Natalie. He wasn't limping now.

He had been so smooth, conveniently mistaking them for college girls, a fiction Nat had been only too eager to embrace. Then he had lured them out of the restaurant with a promise of showing them artifacts he'd discovered in a burial cave on the North Shore. Not just her and Natalie, but the boys, too—her younger brother Tim, and Nat's kid brother Jack. Tim had been suspicious. Jack, too. But they had ignored their instincts, let down their guard. Then C.J. had dosed her and Nat with something, while C.J.'s ugly friend—

Lee. C.J. called him Lee.

—had overpowered the boys. Now they were in this ratty shack, bound and gagged. She had been feigning sleep but she didn't think C.J. was buying it.

There was a flash of movement across the room and the crunch of Jack's boot soles slamming into Lee's face.

"Damn it!" Lee spat the curse along with a mouthful of blood as he staggered back, then dropped to his knees with a grunt as Tim struck out with his legs, ankles still bound together with silver tape, and drove his feet into Lee's crotch. The commotion was enough to distract C.J.

Now!

Paula thrust her own feet at C.J.'s head but even as she did, his gaze swung back to her. He knocked her kick aside with the same disdain he might have shown shooing a fly, but her attempt had given Natalie a chance to strike. She jammed both feet against his right ankle.

He reeled around and swung his fist down at Natalie. There was a loud crack as his punch connected with her jaw, and then another as her head bounced off the floor.

Paula screamed into the strip of tape covering her mouth and kicked again, wildly, blindly, striking nothing but air.

C.J. took a step back, his nostrils flaring, eyes red with rage. "Oh, you want to play. Let's play."

Paula's blood turned to ice in her veins, but then, in the corner of her eye, she saw Tim moving, levering his body up for another thrust at C.J. His feet struck C.J. in the small of the back, staggering him, and then Tim was up, hands free, bits of torn silver tape still clinging to his wrists above his balled fists. There was a look of deadly resolve in his eyes as he started toward C.J. and for a moment, Paula thought that she was wrong, that it wasn't Tim at all, but their father, come to rescue them.

Then the air rang with the noise of a shot and Tim's determined expression vanished in an eruption of blood and gore.

Paula screamed again, the cry rebounding against the gag.

Tim's lifeless body pitched forward, collapsing onto her, splattering her with gray matter. Behind him, Lee was brandishing a revolver. Smoke was curling up from the end of the barrel. Paula felt her gorge rise. She was going to vomit and, if she did, she would choke on it and die.

C.J. stepped into her view. His hands were clenched into fists, but after staring at her for a few seconds, he opened them and then began slowly unbuckling his belt. She could see his lips moving, recognized the shape of the words he was speaking, but could hear nothing but the pounding of blood in her ears and the ringing echo of the shot that had killed her brother.

There was another report. Paula couldn't see past C.J. but she knew that Jack had just died.

No!

Paula twisted and struck at C.J. with her feet, but her attack was about as effective as trying to kick down a tree. He hooked a thumb in the waistband of his jeans, yanked them down, and then reached out for her....

Chapter One - **Paula**

Paula Rourke jolted in her seat, striking her knees against the back of the seat in front of her. The pain brought her fully awake, but she remained disoriented, part of her still trapped in the memory of that awful shack.

"Hey!" A head appeared above the back of the seat she had just struck. "Do you mind?"

It was Jack—John Michael Rubinstein—still very much alive, just like her brother Tim, who sat beside Jack in the row ahead of her.

She hid her relief at seeing him behind a perturbed frown. "Well maybe if you hadn't reclined it back so far, I'd have room to move."

A hand—Natalie's—gripped her right forearm and gave a reassuring squeeze. "Paula honey, you okay?"

Paula worked her jaw, felt her ears pop. Her mouth was as dry and fuzzy as an old sweater, but she faced her seatmate and managed a smile. "I'm good, Nat."

Natalie returned the smile. "You should know better than to try to sleep on a plane."

Paula laughed. "There's not much else to do."

"No kidding." Natalie rolled her eyes. "This is such a drag. I can't believe they're making us do this."

Paula gave a non-committal nod. When their parents had first proposed the idea, she had felt much as Nat now did. She had balked at the idea of spending the balance of their school break out in the middle of nowhere, away from their friends, away from everything. But part of her understood the reasons for it. This wasn't about having fun. It was about being *ready*.

The kidnapping always ended differently when she dreamed about it, as if her mind was running the scenario again and again, trying different variations in the search for a better outcome but, perversely, always finding one worse than what had actually happened. In reality, their failed escape attempt had ended with Lee threatening but not actually firing his revolver. Shortly thereafter, the Honolulu Police had raided the shack, critically wounding their captors and rescuing the four of them more or less unharmed. Physically, at least.

Although the kidnappers had not violated her body, the mere fact of the abduction was an assault on her psyche that had not yet healed. C.J.—a.k.a. William Alan Davis—and Lee McAllen had made her feel helpless. They had made her feel afraid. They had taken her freedom, and even though the police had rescued her, she did not yet feel free.

I should have seen what was happening.

That was the worst part. She was embarrassed by her failure to recognize the warning signs… No, that wasn't quite right. She had seen the signs but had willfully ignored them. She had not even lifted a finger to stop it.

She was still a little angry at Natalie for having been so easily taken in by C.J.'s flattery. Nat was beautiful, just like her mother, and while she was not stupid by any means, she never grew tired of attention from boys and that sometimes compromised her judgement. It had certainly done that on the night of the kidnapping. But blaming Natalie in no way lessened Paula's own sense of failure, nor did she want it to.

We all came up short that night, she thought.

Tim and Jack had known that something was wrong, but had kept silent, trusting their older siblings to make the right call. She and Nat had done the same thing, really, eschewing responsibility, assuming that, if no one spoke up, there was nothing to worry about. It had been a nearly fatal mistake.

"The only real mistake," her father had often told her, "is the one from which we learn nothing." The words were not his own, but a quote from someone named Ford who had lived and died six hundred years before Paula's birth.

Paula would never forget the lesson learned from this mistake. Survival was ultimately her responsibility. Not Natalie's or her brother's, not her parents', not the police or the government or anyone else. Hers. That too was something her father had tried to teach her, though she had not actually learned it until the kidnapping.

It was a practical lesson, not a matter of morality. A life-or-death struggle did not care whether you deserved what was happening to you, or check to make sure you had reached the legal age of responsibility. Bad things sometimes happened to good people. Period. And whether or not someone else should have or could have done something to stop it, dead was dead.

Period.

Taking responsibility did not just mean fighting back when a crisis came along. That was another lesson she had learned the hard way. In the shack, they had tried to fight back against C.J. and Lee, and all they had gotten for their efforts was a beating.

Taking responsibility meant being ready ahead of time. It meant being prepared.

That was perhaps the most ironic and, in Paula's mind, humiliating aspect of that ordeal. She and Tim were the children of John Thomas Rourke, unquestionably the world's foremost expert on survival. Nat and Jack were Rourke's grandchildren. To say that Rourke had literally written the book on survival was to woefully understate both his output as a writer and his actual experience as a survivor.

John Thomas Rourke—her father—had survived the end of the world. He had been born in the 20th Century; a world not unlike their own, where people went about their daily lives and rarely stopped to consider just how fragile the connective tissue of civilization really was. Rourke was a rare exception to the norm. Although trained as a medical doctor, he had chosen instead to become a government intelligence operative, and subsequently an instructor in survival and combat techniques. He had foreseen the end, the inevitable breakdown of society which would occur following a global nuclear war or some other apocalyptic disaster—natural or manmade—and he had prepared accordingly, building the Retreat—a secret refuge in the mountains of Georgia. And when the war had finally come, he had survived.

In the immediate aftermath, he had journeyed across half the country, battling mobs of armed brigands and invading enemy troops, eventually gathering his family—his first wife Sarah and their children Michael and Annie into the Retreat, where they, along with Rourke's friends Paul Rubenstein and Natalia Tiemerovna, had all gone into cryogenic stasis. Five hundred years of suspended animation, long enough, or so Rourke hoped, to allow the earth to heal from the grievous wounds of that awful war.

Rourke's obsession with survival preparedness, and making sure that his loved ones were both safe and prepared, had prompted him to schedule an early wake-up for both himself and his two children—Paula's half-siblings. The world outside the Retreat would be far too dangerous a place for youngsters. What he would need most of all when going forth to meet a world five centuries removed from oblivion would be fully mature and, more importantly, fully combat capable adults, so Rourke spent several years with young Michael and Annie, teaching them everything he knew—everything they would need to know—then returned to cryosleep for another decade.

Upon awakening to discover that her two young children were now fully grown adults, almost as old as her, Rourke's wife Sarah had been inconsolable, blaming Rourke for stealing their childhood from her, but to Rourke's eminently logical way of thinking, preparing his children to survive was worth any price, even his wife's affection.

She had divorced Rourke, and they had both eventually remarried. A grown-up Annie had married Paul Rubinstein, which meant that, technically speaking, Paula was an aunt to Nat and Jack, but that was kind of weird, so they all just called each other cousins.

The point however was that Rourke had sacrificed everything to make sure that his kids would be able to survive, and it had worked.

Maybe a little too well.

The survivors from the Retreat had eventually joined forces with other groups and rebuilt the civilization they had lost. While the global population was only a fraction of what it had once been—millions instead of the billions that had occupied every corner of the pre-war earth—law and order were restored, and survival was something everyone took for granted, just as they had in the days before the war.

That was all ancient history to Paula. She was the daughter of Rourke's new wife, Emma, a child of the new world. Rourke and the other parents had tried to instill a sense of preparedness in the children, but the idea of having to survive a crisis had seemed so remote. A worry for another day, another year. She had a double-course load to contend with—high school classes *and* college-level pre-med. She barely had time for a social life, much less to get ready for a worst-case scenario that might never happen.

But it had happened, and it could happen again. Her father had another favorite old quote from before the war: "Anything that can go wrong probably will."

A lot of things had been going very wrong lately. Just a few days ago, she had attended the state funeral for her step-father, Wolfgang Mann, the President of Germany, who had been assassinated in a rocket attack that had leveled the German Presidential residence in New Brandenburg. A few weeks before that, Paul Rubinstein had been taken hostage briefly by agents of the Russian government. Her half-brother Michael, who just happened to be President of the United States of America, had barely survived an assassination attempt and had spent several weeks in hiding. Even closer to home, John Rourke was overdue in returning from a secret assignment somewhere, and although her mother wouldn't admit anything, Paula sensed that her father might be in trouble.

Outside the family circle, there had been an increase in terrorist attacks and rumors of a plague outbreak—possibly a biological weapon. More and more disaffected citizens were being drawn to the Neo-Nazi movement and other radical groups. Michael Rourke had put it succinctly: the world was starting to shift and the newest generation of the Rourke clan was unprepared to meet the challenges that shift would bring.

Which was no small part of the reason why the four of them—her and Tim, Nat and Jack, along with their younger cousins, John Paul and Sarah Ann—the son and daughter of Michael Rourke and his wife Natalia—were on a jet plane bound for the Texas Panhandle and the John Thomas Rourke Survival Academy, a school founded by her father—though she had only recently learned of it—with the sole purpose of equipping young people like her with the skills to survive a worst case scenario.

A prep school in a literal sense, preparing for the end of the world.

A chime sounded and the "Fasten Seat Belt" light flashed on above Paula's head. She felt the plane shifting and her ears popped again. A moment later, the head flight attendant's voice came over the PA. "Ladies and gentleman, we're beginning our descent into El Paso…"

Chapter Two - **Jack**

"Welcome, survivors!"

The young woman's electronically amplified voice floated above the crowd, rising in pitch with each syllable uttered, like a cheer at a sporting event.

John Michael Rubinstein—Jack, to his friends—raised his head in the direction of the sound, peering over the tops of the heads of his fellow…students? Classmates?

Survivors didn't really seem like the right term. So far, all they had survived was a long flight and a long, but not quite as long, bus ride. They were more like prospective survivors or survivors-in-training.

He located the young woman with the bullhorn just as she triggered the device again. "Okay, I need you all to form a horseshoe around me," she said, with only slightly less enthusiasm than before.

"Here we go," Jack said, hefting his backpack onto his shoulder and starting forward with an irrepressible grin.

Around him the group shifted to comply. Jack glanced over at Tim who was standing behind the "kids"—their younger cousins, John Paul and Sarah Ann. Tim's hands were resting, protectively, on the shoulders of the youngest members of the Rourke clan. Nat and Paula were already moving into the loose formation, as directed by their greeter, but none of them seemed to share Jack's eagerness to begin this adventure.

They were all here primarily because their parents wished it, and given the recent troubles that had touched the family directly, and which seemed to be only a foreshadowing of things to come, it was hard to argue with their wisdom. Nevertheless, the children, Nat, in particular, made no secret of their mixed feelings about attending the survival academy. Jack could understand why the girls were less than enthusiastic. They were girls, after all, more interested in being with their friends, shopping for shoes and make-up, and talking about boys. The kids were probably overwhelmed by the prospect of being away from their mom and the comforts of home. But Jack couldn't understand why Tim wasn't more excited.

Must be that trademark Rourke seriousness, he decided.

Jack was positively ecstatic about being here. It was going to be tough; physically and emotionally demanding like nothing he had ever done before. As Nat had put it, whispering so that their parents wouldn't overhear, it was going to *suck*... And Jack could not have been happier.

His elation in no way diminished his respect for the practical considerations that had prompted their parents to send them to the academy. The world was getting crazier every day, and danger had already touched the Rourke children. Twice in his case. His father had been taken hostage in their home shortly before the kidnapping. Jack had been in the attic through the ordeal, and while he had not simply been a frightened bystander—he had been able act as eyes and ears for the rescue team outside, helping to effect his father's escape—he wanted to be able to do more if such a situation ever arose again.

But that wasn't the real reason Jack was excited about getting started.

He was here for the adventure.

He had grown up on his father's stories of the Night of the War, of accompanying John Rourke across the war-torn landscape of America. While he never would have believed—at least, not back then, when he was just a kid—that the world would ever get that bad again, in his daydreams, he was the hero, fighting Neo-Nazis and bandits in the wasteland, trekking across the wilderness, living off the land, climbing mountains and exploring caves.

He loved hearing his father's stories, and when they were burned into his memory, he went looking for more. A voracious reader, he devoured real-life accounts of explorers and soldiers and the pioneers who had helped rebuild the world. Fictional adventures were fine, too. In fact, not only had he developed an appetite for adventure novels, he had even tried his hand at writing some. During a recent visit to John Rourke's Retreat in the mountains of Georgia, he had come across a collection of well-thumbed paperback novels, relics from before the war. The books, which together comprised the Sean Dodge series, were written by a guy named Josh Culhane, who according to the author's biography on the back page, made it a point to actually go out and do all the crazy stuff his hero did in the stories. Jack had stayed up all night reading the first book in the series by flashlight, and when he was finished, he knew what he wanted to do when he grew up.

He was going to be an action-adventure novelist.

He hadn't told anyone yet, not even Tim, and he was a little apprehensive about revealing his most cherished dream to any of his relations. He had lived his entire life in the spotlight of the Rourke family legend, and while there were no explicit expectations laid upon him or any of the others, the pressure to do something meaningful, something important, was there nonetheless. Paula was already working toward her goal of being a medical doctor. Tim wanted to be an archaeologist. Nat was vacillating between a career in journalism or politics, and because she was ideally suited for both, it was probably not a matter of which she would pursue, but rather which she would do first. Compared to those vocations, making up stories seemed kind of frivolous.

Maybe he would be a journalist, too. That would at least mean he could make a career of writing and then pursue his true calling in his spare time.

What made being here at the survival academy such a thrill for him was that he would be getting a comprehensive hand's-on education in the full spectrum of adventure skills. The experiences he would have at this school would inform his stories for years to come.

He couldn't wait to get started.

He pushed to the front of the group and got a better look at the young woman with the bullhorn. Almost as tall as Paula, but thinner, with short auburn hair, cute elfin features and a smattering of freckles, she wore baggy black running shorts, emblazoned with the letters JTRSA on the right thigh, and a tan T-shirt with the same logo in black across the chest. Jack couldn't begin to guess at her age; she might have been sixteen or twenty-three.

"I hope all the teachers look like you."

The statement came from a boy standing to his left. Jack had first noticed the stout ruddy-faced older youth in the boarding lounge at the airport in Hawaii, and then again when they had boarded the shuttle at the airport that had brought them here. Jack had actually been a bit surprised by the number of young people he had seen on the plane who were now here gathered alongside him, and even more so by how many people were actually present—at least two dozen in all. He had been under the impression that it would be just the six of them, but evidently the John Thomas Rourke Survival Academy was not exclusively for the Rourke family. Jack wasn't sure how he felt about that.

The cute girl lowered her bullhorn and raised an eyebrow at the boy. "I'm actually a student-instructor. That means I've completed all the beginner level courses you're here for, and now I'm helping the instructors."

"Like an apprentice," Jack said.

Her eyes found his. "That's right. One of the best ways to master a new skill is to teach it to someone else. That's one of the things you'll learn here."

She raised the bullhorn to her lips again. A strident electronic hiss preceded her words. "And now that I've got your attention, ladies and gentleman..." She stepped aside and made a sweeping gesture toward the open end of the horseshoe.

Jack half-expected the group to break into applause, but evidently everyone else was as uncertain about what to do next as he was.

A tall, broadly-built man, wearing tan military-style fatigues with trouser legs bloused over brown combat boots, strode into the midst of the U-shaped formation. He waved away the offer of the bullhorn, and then crossed his arms over his chest and demonstrated to the group why he had no need of it. "Welcome to the John Thomas Rourke Survival Academy, my name is Mr. Dickson."

Mister Dickson? Jack mused. *Not Sergeant or Colonel?*

A voice from the crowd—Tim's voice—summarized what Jack was thinking. "You're not military?"

Dickson smiled. "No son. We have some military instructors you will meet but they are on loan to us for specific topic instruction."

Based on the man's bearing alone, Jack was sure that Dickson had to be former military, but he understood the importance of the distinction. Military training, or even private paramilitary instruction, was not the purpose of the Academy. There was bound to be some cross-over of course. Soldiers learned survival skills, and Jack already knew that the course would include weapons familiarization and self-defense training. But a major component of soldiering was learning to follow orders and work as part of a highly-disciplined unit. The purpose of survival training on the other hand, was to prepare for what happened when discipline broke down and there was no one around to give orders. A soldier needed to learn how to be part of an army, but he was also taught to rely on that army. Survival was a solitary affair.

As Dickson detailed the agenda for the rest of the day and provided an overview of what to expect from this, the basic or "zero" phase of the academy, Jack surreptitiously studied the rest of the group.

His earlier count had been right on the mark. Aside from himself and the rest of the Rourke scions, there were eighteen other young people in civilian attire. Most appeared to be in the same age cohort as Jack and his sister, though there were two—one male, one female—who looked old enough to be in college. Jack had noticed both of them on the plane, though they had not sat together then, and did not appear to be together now. There was one boy who Jack thought might be the same age as John

Paul—twelve years—but no one else as young as the nine-year old Sarah Ann.

Good thing, Jack thought. He understood the logic behind their parents' decision to send the kids along. Sarah Ann was now older than Jack's mother Annie had been when the world ended the first time, but the Survival Academy was supposed to be an adventure, not day care for rug rats.

Dickson was enumerating the set of skills they would be learning, which began with a foundation of basic trail craft—hiking and camping—and then progressed into foraging, setting snares and so forth. "We will supply your equipment which for the basic course will be a knife, mug, sleeping bag and liner, sleeping mat, rucksack and liner, head torch, water bottle and all technical safety equipment."

He drew a large knife from a sheath attached to the pistol-belt he wore on the outside of his uniform blouse. Jack recognized the blade immediately; his grandfather had one just like it. The weapon looked like a short sword; a hefty single-edged blade, made from quarter-inch high carbon steel, with serrations on the back edge, a hilt designed to be held in either upright or reverse-grip, and a heavy duty "skull crusher" pommel.

"On completion of the course," Dickson went on, "you will receive the coveted John Thomas Rourke Fighting Bowie designed by John himself."

He held the blade up for their inspection. There were some appreciative murmurs from the group, and the boy who had spoken out earlier nudged Jack's arm. "Sweet. How much do you think that's worth?"

Jack answered with a stern look which he hoped would pre-empt further comments from the older boy.

Dixon sheathed the blade. "Right now the cadre will get you settled in and your equipment issued. We will meet back up in the training room at 1400 hours so you can meet your course leaders and teammates and ensure you have all of the required items and equipment. Then you will be released until 0600 hours tomorrow morning."

He went on to outline the rest of the week's schedule. Jack was relieved to learn that almost all of the instruction would take place in the field, rather than in the classroom, and that they would be camping out rather than sleeping in a barracks or bunkhouse.

"Day two will start with field physical training and we'll move into self-defense, self-preservation, wilderness navigation and compass reading over difficult terrain. When each team thinks they are ready, you will head across country on foot to an overnight wilderness campsite. On the way, you'll be shown how to collect, filter and purify water, forage for food, make and put out fishing drop lines and various traps and snares in the hope of catching your first wilderness meal."

The apple-cheeked boy next to Jack stuck his hand up and started grunting to get Dickson's attention. When that didn't work, he blurted out, "If we don't catch anything, you'll still feed us, right?"

It had not escaped Jack's notice that the senior instructor had twice mentioned "teams." He hoped he didn't get put on *that* kid's team.

Chapter Three - **Sarah**

The pack was big but not as heavy as it looked. In fact, Sarah Ann Rourke thought it was actually lighter than the suitcase she had brought along with her from Hawaii, and she had carried that on her own with no problem. The equipment they had all been issued was made from special materials that were tough and durable but weighed almost nothing. Still, Sarah didn't see how she would be able to carry the rucksack on her back for hours and hours. She was only nine years old; she didn't know how she was going to do any of this.

Like the others, Sarah had changed into the camp uniform, which had been issued along with the rest of the equipment. The clothes she had been wearing, along with everything else she had brought along from home, were locked up in the storeroom. She had not even been allowed to keep her teddy bear, a gift from her grandmother, who was also her namesake.

They hadn't been mean about it. Madison, the nice student-instructor who had met them in the reception area, had explained gently that teddy bears were domesticated and didn't do very well in the wild, which was a silly thing to say about a toy. Sarah wasn't stupid and she wasn't five years old.

I'll be okay without teddy, she told herself. *I only keep him for senitem…sentimental reasons.* She had brought the stuffed bear as a little piece of home to keep close in this strange place, but she would do just fine without it. Her mom had explained that the survival academy would be sort of like a fire drill; a practice session for how to respond when something bad happened. In a real fire, you didn't waste time gathering up your things, you just got out as quickly and safely as possible, so that was what you did in the drill when it was just make-believe.

She was getting the feeling that this was going to be a very long fire drill.

If they weren't going to let us use our stuff, she thought, *why didn't we just leave it all home?*

She stayed close to her brother John, though judging by his frown, maybe she was too close. He had already made a friend, a dark-haired boy about his age named Philip. The two had struck up a conversation over lunch—hot dogs, potato salad and lemonade to wash it all down—and two hours later, they were still talking whenever their attention was not required by the instructors. Their discussion moved randomly from favorite movies to football teams to video games, and back again. Boy stuff, but Sarah liked those things too, some of them anyway. The boys however did not seem much interested in her opinions.

She sighed and looked around for her cousins. Tim had stayed with her and John when they had first arrived, but as the day progressed and they had all settled in to some extent, he had drifted away, preoccupied with getting his gear in order and meeting new people. Just like everyone else.

"You don't look like you're having any fun, sweetie."

The voice from behind startled Sarah and she whirled around, ready to cry out or flee. The reaction was a reflex, and an embarrassing one at that. She was safer here than almost anywhere on earth, although, given some of the things that had been happening lately, she wasn't sure anywhere was really safe. But there was no reason for her to panic. The young woman speaking to her was wearing the camp uniform, just like her—a fellow student of the John Thomas Rourke Survival Academy. Sarah recognized her from the plane and the shuttle ride from the airport. She looked older than most of the others, like she might already be grown-up.

Sarah shook her head. "I'm okay."

The young woman smiled. She had long brown hair, pulled back in a pony-tail, with bangs hanging down almost as far as her dark eyes, and curving down to frame her face in a half-circle. "If you say so, sweetie. But we girls gotta stick together, right?" She raised a finger in the air as if testing to see which way the wind was blowing, and then drew a circle. "We're outnumbered you know."

Sarah looked around. She had not realized it before, but the woman was right. Most of the students were boys. There were just eight females in all, and three of them were from the Rourke family.

She turned back to the young woman. "It doesn't matter. Boys are dumb."

The woman smiled. "You're not wrong about that, sweetie." She stuck out her hand. "I'm Alma."

Sarah shook the proffered hand. "That's a pretty name. I'm Sarah Ann."

"That's a pretty name, too. Did you know that 'Sarah' means 'princess?'"

Sarah nodded. "Does your name mean anything?"

"As a matter of fact, it does. Alma comes from a Latin word that means 'nourishing.' You know what that word means?"

Sarah nodded.

"And in Spanish," Alma continued, "my name means 'soul.'"

"I'm learning Spanish in school," Sarah volunteered.

"Good for you."

"Why are you here?"

Alma smiled again. "Got to be ready in case things go bad, right?"

"That's what my parents said. They made me come here."

Alma reached out and squeezed her shoulder. "I'll bet that's because they love you very much and want you to be strong enough to deal with whatever happens." She looked away for a moment as the senior instructor, Mr. Dickson, walked into the room, calling for their attention, and then returned her gaze to Sarah. "Like I said, we girls need to stick together, so if you need anything, or just want someone to talk to, don't be afraid to ask. Sound good?"

Sarah nodded.

"Survivors," Dickson bellowed. "Listen up. I would like to introduce your primary trainer for this week, Sandy Tempest."

Tempest? Sarah knew that was another word for "storm." She looked around, expecting to see someone as hard and blustery as the name.

"We call her 'Ma,'" Dickson added, chuckling as if he had made a joke.

It *was* a joke, Sarah realized. There was a name for jokes like that, where a word meant the opposite of what it really meant, but she couldn't remember what it was. It would come to her eventually.

There was nothing motherly about "Ma" Tempest. She was a woman of average height, with short graying hair and a gruff scowl on her face. She took Dickson's spot and then gave the students a long hard look before speaking.

"Not what you expected, huh? That's okay. It's the usual response when I'm first introduced. And don't think them calling me Ma means I'm gonna be soft on you. I'll kick your butt if I have to."

Sarah swallowed nervously as she imagined the grumpy woman's boot connecting with her backside.

"We'll just have to grow on each other I guess," Ma said, with a short harsh laugh. "Alright, here is the schedule of training for this week. Day two starts with a field physical training session and a lesson in self-defense, self-preservation and primal instinctive training."

The more Ma said, the more confused Sarah became. Even though she understood a lot of the words—and there were several she had never heard before, like "abseil" and "Tyrolean line traverse"—the way Ma put them together made Sarah's head hurt.

"During the fourth and fifth days… We'll call these your final exercise. For the next thirty hours, you will move by foot, four-by-four land rover and speed boat to the island. There you will climb, scramble, swim, wade, jump and crawl. Food and water? Who knows, let's just say you'll need to be putting all your new found skills to good use." Ma checked her watch. "Yeah, we got time for your first weapons class. Alright, let's go."

Without another word, and without looking back to see if the group was following, she turned on her heel and marched from the room.

Sarah felt a hand on her shoulder. She looked up and saw Alma nodding, as if to say, *You can do it. We'll do it together.*

Chapter Four - **Natalie**

"Good morning, survivors!"

Natalie groaned and pulled the pillow over her head to shut out the sound of Madison's too-cheerful voice, amplified by the bullhorn to an insanity-inducing volume level, and the overhead lights, which had snapped on with the abruptness and severity of a guillotine.

"Rise and shine," Madison went on. "Your adventure begins today! Accountability formation in five minutes."

Begins? Natalie thought. *Then what the hell was last night about?*

She pressed the pillow tighter, in a futile effort to shut out the light that seeped in around the edges. The previous evening's activity had gone on way too long.

Firearms familiarization.

That was the term Ma Tempest and the weapons instructor, Terry Hickok, had used. It sounded like an official term, a military euphemism. The boys had eaten it up. Why was it that boys were so fascinated with guns? And not just any guns, but the old fashioned kind that used bullets and were soooo loud.

Hickok, a tall, wiry guy that looked as tough as gristle—and probably was—had not really talked much about shooting technique. The emphasis had been on safe handling procedures, but Hickok had talked a lot about why he thought guns were so great. In fact, no one had been allowed to even touch the array of guns laid out on a table at the firing range until they could quote back Hickok's rules of surviving a gun fight.

"Rule one," he had said, sounding a little like a cross between an Army drill sergeant and a wizard from one of those old movies from before the war. "Guns have only two enemies: rust and politicians. Number two: It's always better to be judged by twelve than carried by six. Number three:

Cops carry guns to protect themselves… not you. The average response time of a .357 is fourteen hundred feet per second."

Natalie had to fight the urge to protest the comment. She owed her life to the quick response of the Honolulu police department. The officers who had stormed the shack to rescue them from the kidnapers had definitely been shooting as much to defend her and the others as they had been to protect themselves.

"Rule four," Hickok went on. "Never let someone or something that threatens you get inside arm's length and never say 'I've got a gun.' If you need to use deadly force, the first sound they should hear is the safety clicking off."

She couldn't help but wonder what might have happened that night if they had been armed. Would C.J. and Lee still have gotten the drop on them? Probably, and given the swiftness with which the four of them had been subdued, any guns they might have had would have been taken away and possibly used against them. Just having a gun wasn't enough. Firearms weren't magic talismans; just having them didn't make a problem disappear. Without adequate training and perhaps even more importantly, the instincts to know when a situation was about to turn dangerous, all the guns in the world couldn't save you.

She knew that was why their parents had sent them here, to get the training to deal with the unexpected, but the kidnapping had been a fluke. The odds of something like that happening twice in one life were astronomical.

"Rule five. The most important rule in a gunfight is: Always win. There is no such thing as a fair fight. Always. Win. Cheat if necessary."

As the presentation moved into the Q-and-A portion, Natalie had made the mistake of speaking her mind. "Kids at school say a person that carries a gun is paranoid."

"Nonsense," Hickok countered, "Nonsense! If you have a gun, what do you have to be paranoid about?"

That didn't seem like an answer, but she realized she had already drawn the wrong kind of attention, so she quickly clammed up.

"Are we supposed to holler 'stop' or 'halt' before we start shooting?" Tim had asked.

Hickok shook his head, "The police do it. You won't here. Just remember, you can say 'STOP' or any other word, but a large bore muzzle pointed at someone's head is pretty much a universal language. And if you have to shoot, shoot to kill. Never leave an enemy behind.

"If you have to shoot," he repeated. "Shoot to kill. In court, yours will be the only testimony. Remember, this course is not designed to save the planet, but you may be able to save yourself and your family."

Wow. This is gonna be great.

Paula's voice, though somewhat muffled by the pillow, reached her. "C'mon, Nat. Get a move on."

Reluctantly, Natalie removed the pillow and sat up. Paula was already dressed and the other girls in the dormitory room were all in various stages of rising. There were only eight of them all together—five that weren't from the Rourke clan. With the possible exception of Alma, a tom-boyish young woman who claimed to be a teenager but looked like she was in her early twenties, the girls were about the same age as her and Paula, give or take a year.

A couple beds down seventeen-year-old Heather was pulling on her boots. The most charitable thing Natalie could say about her was that she was probably an ugly duckling. She was tall, but like a lot of tall girls, seemed embarrassed by her height, and slouched her shoulders forward in an effort to look smaller. This made her seem a little masculine, but Natalie was pretty sure that, with just a little effort, Heather might transform into a strikingly attractive woman. A shy girl, she had said little during the introductions; only that coming to the Survival Academy had been her grandfather's idea. Natalie couldn't tell whether the girl was actually happy about being at the school or not.

Across the aisle, Holly and Devra—both fifteen-year-olds—were fully dressed and sitting on Devra's bunk, conversing softly. The two appeared to be fast friends, though they had met for the first time on the flight to Texas. Both were slender, looking more like the girls they had been than the women they would someday be, and both had long straight black hair. They looked enough alike to be sisters, and Natalie and Paula had already decided to start calling them "the Twins." The only noteworthy difference was that one of them—Natalie thought it was Devra—had rounder cheeks and porcelain white skin, while the other had a smattering of freckles on her nose. Even their stories were almost the same. The daughters of successful businessmen who, much like Natalie's own parents, were worried about where the world was heading and wanted their kids ready to deal with whatever uncertain future lay ahead. The two girls appeared to be enthusiastic about being at the academy, which was certainly more than Natalie could say about herself.

The last remaining girl who had introduced herself as "Jennifer, uh, I mean, Jenn," was still in bed, the blankets pulled up over her head as if refusing to get up. She was thirteen and short, with curly blonde hair and big round cheeks, baby fat that would turn into proper chubbiness if Jennifer, uh I mean Jenn, didn't watch her diet and get plenty of exercise. The night before, she had been trying very hard to act like she was mature enough to hang out with the older girls, but had come across as an insufferable know-it-all, always trying to one-up everyone else. When Devra and Holly had mentioned that their fathers were both successful businessmen, Jenn had bragged about how wealthy her parents were. When Paula had mentioned that her father was "sort of a life-skills instructor"—the Rourke clan had all agreed that it would be a bad idea to reveal that they were related to the founder of the Survival Academy, to say nothing of the President of the United States—Jenn's parents had magically transformed into college professors.

"Which college?" Natalie had asked, innocently.

Jenn had dissembled for a while until someone had changed the subject to... what else? Boys.

Remembering that was enough to get Natalie moving. If there was one thing that just might make the Survival Academy tolerable, it was the two-to-one ratio of boys to girls. One boy in particular had caught her eye. Seventeen-year-old, dark-haired, dark-eyed Matthew Kestrel looked like... well, he looked perfect. With the physique of a star quarterback, a boyband handsome face, and a smile that made her feel a little weak in the knees.

She wasn't actually looking for a boyfriend, at least she didn't think she was, but a little attention from a good-looking guy was never a bad thing, especially when there wasn't much else to look forward to.

And if something like true love did happen? Well, that wouldn't be such a bad thing either. The boys at her school were sooo boring. If nothing else, survival camp would be a great place to meet some new prospective friends.

She got ready and straightened the bed, somehow managing to make herself presentable in the allotted five minutes. "How do I look?" she asked Paula.

"Better than you have any right to," Paula replied. "I'm jealous." She looked down the row of beds. "Looks like Sarah has a new friend?"

Natalie glanced at her younger cousin. Sarah was conversing with Alma as she got ready. "That Alma girl," Natalie said. "There's something..."

"Weird?"

"Yeah. I don't think she's a teenager. Do you think we should tell someone?"

"I'm sure the Academy did their homework, but..." Paula shrugged. "I don't like how quick she buddied up to Sarah. Let's keep an eye on her."

Natalie nodded, but Paula was right. There was no way the Academy would have let someone suspicious in, especially not with the President's children there.

They filed out into the courtyard between the boys' and girls' dormitories, where Madison was waiting, bullhorn in hand. Most of the boys were already there, milling about in little groups. Jack and Tim were together in a group that included the obnoxious red-haired boy that had kept running his mouth the night before—Clayton was his name. Clayton seemed to have taken a liking to Jack, and Natalie felt sorry for her brother. The boy was almost as irritating as Jennifer, uh, I mean, Jenn.

Speaking of whom, Natalie thought, doing a quick check of the girls. *Where is she?*

Madison raised the bullhorn. "Listen up, survivors. When one of the staff calls for an accountability formation, you need to line up in an orderly fashion. Later today, you'll be put into teams, but for now, give me two groups. Boys here." She pointed to her right. "Four by four. And girls over here." She pointed to her left. "Two rows of four."

As the groups shuffled into place, Kevin, the oldest boy, took charge, directing the boys to line up four abreast. Natalie wondered if he had some kind of military training, maybe a school ROTC program or even Boy Scouts. Most of the boys seemed to catch on quickly, though Clayton couldn't seem to grasp what was expected of him.

"We're not in the Army here," Madison went on, "and we don't expect perfect discipline, but try to keep it neat."

Paula moved to stand behind Alma, and Natalie took the spot behind Sarah. She immediately noticed that Jenn was not present. Madison noted it as well and began moving toward the incomplete formation with a wry smile on her lips.

Uh, oh.

"I could have sworn there were eight girls last night," she said. "Did you lose someone?"

One of the boys, probably Clayton, snickered.

"Jenn's still asleep," volunteered one of the dark-haired Twins. Natalie couldn't tell which one.

Madison nodded slowly, then turned and walked back to her original spot. "This is what we call a 'teachable moment.' One of the things you will learn here is that survival is an individual responsibility, but that doesn't mean that all you care about is saving your own butt. In a survival situation, you might need help from other people, and you might not get to choose who those other people will be. Learning to work together as a team is just as important as being self-reliant. That means looking out for each other."

Still holding the bullhorn in her right hand, she crossed her arms and stared at the girls. "Isn't there something you should be doing?"

Natalie looked down, trying to avoid eye contact with the student-instructor. To her complete astonishment, Paula spoke up. "I'll go get her."

Madison nodded. "Better hurry. Breakfast is getting cold."

Then, as Paula jogged back to the dorm, Madison held the bullhorn up again. "I just hate standing around and waiting, don't you?"

There were a few nods and a few laughs.

"That's what I thought. I've got an idea. Let's do some push-ups while we wait."

The laughs became groans, but several of the boys immediately dropped to hands and knees, and started doing the exercise.

Show offs, Natalie thought.

"Why are we in trouble?" Clayton whined.

Natalie was inclined to agree, but grudgingly assumed the front-leaning rest position along with the rest of the girls. She realized now that Paula had made the smart choice by taking the initiative to look after Jenn.

There's my teachable moment, she thought.

"Trouble?" Madison laughed. "Believe me, if you get in trouble, you'll know it. Everybody, get down, start pushing."

"Stupid girls," Clayton said.

"Come on, Clayton," Matthew Kestrel said. "A little exercise before breakfast is a good thing."

In front of Natalie, Alma was offering quiet encouragement to Sarah. "Rest on your knees, sweetie. When you get stronger, you'll be able to do them just like the boys."

It had been Natalie's intention to do "girl push-ups" as well, but then she saw that Alma was doing regular push-ups, her lithe body fully extended in plank position. The Twins were doing the same.

Okay, Natalie decided, *if that's how we're gonna play this.*

She straightened her knees and back, and lowered herself to the ground. Push-ups weren't so hard, and she was in pretty good physical condition.

"Down," Madison sang out. "And up! One. Count with me. And down."

The torture was mercifully cut short when Paula emerged from the dorm with a slightly disheveled Jenn in tow. Clayton, who had stalled out after the first "down" and was flat on his belly, looked up and snarled, "Nice of you to join us."

Madison ignored his outburst just as she ignored his evident laziness, and kept singing out her two-note cadence until Paula and Jenn were back in the group. "Jump in, girls. Let's do five more, and then we'll head to breakfast."

Five more? Natalie groaned. Her arms were quivering and her back was starting to ache, and she was having trouble keeping up with Madison's rapid-fire. "Up. Down." *Maybe I'm not in such great shape after all.*

She dropped to her knees, but kept pushing until Madison, mercifully, shouted: "Recover!"

Ugh.

Natalie dropped flat and then got up slowly, like an old man getting up after a fall. She glanced over at the boys and saw Matthew, already on his feet, swinging his arms back and forth, turning his head this way and that, limbering up for the next challenge. Then his eyes met hers and he smiled.

Her heart fluttered a little. She looked away quickly and did a few quick stretches of her own.

"Now that we're all present and accounted for," Madison said, "let me just reiterate what I said earlier. Survival is an individual responsibility. If you die waiting for someone to come along and rescue you, you've got no one to blame but yourself. So, can anyone tell me why I want you to look out for each other?"

There was a long pause until Tim raised his hand. Madison nodded to him.

"Because it's the right thing to do?"

A smile flitted across her lips. "It may be that, but in a survival situation, your primary consideration is just that: Survival. And as I just said, survival is an individual responsibility." She looked around. "Anyone else want to take a stab at it?"

One of the other boys—Natalie didn't recall his name—raised his hand and then spoke without waiting for a prompt. "Strength in numbers."

"That's right. Even though you may not always be able to rely on that other person..." She stared pointedly at Jenn. "Your chances of survival increase when you're part of a group. Every person on your team will have unique skills to contribute. One person can forage while the other builds a fire or a shelter. You can trade off keeping watch at night. And sometimes you just need an extra pair of hands. Keeping that other person alive is part of keeping yourself alive.

"Your instructors will go over this in more detail, but I want you to start thinking like survivors right now." She paused a beat, then smiled again. "Okay, who's hungry?"

Natalie thought she was hungry until she reached the serving line in the chow hall where they had eaten the night before, and got a look at the fare that was being offered. Biscuits and country gravy, sausage patties, scrambled eggs, hash browns...everything glistening with grease.

"Yuck," she muttered and turned to Paula. "Want mine?"

Paula laughed. "It's not that bad."

Natalie rolled her eyes. Her idea of breakfast, when she chose to eat it which wasn't often, was usually just a toaster pastry or a bowl of cereal. "Just looking at all that grease is giving me zits."

The biscuits looked almost tolerable so she took one and then stepped out of line, heading for the table where the Twins were already seated. They acknowledged her presence with nods, but kept eating. Natalie noted that their plates were almost overfilled and that they were eating quickly, as if trying to beat a deadline.

They won't stay skinny if they keep eating like that, Natalie thought as she took a bite of the biscuit.

Paula sat down beside her, and then Heather and Jenn joined the table, the latter jabbering away about the superiority of her mother's cooking to what had been served thus far. If she felt any remorse for having been the cause of the earlier group punishment, she gave no indication, though Natalie wondered if the constant talking was her way of trying to avoid recriminations.

God, I wish she would shut up, Natalie thought. Even being around hunky Matthew Kestrel wasn't enough to make up for having to put up with Jennifer, uh, I mean Jenn.

There was a loud thunk as someone set a plate down on the table next to Natalie. She looked over, wondering who was joining them, and jumped a little when she saw Ma Tempest standing beside her, arms folded across her chest.

"I noticed you forgot to put food on your plate," Ma said. "So I got some for you."

"Uh, thanks, but this is enough." Natalie waggled the biscuit.

"Enough for what?"

Natalie blinked at her. "Ummm…"

"Worried about your little figure? This is survival school, honey, not high school." Although she was looking at Natalie, Ma spoke loud enough for everyone in the dining hall to hear, which wasn't difficult since everyone had gone completely silent. Natalie felt her cheeks go hot in embarrassment.

Ma took a step back. "You've all probably heard that a person can survive for several days without food. Well, that's true, but here's something that you probably haven't heard. In order for your brain to function, it needs fuel. Food. Your brain is the most important survival tool you possess. If it stops working, you will die.

"The average teenaged girl needs a minimum of 1,800 calories a day just for normal bodily function. Boys need more. In a stressful situation like a survival scenario, that number can increase to as much as 6,000, and guess what? The only food you're going to have is what you can forage or hunt for yourself. If you can't find enough food, your body will start devouring your reserves. Some of you have a little more reserves than others."

She looked around the room, staring intently at a few of the students who were a little on the stout side, which only made Natalie feel a little less mortified.

"Trust me when I say this," Ma went on, returning her attention to Natalie. "When you're sucking on jackrabbit bones in a couple days, there's going to be just one thought going through your pretty little head." She paused a beat for dramatic effect. "I wish I'd had another helping."

Fuming, Natalie pulled the plate to her, scooped up a heap of the thick sausage gravy on her biscuit and shoved it into her mouth. She swallowed the whole mouthful down without even tasting it, and scooped up another.

"Atta girl," Ma said with a triumphant grin, and then walked off without another word.

Natalie kept her gaze fixed on the plate as she shoveled the food into her mouth. It wasn't actually as bad as it looked, but the only reason she ate it was to avoid further humiliation.

Lesson learned, she thought. *Avoid that old hag like the plague.*

Survival school had not even really started yet, but the teachable moments were already coming in hard and fast.

Chapter Five - **John**

John Paul Rourke stared out the side window of the Jeep in astonishment. The old trail creeping up the side of the mountain was so narrow, and the slope so steep, that he couldn't even see the ground beneath them. It was like being in the plane again, only now they were flying just a few feet above the earth. Even with his face pressed to the glass, all he could see was the cliff face falling away beneath them for hundreds of feet, into a rocky canyon dotted with wild grass and trees.

It was beautiful, but the really cool part was riding on the trail. As it rolled over the uneven terrain, the Jeep dipped and tilted crazily, and John was sure that, at any moment, the vehicle would roll over completely and go tumbling down into the canyon.

It was scary as hell. Better than any roller coaster he'd ever ridden.

"This is so cool!" he shouted as the right side of the four-wheel drive vehicle rose up yet again. His exclamation was cut short when the boy next to him, his new best friend, Philip Kestrel, half-slid, half-fell into him. "Oof."

"I know, right?" Philip chortled. "I just wish we could go faster."

Faster would be better, John thought. *But scarier, too.*

The convoy of multi-passenger off-road vehicles seemed to be just creeping along, barely faster than he could walk, and sometimes—like when a section of trail had washed out and they had to ride up along the cliff wall—slower than an actual crawl. In fact, he was pretty sure that if they went any faster, they probably would go over the side, and that wouldn't be cool at all. The grown-ups driving the off-road vehicles seemed to know what they were doing.

It had still been dark when the convoy, roof racks loaded with rucksacks and other equipment, set out from the survival academy complex and headed out into the wilderness. After about five minutes the paved road had given way to a mostly flat dirt road, and then ten minutes after that, they had begun ascending the mountain trail. John and Philip were in the lead vehicle, along with Philip's older brother Matthew, Kevin, and a couple other boys whose names John hadn't learned yet.

The mood had been subdued for the first half-hour or so. It felt like the first day of school, which John supposed was exactly what it was. Learning the ropes, getting used to the routine, meeting new people and trying to figure out who would be a good friend and who the troublemakers were, and maybe the toughest part, dealing with the teachers. Even Madison, who had seemed really friendly at the beginning, had shown a harder side to her personality, making them all do push-ups just because one girl had overslept, which John complained about during the ride.

"That wasn't so bad," Kevin said. "Just think of it as an opportunity to get stronger."

"I don't mind exercise," John said. "I just don't think it's fair to punish everyone when one person screws up."

"That's what they do in army training," Philip put in. "It teaches you to think of yourself as part of a team rather than always looking out for yourself."

Kevin raised an eyebrow. "That's right, Philip. Where'd you learn that?"

The younger boy grinned. "I love military stuff."

"Well, you're right. Team building is part of the reason for it. But an activity like that also adds to the stress level during training, which can help you remember your lessons when you need them the most."

That made no sense at all to John. "How does adding stress help you remember better?"

"Have you ever heard the saying 'train as you fight'?"

"I have," Philip said quickly.

"Combat is stressful. You can read all the books and watch all the war movies you want, but when you're surrounded by the noise and confusion of battle, with people trying to kill you, you'll have a tough time trying to access the part of your brain where that knowledge is stored. That's why military drill instructors are always shouting and making new soldiers do lots of physical exercise. It keeps them in a state of constant stress while they're learning the skills that will save their lives in a real battle.

"Survival training is the same way. You can learn everything you need to know about survival from reading a book, but when you're in a high stress situation, all that information you've got filed away in your brain gets jumbled like a deck of playing cards scattered on the floor. But if you learn those skills in an environment of simulated stress, you'll have an easier time remembering them when the stress is real."

"So we're gonna be doing a lot of push-ups."

Kevin grinned. "You'll do fine."

John knew that was probably true, and they were preparing for the end of the world after all. A little exercise wasn't a big deal.

"One other thing," Kevin added. "Just remember that the instructors aren't out to get you. Whatever happens, it's all part of the program. Don't take it personally."

"Unless you're a fat-ass like Clayton," Philip put in.

It was a mean thing to say, but true. From an early age, John had been taught to never judge people based on their appearance, but with Clayton, ugly wasn't just skin deep. The stocky red-haired boy was lazy and abrasive, with a big mouth and no filter. He complained about everything, made fun of everyone, and seemed incapable of doing anything for himself. Clayton's parents—he claimed his father was the CEO of a leading energy weapons manufacturer, but John suspected he was either exaggerating or outright lying—had probably sent him to the Survival Academy to learn a little self-sufficiency, but John couldn't help but wonder if their real motive had simply been to get rid of him for a while.

Kevin frowned at the comment. "Animals turn on the weakest members of a group, driving them out. Sometimes even killing them. Humans have to be smarter than that."

"Smarter?" John asked.

"A chain is only as strong as its weakest link. It's like Madison said this morning, you don't always get to choose the people who survive with you. If getting rid of a weak link isn't an option, the only thing you can do is try to make that weak link stronger."

Grown-ups were always saying things like that, but in Clayton's case, it sounded like an impossibly tall order. John let the subject drop.

Philip had the final word on the matter. "I just hope he's not on my team."

The trail continued through a series of switchbacks back and forth across the slope and then crossed a saddle between two peaks to reveal a breathtaking view of the wilderness where John and the others would spend the next few weeks of their lives.

"There it is." Their driver, Bob Decker, pointed to a spot on the canyon floor at the end of the serpentine trail. "We call it 'Camp Zero' because that's where you start counting the days until it's over."

A tall, scrawny looking young man, with unkempt sun-bleached hair and a reddish blonde goatee, Decker had been quiet during the long drive. John wasn't sure if he was just a driver or one of their instructors. Decker laughed, and everyone else laughed too, though John wasn't sure he understood the joke.

Camp Zero consisted of four green tents, each the size of a small cottage, arranged in an orderly row. There was a ring of stones around a fire pit but John saw no picnic tables or outhouses.

Camp Zero is right, he thought. *There's nothing here.*

As they piled out of the Jeeps, Madison called for an accountability formation while the other instructors and drivers stood off to one side, watching. There was far less confusion this time since everyone understood what was expected of them, but John could hear some of the kids grumbling about being tired and hungry or wondering where they were supposed to relieve themselves.

Madison ignored the discontented murmurs. "Okay, survivors, you're on the clock now. First order of business is to unload the vehicles. Grab your rucks and line them up right where you're standing. After that, you can help your driver unload the rest of the supplies and when that's done, you can take five for a bathroom break. We'll be passing out food rations in a bit, so make sure you're back here, standing behind your ruck, fifteen minutes from now. If you're not here, you'll probably go hungry."

"Where *is* the bathroom?" asked one of the boys.

Before Madison could answer, Clayton shouted, "I heard about this one survival dude who drinks his own pee. Are we going to do that?"

There was a chorus of disgusted groans but Madison didn't bat an eye. "That's something to consider, Clayton. In a survival situation, you might have to do some gross things to get water and we'll talk about some of the ways to purify your water supply to make sure you don't get sick. Drinking contaminated water in the wild is almost as dangerous as dehydration.

"Now, believe it or not, where you go to the bathroom is just as important to survival as finding fresh water and food. We'll be digging latrines later, but for now, I'd recommend you choose a spot at least fifty yards from the tents. Hygiene is one consideration of course. You'll want to avoid contaminating a possible water supply. Also, consider that urine is one way that animals mark their territory. Your pee might keep small game animals away, and that will have an impact on your food supply. Oh, and when you're traipsing around out there, watch where you step. There are rattlers and other things out here that you don't want to get too close to."

John glanced around the surrounding area. There were no trees or anything else in the suggested fifty yard interval to afford a degree of concealment for modesty's sake. He decided he didn't have to go just yet.

Madison glanced at her watch. "Fourteen minutes," she said. "Better get moving."

They unloaded the vehicles with plenty of time to spare and, as promised, fifteen minutes later, Madison directed them to line up for their food ration, which consisted of three freeze dried meals in plastic pouches. John got Beef Stroganoff, Teriyaki Chicken with Rice, and Cajun Beans and Rice. Almost as soon as the meals were distributed, some of the kids—Clayton foremost among them—began complaining about the choice of menu and asking to swap them out. As the noise grew to a dull roar, Ma Tempest took Madison's place at the front of the formation.

"This is all the food you're going to get from us. You can eat it all for lunch today, or you can try to make it last a couple days… Hell, you can sell it to the person next to you if you want, or throw it away, I don't care. Just know that once it's gone, it's gone. The meals are a safety net. The sooner you learn to procure your own food, the better off you'll be, so pay attention to this next block of instruction."

Ma provided the instruction herself, giving them an overview of strategies for finding safe drinking water, foraging for edible plants and roots, and setting snares for small game.

"Finding potable water," she said, "is one of your top priorities, and your body will definitely let you know. In fact, if you're thirsty, you're probably already starting to get dehydrated. We brought along a few five gallon cans of potable water, but once you move to your wilderness camp, you'll have to find your own water.

"Now, unless you're in the Sahara desert, finding a source of water won't be too much of a challenge. We'll get into more advanced methods of water collection later on, but for now, here are some basic tips.

"Water flows downhill and always follows the path of least resistance, so start by heading down and keeping your eye out for natural drainages.

If you look around you, you can see how water has shaped this entire region. You'll see channels where the water has flowed down the slopes. Your best chance of finding water is at the bottom of those channels.

"Vegetation is another good indicator. Plants need water. Some plants more than others. Reeds and cattails grow in saturated soils. If you see those growing, you've found water. You can also follow the animals to water, though that may take a bit more patience.

"The water is there if you know where to look. You might have to dig down a few inches to actually get at it, and what you get might look more like mud than what you're used to seeing from the kitchen tap, which brings us to the second, and actually most important part of finding water in the wilderness: Purification. How can you tell whether a water source is contaminated?"

Ma paused, indicating that the question was not rhetorical, and after a few seconds, hands started going up. Ma pointed to one of the boys. "You. How can you tell clean water from dirty water?"

"Look for particles."

"Particles," Ma echoed, then pointed to a girl with reddish-blonde hair. "You."

"Smell it. If it smells nasty, don't drink it."

"Smells nasty," Ma said. She pointed at Paula. "You."

"You can't tell," Paula said. Her tone was hesitant, uncertain.

Ma raised an eyebrow. "Is that so?"

Paula straightened a little, and when she spoke again, the uncertainty was gone. "The stuff that can make you sick is microscopic. Bacteria and protozoans. Stuff like that."

Ma continued to stare at her. "Who agrees with Paula, here?"

John stuck his hand up right away. Paula was going to be a doctor someday; she knew what she was talking about. He was pleased to see most of the other kids raise their hands as well.

Ma nodded. "Paula is absolutely correct. In a survival scenario, you should assume that water from any source is contaminated, and treat it before you drink it. Out here, we're primarily worried about biological contaminants. Those are easy to kill. Chemical and radiological contaminants are a little trickier. We'll talk more about those later on, but they won't be a problem out here.

"There are a variety of methods for treating water. You can add chlorine or iodine tablets. You can run it through a charcoal filter. But if you don't have the means to do that, your best bet is boiling the water before drinking it. Ten minutes at a boil will kill one hundred percent of biological contaminants. You're going to be boiling all your own drinking water from here on out.

Ma clapped her hands together. "Okay, that takes care of water. Now let's talk about what you're going to eat." Her gaze settled on Natalie and she gave a wry smile. "Remember what I said at breakfast? You all need anywhere from 2,000 to 6,000 calories a day depending on your activity level. Now you might think it's impossible to find that much food out here, but the animals that live in this wilderness do just fine. A black bear may consume as much as 15,000 calories a day when they're storing up energy for hibernation." She gestured at the landscape. "It's all out there. A regular all-you-can-eat buffet, if you know what you're doing.

"Bears are omnivores, just like us, but their digestive system is better adapted to wild food than yours or mine. They can thrive on foods that would make us sick. There are two basic sources of food out here: plants and animals. Ideally, you're going to want a little of both. The more diverse your diet, the healthier you'll be. Animal protein is a better source of calories, but hunting burns up a lot of energy, too. We're going to take an all-of-the-above approach to food out here: trapping, hunting, foraging and even cultivation. There's a reason our ancestors developed agriculture: it takes a lot less energy to harvest plants from your garden than it does to roam the woods looking for edible plants.

"In the first few days of a survival scenario however, you're just trying to get by, so we'll start with foraging. The most important thing you can do to prepare is get familiar with what's edible and what isn't. A toxic plant will kill you a lot faster than starvation.

"I'd strongly recommend you pick up a guidebook to edible plants in your home area and practice a little foraging on your own, but be careful. Sometimes, even the guidebooks have bad or incomplete information. There's an old story, from before the War, about a young man who decided to try living off the land in Alaska. He read all the guidebooks and thought he had all his ducks in a row, but when he actually got out in the wilderness, he wasn't able to find enough food to keep his strength up. To make matters worse, the one wild plant that he found in abundance and which made up most of his diet, contained trace amounts of a chemical that ordinarily wouldn't have been a problem to a healthy person, but to a person in a weakened state, it was toxic and left him too weak to even go out and forage. He did everything right—by the book—but he still starved to death.

"The takeaway here is that this isn't a game. We're trying to get you ready for an extreme situation where all the systems we rely on for survival disappear. There are no guarantees, but you'll have a better shot at surviving it if you're prepared. Guidebooks are a great way to get started, but there's no substitute for real experience." She got to her feet. "Let's take a walk and I'll show you what there is to eat around here."

Ma led them across the valley floor to a nearby tree with a stout main trunk that branched into several thick limbs to produce a broad overhead canopy. The leaves were thin but clustered together like the quills on a feather, and interspersed with them were long green pods that looked like peas.

"This is a honey mesquite tree," Ma said. "It's one of your best friends out here. The pods and the leaves are edible." She snapped off a branch

42

and handed it to Tim, who happened to be standing closest to her. "Go on. Give it a try. Watch out for the thorns.

"The wood is great for fire and for smoking meat. It's also very hard, which means you can make spears and arrows from it. You can make needles and fishhooks with the thorns. We'll be making some twine from the fiber, which we'll use for our snares. And, as you can see, it's a great source of shade."

The branch was passed around. When it came to him, John took a single leaf and put it between his teeth. It wasn't horrible, but it reminded him that it was nearly lunchtime.

When everybody had sampled the mesquite leaves, Ma showed them other edible plants. John recognized several of them but had no idea they were edible; dandelions and clover leaves, oak acorns and seeds from pine cones.

"Okay, that's just a quick overview of edible plants," Ma said at length. "When planning for long-term survival, you'll want to set up your permanent shelter in an area with lots of plants, not only because you need them for food, but because game animals will be drawn to them as well. That brings us to setting snares."

"Traps are cruel," one of the girls said. It was the same girl who had overslept and gotten them all in trouble.

Ma raised an eyebrow. "I hate to break it to you honey, but life is cruel. That's something we lose sight of when we get all our food from grocery stores and restaurants. I don't care what you think about hunting or eating meat. My job is to teach you how to survive. Maybe you've heard the old saying about how there are no atheists in foxholes…well believe me, there are no vegetarians in a survival situation. Not for long. They either get over it or end up dead. Meat for some other animal."

She paused as if waiting to see if the girl would say anything more, then went on. "I'm going to show you how to make a basic noose snare. Tomorrow, you'll each have a chance to set your own snares and do some foraging. Pay attention because after tomorrow, the only food you're going to get is what you catch for yourselves."

John swallowed nervously at the thought. He wasn't too bothered by the thought of preparing and eating wild game, but what if they couldn't catch anything? Surely the instructors wouldn't let them all go hungry.

He glanced over at Philip who just smiled and whispered, "Yum."

Chapter Six - **Tim**

As Mr. Dickson had promised, the first day at Camp Zero was busy and exhausting, and Tim Rourke felt like his brain might pop if he tried to cram one more bit of obscure outdoor survival lore into it. Ma had shown them dozens more edible plants, guided them through setting noose snares and fishing lines, and even given them a crash course in how to skin and cook small game animals. Tim doubted he would be able to recall half of what he had been taught. Fortunately, he wouldn't have to do it all on his own.

He was part of a team now, Alpha team.

Tim had mixed feelings about this development. Alpha was a strong team, possibly the strongest of the three. Although they had not been required to choose a team captain, that job had gone by default to Matthew Kestrel, a smart, athletic charismatic seventeen-year-old who the other boys just seemed to naturally want to follow. Alpha was also made up mostly of older boys; in fact, Tim was the youngest boy on the team. There were only two females, and while some of the boys had quietly complained about getting stuck with Tim's cousin, Sarah Ann, the youngest person in the whole camp, there was no denying that, on balance, they still had a physical advantage over the other teams. The other female, Alma, was not only strong and confident in her own right, but had taken it upon herself to look out for Sarah, a job that her teammates were only too happy to let her take.

And therein lay the root of Tim's misgivings. On the one hand, he felt a measure of relief at not having to be the one to take charge. Even though Paula and Natalie were both older than he was, he felt like looking out for them all was his responsibility. His failure in that regard on the night of the kidnapping stung like an open wound. He had missed the warning signs— no, that was wrong. He had not missed the signs. Rather, he had ignored them, and they had all paid dearly for it. And then, when the chance came to fight back, he had failed a second time, letting the kidnappers overpower him. He would not let that happen again, and that meant never letting his guard down. So while it was kind of nice to just be a kid again, no expectations, he could not help but feel like he was shirking his duty to his family. It didn't help that they had all been split up.

He and Sarah were on Alpha team. Jack and Paula were on Bravo team. Nat and John were in the third team, Charlie.

Tim felt a little sorry for Jack and Paula. Somehow, both of the camp's troublemakers—Clayton Reynolds and Jenn Hargreaves—had been assigned to Bravo. On the other hand, that pretty, dark-haired girl, Devra Merlin, was on Bravo team, too, so maybe Jack didn't have it so bad after all.

Tim understood the logic behind breaking up the family group, but it still felt a little weird. As long as he could remember, the Rourke kids had always been a close-knit unit. The family bond had always been the most important thing to John Thomas Rourke. It was the strong foundation upon which everything else depended. Rourke had crossed the post-apocalyptic landscape, fought brigands galore, and even taken on an invading army, all to reunite with his family. It was not an exaggeration to say the modern world owed its existence to the strength of the Rourke family connection.

When their parents had collectively decided to send them to the Survival Academy, Tim had just assumed they would go through the course the same way they did everything else: Together. He wondered now if this had been their parents' intention all along.

As he sat with his teammates that evening around the open bonfire, eating the dinner Ma had prepared in a Dutch oven over that same fire, Tim pondered the question of whether to fully embrace his new team, or try to maintain the cohesiveness of the Rourke clan. One look at Sarah, who was chatting with her new friend, the too-friendly Alma, was enough to bring him to a decision.

Family comes first, he decided.

A loud banging pulled him back to the moment. Ma was standing near the fire, rapping a spoon on the lid of the Dutch oven to get everyone's attention. "Okay, survivors, what do you think of your dinner? Not too shabby, huh?"

There were murmurs of agreement and Tim nodded absently. The meal reminded him of chicken and dumplings, though there was something slightly off about the way it tasted. It was not horrible by any means, just different.

"We call that Alpine style cooking, but that's really just a fancy way of saying that we're working with just the bare minimum of supplies and equipment. Self-sufficiency is our watchword. We don't keep a store of food here at Camp Zero, and we won't be getting any deliveries. I used just a few ingredients that I brought along—mostly just a few spices—and the rest of it I gathered myself this afternoon."

This comment prompted some of the kids to exchange nervous looks. Tim distinctly heard someone say, "You mean that wasn't chicken?"

"Now you see that living off the land doesn't have to be a horrible experience," Ma went on. "By the end of the course, you'll be regular wilderness gourmets.

"Okay, that's all we have planned for you tonight. Tomorrow we're going to pick up the pace a little, so make sure you get a good night's sleep. Each team has an assigned tent and you'll all be bunking together co-ed from here on out. I expect you to behave respectfully toward one another. Does anyone need me to explain what that means?"

The only sound was of crickets in the distance.

"Good. Now, it's about 1900 hours right now—seven o'clock if you still tell time the old fashioned way—so you've got a couple hours to yourself. Finish your dinner, clean up, brush your teeth, do some star-gazing, and get all the chatter out of your system, because I don't want to hear a peep out of you after 2100.

"I highly recommend that you draw up a schedule for keeping watch through the night. There are eight of you per team, so everyone can pull a one-hour shift. The last person on the schedule will be responsible for waking everyone up and getting them to the accountability formation at 0500 hours. Believe me; you don't want to be late." Ma put her hands on her hips. "Maddie will help you get that all sorted out, but don't waste her time with a lot of stupid questions. Self-sufficiency starts right now. See you bright and early."

With that, Ma turned on her heel and headed for the fourth tent in the row, followed by the other instructors. Even before she got there, Matthew was on his feet, addressing Alpha team. "Okay, you heard her. We need to organize our watch schedule. First watch will be the easiest, so if no one has any objections, I think we should let Sarah take it." He turned to Sarah and grinned. "Think you can handle it?"

Sarah looked back at him like a deer in the headlights. "I don't even know what I'm supposed to do?"

"There's really nothing to it," Matthew went on. "Just keep an eye on the tent and make sure that we don't have any unwanted visitors in the night. If we have a fire, make sure it doesn't go out. Other than that, the only important thing is to make sure that you stay awake, and wake your replacement up when your shift is done.

Alma patted her on the shoulder. "How about I stay up and keep you company tonight, okay?"

Sarah nodded.

"Then why don't you take the second shift," Matthew told Alma. "And we'll go in age order after that, youngest to oldest."

Tim felt everyone else's eyes on him. After Sarah, he was the youngest person on the team.

"Perfect," Matthew went on. "I'll write up the list."

As if by some unspoken accord, the older boys crowded around Matthew, leaving Tim, along with Sarah and Alma, outside the circle. Tim didn't think they had intended to exclude him, but it felt that way all the same. He turned and found Alma kneeling beside Sarah, offering encouragement in a low voice.

Tim suddenly felt very alone. He glanced across the fire to where the other teams were similarly getting organized. Jack was staring at the fire while Clayton, sitting on the ground beside him, was jabbering away. He didn't see Paula, but he did see Devra Merlin. She was talking to one of the older boys on her team, but then, as if feeling Tim's eyes upon her, she turned her head, looked directly at him, and smiled.

Tim looked away, embarrassed, and then turned to Charlie team. He spotted Natalie immediately. Despite being younger than some of her teammates, and a girl to boot, she seemed to have taken charge. That didn't surprise Tim at all. Nat was charismatic and a good organizer, even if her judgment was sometimes suspect. Like it had been on the night of the kidnapping.

The thought made his heart race a little faster.

He spotted John Paul, sitting beside and speaking to Matthew's brother, Philip and an older boy named Kevin.

Tim had noticed Kevin when they first arrived. He said he was eighteen, but he looked older than that, maybe old enough to be in college. And now he was buddying up to John Paul.

You're being paranoid, he told himself, and yet if he had heeded that instinctive wariness on the night of the kidnapping, things might have ended very differently.

Before he quite knew exactly what he was doing, he was moving toward Sarah. "Hey, I was thinking we should have a little family pow-wow."

Sarah looked up at him, and then looked at Alma, who nodded approvingly. That bothered Tim, but he didn't let it show.

"Okay," Sarah said. "Mom and Dad would probably like that."

He took Sarah's hand and walked her over to Bravo team's area. Jack saw them first and eagerly broke away from Clayton to join them. A few minutes later, the Rourke clan was gathered together in a cluster away from the bonfire and out of earshot from the others, waiting for Tim to explain why he had asked for the meeting.

"I was just thinking," he began, haltingly, "that our parents would want us to look out for each other, and now that we're all on different teams, that might be harder to do."

There were nods of agreement.

"So…uh, how is everyone doing?"

For a few seconds, he got only more nods and shrugs, then Jack finally came to the rescue. "The camp is great, but that Clayton kid is driving me nuts."

Suddenly, they were all talking, as if Jack's comment had given them permission to finally say what they were thinking and feeling. It all came out in a rush, from the things that made them miserable to the things they were really enjoying. All their fears and concerns, and their hopes, too. How much they missed their home and their parents, and how exciting it was to be somewhere new, making new friends and doing amazing things.

Tim breathed a quiet sigh of relief. He had been worried about how the others would respond to his request for a family meeting, but now he knew that he had made the right call. "Listen," he said. "I think we should do this every night. Get together after dinner and check in with each other."

A round of nods greeted the suggestion.

"Cool. There's just one other thing I wanted to bring up." He gave Sarah a long hard look, then did the same to John Paul. "Those two older kids, Kevin and Alma. Something about them seems a little fishy."

Sarah's eyes went wide in shock, and John began to sputter in disbelief, but Tim noticed that the others were nodding in agreement.

"I thought so, too," Natalie said. "No way are they teenagers."

"If they're lying about their age," Jack added, "what else are they lying about?"

"Alma's nice," Sarah said, loud enough to make Tim cringe and hold a finger to his lips to hush her. "She's my friend. She's not lying."

"Kevin's a cool guy," John said. "You're wrong about him."

Tim raised his hands in a placating gesture. "Look, maybe they are okay. I'm just saying, be careful. Trust has to be earned. You can be friends with them, but don't tell them who your dad is."

Sarah shook her head. "I won't," she said, but her tone was abrupt, as if Tim had insulted her.

"It's good advice for all of us," Paula put in. "We don't really know if anyone is who they say they are. Except for the six of us, of course. If we stick together and watch each other's backs, we'll make it through this."

Chapter Seven - **Paula**

The sound of voices roused Paula from her slumber. It was not a deep sleep. She had been unconsciously ignoring the urge to go the bathroom but the slight pressure had kept her near the threshold of wakefulness. The voices simply brought her the rest of the way up.

Crap! She thought. *What time is it?*

She looked at the luminous dial of her wristwatch. Five a.m.

"Crap!" She sat up, switched on her headlamp, and saw a couple of her teammates likewise stirring, and struggled out of her sleeping bag. "Everybody up! We're late."

Her shout threw the tent into chaos. Lights flashed on, and accusations and recriminations flew through the air.

"Why didn't someone wake us up?" Jenn complained. "Who was supposed to be on watch duty? Dustin? You had last shift. Did you fall asleep?"

"Nobody woke me up," Dustin shot back. He looked around the tent. "Who had the shift before me?"

"It doesn't matter," Devra said, her tone sharp enough to curtail the discussion. "We'll sort it out later. Right now, we need to get moving, or we'll all pay the price."

Paula had slept in her uniform, and needed only to pull on her boots and straighten her sleeping bag, which took all of ninety seconds. Jack and most of the rest of her team seemed to be moving with similar urgency, but the two troublemakers, Jenn and Clayton, seemed more interested in fixing the blame than dealing with the immediate crisis. Devra stood over them, hands on her hips in a fair imitation of Ma Tempest, and shouted, "I'm going to count to five, and if you're still here, I will drag both of you to formation by the hair. One...Two..."

That got the pair moving, but as the team emerged from the tent, Paula saw that it was already too late. The other teams were lined up in neat rows, a conspicuous gap between them where Bravo was supposed to assemble. Madison stood at the front of the formation, bullhorn tucked under one arm, and a wicked smile on her lips as she watched the tardy team line up.

When they were all finally where they belonged, she glanced at her watch, then shook her head sadly. "You're late. You were told not to be late, but here you are. Late. If your survival depended on being punctual, you would all have died ninety seconds ago." She pointed to the ground. "Go on. Lie down. You're all dead."

Paula stared back Madison, waiting for the laughter, but Madison did not appear to be joking.

"You heard her, Bravo," Devra said. She dropped to her knees and then assumed a prone position. "On the ground."

With a sigh of resignation, Paula followed suit. She had a feeling she was going to be spending a lot of time being humiliated for the sins of her teammates, particularly Clayton and Jenn. The odds were good that one of the two was responsible for the breakdown of the night watch schedule. On the plus side, Paula had missed her one-hour shift, which meant that she had gotten a full night's sleep.

"Oh, what have we here?" Ma's familiar voice crooned from behind the formation. "Looks like some campers didn't make the *dead* line. I warned you not to be late to my formation."

Paula kept her eyes forward, dreading what would happen next. Ma did not disappoint. "On your feet, Bravo."

Paula got up, but no sooner was she standing erect when Ma sang out, "Too slow. Get back down and try again."

When this signal came to get up, Paula sprang to her feet like a jack-in-the-box, but not all of her teammates were as nimble, and a moment later, they were all face-down again.

"Slow risers," Ma said. "That seems to be a problem for some of you. Let's practice it. Up… Down…Up…"

Someone in one of the other formations made the fatal mistake of letting a snort of laughter slip out. Ma seemed to have been waiting for that opportunity. "What's that? Does someone here think this is funny? Everyone, get down."

There was a collective groan as the other two teams went to the prone.

"Survival is about self-discipline," Ma went on. "Up. Of course you want to sleep in a few extra minutes. Down… Up. I do, too. And maybe it doesn't matter if you're a few minutes late to the breakfast table. Down… Up. Maybe the worst thing that happens when you're late is that you get marked tardy by your teacher, or miss the bus and have to ask Mommy for a ride. Down… Up. But in a couple years, you show up late to your job and get fired. Now it's about survival. Down… Up. Self-discipline *is* the first key to survival, and I'm going to make sure you learn it. Down…"

Paula was starting to feel a little light-headed from all the up-and-down, but she had quickly figured out not to go completely flat on the ground, but to hold herself up a little.

"Push yourself up to your knees," Ma said, her tone marginally more sympathetic. "Now, get up slowly so you don't get a headrush."

"Too late," someone complained.

"If you're feeling dizzy, take a moment. Part of self-discipline is knowing your limitations. We're going to find out what those are, and then we're going to push past them."

Over the course of the half-hour that followed, Ma did exactly that, running them through a series of callisthenic exercises at a brutal pace. Jumping jacks, push-ups, mountain climbers, and a particularly nasty exercise called a "burpee." Paula was seldom able to do more than a few repetitions before her quivering muscles gave out, forcing her to go to her knees for a few seconds before trying again. Ma, who was strolling back and forth through the midst of the formation, didn't seem bothered by the frequent breaks that Paula and some of the others were taking, but if she spotted anyone lingering too long in a rest phase, she would single them out for special harassment. Clayton and Jenn were, not surprisingly, repeat offenders, which meant that all of Bravo was under Ma's microscope.

Mercifully, the torment eventually ended. Ma brought the sweaty exhausted group to their feet. "Wasn't that refreshing?" she asked with a grin. "Better than a cup of coffee, am I right? Who here isn't energized and ready to go?" She paused and eyed them all with a mischievous gleam in her eye.

Paula braced herself for Clayton or one of the others to say something stupid, but thankfully, nobody took the bait.

"I'll bet you're all hungry," Ma went on after a moment. "Let's go see if any of you managed to catch some breakfast."

She led the group out across the valley floor to the spot where they had set their practice snares the previous afternoon. The noose Paula had set was empty, as were most of the others, but one of them held a rabbit, and two others had caught squirrels...or maybe they were something else... chipmunks or prairie dogs...Paula wasn't certain of the difference. In fact, when she looked at the traps, all she could really see were cute furry little dead things, and her appetite deserted her. Judging by the reaction of some of her teammates—mostly, but not all girls—she wasn't the only one who felt that way.

"Not a bad start," Ma said, ignoring the subdued response. "Altogether, you set twenty-four snares and got enough for a meal for one, maybe two people. Just think about that going forward. I showed you a basic fixed-loop snare. Honestly, I wouldn't have been surprised if you'd come up empty. There are better snares and techniques for how and where to place them to increase your chances of success, but no matter what you do, luck plays a huge role. Snares are just one part of a multi-pronged strategy for gathering food. You'll be foraging and fishing and, later on, you'll make weapons for hunting larger game.

"Okay, we'll dress our game right here. One thing we definitely don't want in our camp is a lot of blood and rotting scraps stinking up the place. Each team will skin and cook one animal. That way everyone can get a taste. After that, we'll do some arts and crafts with the parts you won't be eating."

Bravo team gathered around their designated animal—a squirrel—and followed along as Ma took them through the process of skinning and gutting the animal. Somehow, she managed to break it down into several steps so that everyone had the dubious privilege of a chance to use their knives.

"All right, hold the animal on its back…stretch the legs out. If you're not doing anything, grab hold of a leg and hold it tight. That will make it easier. Take off the head and feet. Now, put the edge of your knife right below his little poop chute and take off the tail."

Paula shuddered at the crunch of the knife slicing through flesh and bone, and had to look away when blood began running from all the various stumps.

"Everyone, reach in and find the breastbone," Ma continued, "right below the sternum." She indicated the corresponding spot on her own body. "Make a very shallow incision in the soft tissue there. You'll have to push a little to break through, but the goal is to just cut through the skin and the belly muscle, without piercing the stomach or intestines."

Paula felt her gorge rise at the visual image those words evoked, but reminded herself that this was no different than the dissections she had done in biology class. If she was going to be a doctor, she would have to get over being squeamish about such things. "Let me do it," she told her teammates, drawing her knife from its sheath.

They had all been issued identical knives which according to Jack, who was obsessed with knives, were "full-tang, fixed blade with a drop point, hardwood handles and a finger indent below the choil." Paula thought they looked a little like the big chef's knife from the kitchen at home. She placed the point against the squirrel's breastbone and pushed, tentatively at first, then harder until she felt it break through.

Just like dissecting a specimen in biology class, she kept telling herself. It was easier to think of the animal that way with the head and tail removed.

Ma paused a few seconds to make sure that everyone was keeping up. "Now, make a shallow vertical cut all the way down to the cut you made to remove the tail."

Paula pulled down on the blade, trying to make the cut, but instead of slicing through with surgical precision, the blade simply popped out and slid along the exterior. She muttered a curse under her breath and tried again, this time angling the blade to keep it underneath the belly muscle. It wasn't as easy as Ma made it sound, but after a bit of tugging and sawing, she completed the cut.

I did it!

She was actually a little disappointed when Ma instructed them to switch off again. The next step involved removing the guts, which was about as gross as it sounded and was accompanied by a chorus of disgusted groans, followed by another cut up the chest to expose the heart and lungs.

Ma came to each group and pointed out the various organs. "The heart, lungs, liver and kidneys are all edible. Rinse those off and put them in your mug for now."

The stainless steel "mugs" were actually more like all-purpose mini-cooking pots. They had used them to boil water the previous night, and now it seemed they were going to serve as field-expedient food preparation containers. Probably soup pans, too.

"In a pinch, you could clean and boil the stomach. We're not that desperate, but the tough tissue has other uses that might come in handy. Just remember that the intestines are full of bacteria that you *do not* want contaminating your food.

"Now work your knife under the belly skin where it's already loosest and start peeling off the hide. Once you get enough for a handful, a good pull will take it the rest of the way off."

There were more *eeeews* and *ughs* as well as a "cool" from one of the boys…it might have been John, and then they were done. Instead of furry forest creature, there was something not much different from what might be found in the meat section at the supermarket.

Ma directed them to rinse everything off and then meet back at the camp. With the addition of a few mesquite branches, the smoldering embers of the previous night's fire were stoked to life, whereupon Ma showed them how to cook the meat on a spit and boil the organs to make a soup. "Go ahead and prepare one of your freeze-dried meals," she said. "You'll need the calories for the rest of the day, but I want everyone to get a taste of your first wilderness kill."

The thought of sipping squirrel liver broth made Paula grimace, though the meat sizzling over the fire actually smelled pretty appetizing. But as she rooted in her rucksack for one of the dehydrated camp meals, Jenn's whiny voice reminded her that some things were even more unpleasant than killing, gutting and skinning small animals.

"Where's my Chicken Enchilada?"

Paula didn't even give Jenn a cursory glance. Her own meals were right on top, easy to reach, but Jenn did not strike her as the kind of person who put much thought into anything.

"It was here last night." Jenn's decibel level was keeping pace with her frustration. "Somebody stole my Chicken Enchilada!"

That got Paula's attention. She stopped what she was doing and hurried over to help Jenn look. Devra evidently had the same thought, and reached Jenn's side first.

"Keep it down," Devra said in a low voice. "Don't make a scene, and for goodness sake, don't make accusations like that."

"But it's gone," Jenn persisted, not making any effort to lower her volume. "Somebody took it."

Ma's voice crackled through the camp like a peal of thunder. "Is there a problem, Bravo?"

"No, ma'am," Paula called out quickly. "Just helping our teammate get squared away."

"That's what I like to hear."

Devra pulled Jenn's ruck to her and upended it, dumping the contents out on the ground. It was, as Paula expected, an incoherent jumble, but as she and Devra sorted through the mess, it became evident that Jenn had only one freeze-dried meal left, and it was not Chicken Enchilada.

"See? I told you."

"Are you sure you didn't eat it?" Devra asked.

"No. I had Yankee Pot Roast for lunch yesterday. I still had two meals in my pack when I went to bed last night. Somebody took it when we were asleep." Her eyes narrowed into accusatory pin-points, staring first at Paula then Devra, and then taking in the rest of the team. "It was one of you. I know it was. Empty your packs."

Devra hushed her with a stern hiss, but then added, "If someone did take your meal, we'll find out, but we're going to handle this ourselves, got it? We don't need to draw any more heat. Unless you like doing extra push-ups."

"Why should I have to do push-ups?" Jenn shot back. "I'm the victim here."

Paula shook her head in disbelief. *Is this girl really that dense?* "Jenn, you really need to shut up. We're going to deal with this, but you need to stop talking."

"She's right about one thing, though," Devra said. She turned to face the others. "Turn out your packs."

The immediate response from the older boys was indignation. "Are you accusing us?" asked Dustin, and Juan added, "Man, this is some bullshit."

"No one is accusing you," Devra said. Her tone was patient but she did not back down. "But either one of us is a thief or Jenn is lying. We can deal with the situation my way, or we can take it to Ma. Your choice."

"I got Chicken Enchilada, too," Jack said. "How am I supposed to prove I'm not the thief?"

Jenn continued to pout. "Maybe whoever stole it already ate it and threw the wrapper away."

Devra gave an exasperated sigh. "Look, just dump your packs out. If nobody has an extra meal, we'll have to figure something else out."

The boys grumbled but assented, turning their rucks over and emptying them onto the ground. Paula watched them all closely, but saw only irritation, not the hesitancy that might indicate guilt.

That was why it was such a surprise when three full meal pouches tumbled from Clayton's pack.

Chapter Eight - **Jack**

It was like watching a volcano erupt in slow motion.

First, a flash of surprise.

Jack felt it, too. Clayton had an extra meal. Jenn's accusation had not been unfounded after all.

Then, disbelief. Denial.

That can't be right, Jack thought. *There has to be a mistake. Clayton is a moron, but he isn't a…thief?*

A thief. It was there, written in bold letters on every face. No, that wasn't quite right. Clayton's expression was still stuck somewhere between surprise and incredulity. The others however were about to boil over with anger.

"Wait!" Jack cried out. "Think about it."

That's what he was trying to do, trying to think of a way to stop the situation from going critical, if it wasn't already too late. He could see that his exclamation had not averted anything, only postponed the inevitable, and worse, cast him in the role of sympathizer, possibly even an accomplice to a thief.

Crap! He looked around the camp to see if anyone outside the group was watching. Most of the other kids were busy with their meal preparations, and Ma was standing off to the side, talking to the other instructors, but Madison was staring right at him, an expression of keen interest on her face. He looked away.

"Just think about it," he said again. "We're already off to a bad start. What if…" He faltered, still trying to find a lifeline to pull himself and the rest of them back from the precipice. "What if this is a test?"

"A test?" Paula asked. Her tone was sincere, and he was grateful for that, but there was some skepticism there, too. If she didn't buy his desperate rationale, none of them would.

"What if they…" He lowered his voice to a conspiratorial whisper. "What if Ma did this to see if we would turn on each other? Survival isn't just about who's toughest or who can eat the grossest stuff. It's about using your head. Thinking before doing."

He was digging deep to sell the idea. Truthfully, he didn't really know if he believed what he was saying, but he also didn't believe that Clayton had stolen Jenn's food. Like it or not, the red-headed boy had latched onto him, which made Jack the closest thing to an expert on Clayton's behavior. The kid was annoying as all get out, but he wasn't a thief.

Which meant that either Jack was right, and the instructors were testing them, or someone else in the team was trying to frame Clayton. That didn't make any sense, either.

Jack put the thought away. All that mattered at the moment was relieving the pressure before they all got in some real trouble.

"That's ridiculous," Devra hissed. "He probably did it last night. When he was supposed to be pulling his guard shift. Then he let us all sleep in to cover it."

This surprised Jack because Devra, who had almost effortlessly assumed a leadership role despite being younger than the boys, younger even than Paula, should have realized what he was trying to do, whether or not she believed in Clayton's innocence.

"Jack may be right," Paula said, just as quickly. "But regardless, this is a test for us. A test of whether we can deal with situations ourselves, like grown-ups."

"I'll deal with it like a grown-up," Dustin said, balling his fists and taking a step toward Clayton. "Two things I can't stand. Thieves and liars."

"You don't know that he's either," Paula said.

Dustin pointed at the meals on the ground. "The proof is right there."

"I didn't take it," Clayton said, breaking his silence. He spoke in gulps, as if he was trying to hold back tears. "I slept all night. Nobody woke me up for my shift."

"Okay," Devra said, raising her hands and making a patting gesture. "Let's take it down a notch. I think we all know what happened, but Paula's right. We have to take care of this ourselves. Beating his ass is just going to get the rest of us in trouble, and we don't need that."

"He stole my food," Jenn said, almost shrieking. "He's the one that should be in trouble."

"I didn't!" Clayton scooped up all three of his meals and threw them at Jenn. "Here. Take it all."

Ma's voice cut through the camp. "Bravo? You need something?"

Jack risked a quick glance over his shoulder and saw Ma on her way toward them.

"We have to take care of this," Devra repeated. "But later. In our own way." She stood up and turned to face Ma. "No, ma'am. Just trying to make sure everyone tries the soup."

Ma did not appear to be the least bit convinced. "Uh, huh. Well, I probably should have told you this sooner, but if you're talking when you're supposed to be eating, I'm going to assume that you're not hungry. We'll call this your one and only warning. Eat up. You're going to need the energy."

She turned away so that she was facing all of the students. "There's an old saying in the military: 'The only easy day was yesterday.' We've got a very full schedule, so right now your mouths should be busy with just one thing, and it ain't gabbing. After we wrap up here, you'll start round robin training sessions. Alpha, you'll go to wilderness way finding, with me. Bravo, you will report to Madison for shelter building. Charlie team, you'll do combatives and unarmed self-defense with Mr. Hickok."

Unarmed self-defense? Normally, Jack would have been thrilled at the prospect. Hands-on experience with close-quarters-combat was just the sort of authentic research that would help him write believable action-adventure stories but, at that moment, all he could think was that Clayton would probably need to know some self-defense techniques if he was going to survive the Survival Academy.

Ma grinned. "You think I was tough on you this morning? That ain't nothing. Mr. Hickok makes me look like a big ol' teddy bear. You're gonna spend a lot of time picking yourselves up out of the dirt, I promise you that. So stop yapping and shovel that food in."

Devra turned back to the team. "You heard her. Eat up." She picked up the packaged meals scattered on the ground, handed one of them to Jenn and returned the others to Clayton. "We'll deal with you later."

Clayton opened his mouth, presumably to make another futile attempt to protest his innocence, but behind him, Dustin spoke in a stage whisper. "Oh yeah. Self-defense training is gonna be fun."

"Hope no one gets hurt," Juan added, his tone nakedly sarcastic.

Clayton got the message. He shrank away from the older boys, and moved closer to Jack. "Thanks for having my back."

"Yeah," Jack muttered.

"I didn't take her food. I'm not a thief."

"Yeah," Jack said again. He noted Dustin and Juan staring at *him* with the same contempt they had shown toward Clayton a moment before. *Wonderful,* he thought. *I guess it's true that no good deed goes unpunished.*

He did not regret having spoken up. It had been the right thing to do, and not just because he actually did believe Clayton. While the others had been letting their emotions rule their actions, he alone had tried to use his head.

"Look," he went on. "I wasn't standing up for you. I was just trying to keep us all out of trouble. But if something like this happens again…" He shrugged. "I don't think anyone's going to listen to me."

"I didn't do it," Clayton repeated, then moved off and slumped to the ground to his meal in sullen silence.

Paula moved closer to Jack. "Do you really think Ma did this to test us?" she whispered.

"I don't know. I don't want to believe that they would, but…" He shrugged. "None of this makes any sense."

"Maybe we should just ask her."

"Ask…you mean Ma? You said we should handle it ourselves. Like grown-ups, remember?"

"If it is a test, then the only way to beat it is to let Ma know that we figured it out. If not, then we really have got a thief on our team. If it isn't Clayton, then someone is trying to make us turn against him."

"Clayton was doing a great job of that already."

"Yeah, I get that. Maybe that's why someone did this. To push him to a breaking point. Maybe the real grown-up thing to do is to get some help before this gets ugly."

Too late for that, Jack thought.

"Or," Paula went on. "We could talk to Madison. It's her job to be a sort of go-between, right? That way, it wouldn't be like we're tattling or anything."

"Makes sense."

"During the shelter class, then you and me."

Jack felt a tingle of excitement at the prospect of talking to Madison, and not just making idle chit-chat, but engaging in an actual constructive dialogue that would show his maturity. It was almost enough to make up for having to put up with Clayton.

"And Jack," Paula said. "What you did…putting on the brakes and getting everyone to calm down. That was pretty impressive. I'm glad we're on the same team."

Jack grinned. "Thanks, cuz. Coming from you, that means a lot."

Chapter Nine - **Sarah**

Sarah gagged and involuntarily spat out the broth. She had never tasted anything so disgusting. Even the lingering aftertaste was enough to make her retch. She hugged her arms around her chest, partly to keep from throwing up, and partly because she wanted to curl up in a ball and hide from everyone.

Alma patted her on the shoulder. "That's okay, sweetie. It's pretty gross, isn't it?"

"I'm sorry," she said, blinking furiously to keep from crying.

"You tried it. That's all anyone expected you to do."

"But if I don't eat it, I'll die." Even as the words came out, she knew how childish it sounded, so she quickly added, "I mean, if this was for real, and that was the only thing…"

"I know what you meant." Alma pulled her closer, hugged her. "You heard what Ma said. There are a lot of other things to eat out here."

Sarah buried her face in Alma's side, but she couldn't help but think about Tim's advice from the night before. *Be careful.*

She pulled back a little, and in the corner of her eye saw Tim looking right at her, his forehead creased in irritation. Tim was wrong about Alma. The older girl was her friend. More than that, she seemed to be the only person to recognize that Sarah was just a kid. Everyone else—from the instructors to her own family—was acting like she could keep up with them, no matter what. She was supposed to exercise like a teenager, and remember all the stuff the instructors said, and eat the grossest stuff on earth….

I'm only nine. It's not fair to make me do all this stuff.

And it wasn't fair for Tim to tell her not to trust her only friend.

Alma handed her a cup full of regular water. "Go on. Wash that taste out of your mouth, then eat some real food." She laughed and Sarah laughed, too. The dehydrated meals might be a little easier to choke down than rabbit liver soup, but it hardly met the definition of *real food*.

Tomorrow, she wouldn't even have that.

Ten minutes later, Ma came over to them. "All right, Alpha. Let's start with a question. Who here can tell me which direction to go to get back to the main facility?"

A few of the students ventured silent guesses with pointing fingers. No two were pointing the same direction.

"Uh, huh. Okay, let's try this." Ma took several folded sheets of paper from the cargo pocket of her uniform trousers. "Pass these around. This is a map of the wilderness area we're in. Take good care of it. You'll need it later."

Sarah took hers and stared at it. The map was mostly green, with lots of reddish-brown squiggles. The whole thing was overlaid with a pattern of one-inch squares outlined in black and there were a few other markings in black and blue.

"This is a topographic map," Ma explained. "The scale is 1:50,000, which means that an inch on the map corresponds to fifty thousand inches in the real world. In case your brain is too fuzzy and sleep deprived to do the math, that's about four thousand feet, or just under a mile.

"You'll see that I've marked the location of Camp Zero with a little blue triangle. I've also marked the location of the Academy HQ with a little blue square."

Sarah found the two shapes Ma was describing, spaced about six inches apart. The square was higher up on the page and to the left of the triangle. *That's northwest*, she thought. *About five miles away. Funny, it seemed a lot further during the drive.*

"Now that you have a map," Ma went on, "can you tell me which direction the HQ is?"

Sarah was about to raise her hand, but Tim and several of the other boys all pointed in more or less the same direction.

"That's right," Ma said. "It's northwest of here. How did you know which direction to point?"

"Because of where the sun is," Tim said. He pointed to the mountains in the other direction where the sun, though still below the horizon, was already lightening the sky. "That's east, and the map says the Academy is to the northwest."

"Very good. Day or night, you can always tell which direction is which, provided you can see the sun or the stars. For precise navigation, you need a compass; but even if you don't have one, or a map for that matter, you can still get where you're going if you know a few basic things. If you had been paying attention yesterday, you might have remembered where the HQ is. Situational awareness at all times will save your butt.

"Let's get back to the map. Find Camp Zero. Now, look at those little squiggly lines and circles. Those are called 'contours' and they denote elevation changes of ten feet. When they are spaced apart evenly, that means you're looking at a slope, like a mountain or the side of a valley. A small circle by itself is a hilltop. Take a look at the terrain around you and then see how it corresponds to the contour lines.

"Now, remember what I said about scale? This is a three-dimensional landscape rendered in two-dimensions, but if you measure the distance between two contour lines, and multiply it by 50,000, you get the distance traveled per ten feet of elevation change. That will give you a general idea of the grade. A 100% gradient means that for every ten feet you travel forward, you gain or lose ten feet of elevation. You really don't want to try walking on a hill like that. A grade of more than about 35% is considered too steep for a vehicle. When planning your route, you want your contour lines spaced as far apart as possible."

Sarah did as instructed and found that it was surprisingly easy to match the two-dimensional representation with the three-dimensional reality.

"You can probably see," Ma went on, "why we had to take such a crazy route to get here. We've got some big mountains between us and the HQ.

You'll also note that Camp Zero is at a higher elevation than the HQ. After your field exercise, we'll be spending entire days on navigation and orienteering, but for now, you just need to know the basics of wilderness travel.

"Okay, let's talk about navigating without a compass. Most of you have learned that the sun rises in the east and sets in the west, but that's only partly true. The sun's position changes depending on the time of year and your latitude. Right now, in summer, the sun is further north than it would be in the winter, but you can still use the sun's position to estimate true north, no matter what time of day it is.

"A simple trick is to take your wristwatch…" She held up her arm and shot her cuff to reveal hers. "You should have a *real* analog wristwatch, preferably one with a perpetual self-winding mechanism. I know you kids like those newfangled electronic phone gizmos, but batteries don't last forever, and this is a trick you can't do with a digital watch."

Sarah didn't know what a 'perpetual self-winding mechanism' was, but she did have a real wristwatch with hands that moved.

"Just point the hour hand at the sun."

Ma held the time-piece up to her eye, twisting her arm a little to line it up with the brightest spot in the sky. Sarah did the same. The hour hand was a little ways past six.

"Now, the point that is halfway between the hour hand and twelve o'clock is due south."

"That's easy," Sarah muttered. "South is three o'clock."

"That's right," Alma whispered.

"This is good for getting oriented if precision isn't that important," Ma said. "Let's say your plane crashes in the desert and you have to find your way to civilization. You may know that there's a road or maybe a river in a certain direction. Once you reach a road or a river, you'll always be able to find your way to civilization. But even if you don't know where the nearest major landmarks are, getting oriented will help you travel in a straight line. As you travel, you'll want to do frequent hasty checks to make sure you're staying on the same heading. If you don't, you're liable to walk in a great big circle and wind up right back where you started.

"Now, once you know which direction is which, you can use terrain features to establish your heading. Mountain tops, big rocks, trees…anything that you can see from a distance and which won't move. Let's say we want to go to the HQ by the straightest route possible. We know south is at our three o'clock, so from this exact position, northwest is going to be roughly between seven and eight o'clock. Look in that direction and pick a terrain feature you can use to guide you."

Sarah found a funny discolored patch on the hillside that was almost exactly in the right spot. "There," she whispered to Alma, pointing it out.

Alma ruffled her hair. "Good job. You're a natural."

Sarah grinned. "This is actually kind of fun."

At that moment, a rowdy cheer went up from the opposite side of Camp Zero. Sarah looked back, along with everyone else, and saw Charlie team, dispersed around the edge of a sawdust pit, cheering on the two boys wrestling inside the circle.

"Don't worry," Ma said. "You'll all get your turn."

Sarah's good mood evaporated. Her queasiness returned, but this time, it had nothing to do with eating rabbit liver soup for breakfast.

Chapter Ten - **Natalie**

"Some of you," Terry Hickok said, "may be wondering why a weapons expert is teaching you about unarmed combat. To tell you the truth, I wonder that myself sometimes." He paused as if waiting for a response. Some of the kids laughed. Natalie did not.

"If you find yourself in a situation where you need to use these skills," Hickok went on, "it probably means you lost your weapon somehow, and that means you've already made what will probably turn out to be a fatal mistake. Maybe you left your weapon at home… Not going to do much good there. Maybe you just thought you wouldn't need it."

Natalie fought the urge to roll her eyes. Didn't he understand that they were all kids? That the decision to own and carry weapons wasn't theirs to make?

The weapons instructor clearly lived in his own world, where danger lurked around every corner, and every problem could be solved with force. That wasn't her world. Her problems involved things like cramming for mid-terms and learning to drive, and those were things that guns and fighting techniques couldn't help with.

Still, that other world—his world of constant danger—*had* found her once. There had been no warning, no time to prepare.

Maybe that was the point of all this. Being prepared for even the remote possibility of violence wasn't the same thing as paranoia. It was just smart.

"Unarmed combat techniques are not a replacement for proficiency with weapons," Hickok said. "Make no mistake. You win a hand-to-hand fight when your buddy shows up with some firepower."

He clapped his hands together. "Now that I've got that out of the way, let's have some fun." He studied them all for a moment, then pointed to Kevin and Ryan. "You two will be my demonstrators. Come forward."

He positioned the two in the center of the sawdust pit. "Either of you fellows have any martial arts training? Or maybe you're on the high school wrestling team?"

Both boys nodded without elaborating.

"That's good. Athletics teach you two things: body mechanics and self-discipline. What they can't teach you though is how to get ready for real sphincter-puckering life-and-death fighting. When things get ugly, there isn't going to be a coach or referee checking to make sure that you use the correct form and obey all the rules. Chances are good that your enemy will be stronger and better trained for the fight than you are. But you will have an edge. Your enemy may be fighting to kill or subdue you, but you will be fighting for your life. That's a powerful motivator. Remember my rules, especially rule five. There's no such thing as a fair fight. Stay alive at all costs.

"In a contest, you're playing defense and offense, trying to protect yourself but also looking for weak spots in your opponent's defenses. The more you train and learn, the better equipped you will be to do both, but for this lesson, we're going to focus on defense."

He posed Kevin and Ryan like mannequins, with Ryan lying flat on his back and Kevin straddling Ryan's chest, with his knees pressing into Ryan's armpits.

"Kevin is in the mounted position here. He can strike Ryan's head..." Hickok nodded to Kevin who proceeded to simulate his ability to punch Ryan. "But Ryan can't hit back effectively."

Ryan pantomimed throwing a few punches up at Kevin, but the latter simply leaned back to avoid the blows.

"This fight will be over for Ryan if he can't get free, and soon." Hickok took a step back and nodded to the two. "Give it your best shot."

There was a moment of stunned disbelief, and then someone on the perimeter of the pit let out an excited whoop. The cheer was just the spark needed to jumpstart the struggle. Ryan began thrashing and squirming beneath Kevin, trying to break free, but nothing he did worked.

"All right," Hickok said after a few seconds. "Let's hold up for just a second. If this was a real fight, Kevin would have to do something with his advantage. He can't sit there forever. Ryan's buddies might show up at any second. So, Kevin needs to kill or incapacitate Ryan. How would you do that, Kevin?"

Kevin considered the question for just a moment and then reached out with both hands for Ryan's throat.

Hickok nodded. "He's going to choke you out, Ryan. What are you going to do about it?"

Ryan immediately seized hold of Kevin's wrists.

"Good," Hickok said, kneeling down. "But you won't be able to hold him off forever. This is the moment where you can turn the tables on your enemy. You only need to trap one arm. Like this…"

Hickok positioned Ryan's right hand over Kevin's right wrist and then placed his left hand up underneath Kevin's arm, gasping him by the elbow.

"At this point, Kevin is vulnerable. He's off balance. Now you can make your move. Ryan, trap one of Kevin's legs with yours."

Ryan lifted his feet and planted them to either side of Kevin's feet.

"Now plant your left foot in line with Kevin's spine and thrust up with your hips."

He did, and Kevin fell forward over Ryan's face.

"Now, roll him over onto that trapped leg."

Ryan did, and just like that, the two reversed position. Kevin was on his back and vulnerable, and Ryan was the one in a dominant position, kneeling between Kevin's legs.

"Okay, hold up there again." Hickok turned to the group. "Think you can remember how to do that? More importantly, do you think you'll remember how to do that in an actual life-or-death situation?"

Natalie shook her head, as did several others.

Hickok gave a satisfied nod. "That's why we're going to practice. Grab a partner and get in position."

Natalie looked around the group, wondering who to choose. John and his friend Philip were already out in the circle, eager to get started. That left the other two girls, Heather and Holly, and a fifteen-year-old boy named Gary Stanton. Of the three, Heather was closest to Natalie's height and weight—she was actually quite a bit taller and probably stronger, too—so Natalie addressed her. "Shall we?"

Almost sheepishly, Heather nodded and they took their place on the ground in the fighting circle. "Why don't you start on top?" Natalie suggested.

Now that she had seen a practical demonstration of the ground fighting techniques, she was actually eager to try it out for herself. She got down on her back and let Heather straddle her. It felt strange having another person in such intimate proximity. Strange and disconcerting. Natalie felt a twinge of panic.

I don't want to do this, she thought. She opened her mouth to say it aloud, but Hickok's voice cut her off.

"A quick safety brief. No striking or punching, and no actual choking. If you're on top, try to grasp your opponent's collar. If you're on the bottom, your only goal is to get on top. Simple as that. Don't give up. Everyone ready? Go!"

Wait….

But it was too late. Heather's legs tightened ever so slightly and Natalie felt her breath go out. The sawdust pit and everyone else in it seemed to dissolve in a gray haze, and suddenly it wasn't Heather sitting on her abdomen, hands groping her chest, but Lee McAllen, dominating her…taking her power…taking whatever he wanted.

She bucked and squirmed, frantic to get away, but nothing worked. She was pinned.

Helpless.

74

Hickok spoke from somewhere beyond the haze. "Trap the arm."

Yes! Natalie clung to the sound of his voice like a lifeline. The crusty old weapons instructor didn't seem so paranoid now.

Trap the arm.

She stopped flailing, and deliberately caught hold of—

Lee's?

—Heather's wrist.

What was the next step?

Grab the elbow. Trap the leg.

As her panic began to ebb, her awareness returned. She could see the others around her, all locked in their own struggles. It was Heather, her face pinched with determination, straddling her chest, staring down at her, not Lee. There was nothing to be afraid of.

Grab the elbow... She did, lifting Heather's hand away from her collar. Heather tried to pull free but Natalie did not let go.

Trap the leg... She rolled her foot across the back of Heather's calf, hooking her foot under the other girl's ankle.

The rest was easy. She planted her other foot and thrust up with her hips, launching Heather forward. The bigger girl fell across Natalie's face, mashing her nose, but Natalie was so focused on the next step, she barely noticed. She twisted sideways, rolling Heather onto her back, and came up in a sitting position.

"Good!" Hickok called out, almost as if he had been watching her and no one else. "Now. Do it again."

Chapter Eleven - **John**

"I think this is the spot," Kevin said, dropping his rucksack on the ground. "Welcome to Camp Charlie."

John checked his map and did a quick survey to make sure the terrain features matched up. He had been double-checking Kevin's navigation throughout the short trek to the wilderness campsite, not because he didn't trust Kevin—he absolutely did, no matter what his cousins all said—but because it was fun.

All the stuff they had done so far was fun, even the really gross stuff like cutting up and skinning the squirrel. He could almost imagine himself as a frontier hero, or maybe a castaway like Robinson Crusoe, living off the land. This was, he supposed, exactly what the Survival Academy was getting them ready for.

Now, the training wheels had come off.

After the morning session and a light lunch—they had decided to extend their food rations by sharing half of their remaining combined supply of dehydrated food—they had been given the coordinates for their wilderness campsite a couple miles from Camp Zero. Getting there, using nothing but the map and skills they had learned that morning, had been their first practical test, and they had passed it with flying colors. But land navigation was pretty easy, comparatively speaking. The real test was just beginning.

"We've got a lot to do," Kevin said, "and only a few hours to get it all done." He used his foot to mark out a circle about three feet across. "We'll put the fire here and build the shelters around it to stay warm. Once those are up, go set your snares. Remember, if we don't catch something, we'll be eating bugs for breakfast."

"Yum," Philip whispered.

John nodded. Eating bugs sounded pretty gross, but also kind of cool. Ma had talked about some of the insects they might encounter, useful both as a protein source and as bait to catch fish. Insects with bright colors— red, orange, yellow, and blue—were best avoided, but most crickets and grasshoppers were perfectly safe to eat, if cooked thoroughly. John had already decided that he was going to try eating one—maybe a cricket—just to see what it was like. He didn't think anything could taste more disgusting than the soup they had made for breakfast, and he had managed to gulp down a whole mouthful of that.

He and Philip worked together to collect several long sticks which they tied together with strips of bark to form the frame of a small lean-to shelter, just as they had done in the practice session that morning. The hardest part was finding sticks that were long and straight enough to suit their needs. Young saplings, growing in the spaces between larger, more mature trees, worked best. Low branches were good too, though many of these were too crooked to be used. Once the frame was built, they wove in several whole branches with the foliage still attached to create a roof to keep the heat in. It wasn't the sturdiest construction, but it would do the trick for one night. In the morning, if there was time, they could make further improvements.

With the shelter finished, they set out to find a good spot to set some snares. In addition to the single loop snare, Ma had showed them several other ways of catching game, which basically fell into two categories: Deadfall traps, which basically consisted of a rock, tilted up and held in place with a stick, that would fall over when triggered, crushing the animal; and snares, which were variations on the noose. Some of the latter were very elaborate, employing stakes driven into the ground, counter-weights, makeshift pulley systems, and spring tension. John's favorite was the twitch-up snare, which used a noose, a trigger stake, and a bent over tree branch for tension. If an animal stuck its head through the noose and jostled the trigger, the tree branch would snap up, tightening the noose and taking the animal with it.

If it worked, which was kind of a big "if."

Location was more important than technique. The traps had to be set in places frequented by the animals. Even then, there were no guarantees. That was something Ma had drilled into their heads. Finding food in a survival situation was pretty much a full-time job, and required an all-of-the-above approach. This was why they had been collecting mesquite pods and edible greens all day, and why he and Philip were going to go catch some crickets as soon as the snares were set, and maybe scout the nearby creek.

There was a lot to do and a lot more to remember, and at the end of the day, John knew he would go to bed cold and sore and miserable, and wake up the same way, but he didn't care. He was having the time of his life, doing stuff that most kids never dreamed of doing and making new friends like Philip and Kevin. No matter what his cousins thought, Kevin was a cool guy. He treated John almost like an equal, instead of dismissing him as "just a kid."

And Philip? John couldn't recall ever having a friend like him.

As the President's son, it was tough for him to have normal relationships with boys his own age. Tim and Jack were okay, but they were older and, even if they didn't mean to, they always seemed to find ways to exclude him. Philip was like the brother he had never had. They liked all the same stuff—music, sports, movies. They even laughed at the same jokes.

After a short trip to the creek, they returned to the campsite to try their hand at starting a fire using the bow drill method Ma had shown them back at Camp Zero. She had warned them that it was an exhausting, time-consuming process.

John had seen it done in movies, but as Ma was quick to point out: "They make it look easy in the movies, but believe me, it's not. If nothing else, this will teach you to never go anywhere without matches or a lighter."

The bow drill method utilized a simple bow, made from a sturdy mesquite branch about two feet in length, bent slightly and strung with paracord, and a drill, made from another straight branch, whittled to dull points at the ends, and stripped of bark in the middle. By looping the bow-string around the drill, and then moving it back and forth, spinning the drill rapidly, it was possible to generate enough friction heat to cause combustion, but there were a few little details that the movies didn't really show, like the V-notch cut into the flat hearth board, or the need for tinder, which was anything that could catch fire quickly. Dried grass, wood shavings, even pocket lint worked well. The notch served to funnel hot black ash from the drill directly onto the tinder, as well as to let air in so the fire could ignite. A second smaller piece of wood was needed in order to press down on the top of the drill.

Despite Ma's warnings, John was surprised to see smoke come from the drill he and Philip were using after only a few back-and-forth strokes with the bow. Nevertheless, getting from smoke to fire took a lot longer. John thought his arm was going to fall off, but then Philip, who had his face down close to the notch, blowing on the faint coals that were starting to glow under the relentless turning of the drill, gave a shout of triumph. Jack looked and saw actual flames dancing in the tinder.

John gave his own hoot of delight, and then Philip gave him a high-five so hard that his hand stung.

"Ow," Philip said, rubbing his own hand, and then they were both laughing.

Chapter Twelve - **Tim**

Although he was bone tired, sleep proved as elusive to Tim as the small game animals that would comprise the bulk of his diet for the next few days. He lay awake, his mind struggling to process everything he had learned, all the strange new sensations his body was experiencing, and all the anxieties that had come along for the ride.

Tomorrow, they would be getting instruction in rock-climbing and rappelling, which was exciting, but also a little scary. He didn't think he was afraid of heights, but what if he was and didn't know it? What if he froze up? That would be embarrassing. He didn't want to make a fool of himself, especially not in front of the girls…in front of Devra.

Performance anxiety, he knew, was probably the last thing he ought to be worrying about.

What if, come morning, the snares were empty? What would they do then? Could they subsist on mesquite pods and dandelion greens?

He had given most of his share of dinner—his portion of the last pre-packaged meal, Cajun Rice and Beans—to Sarah. Despite the gnawing emptiness in his belly, no doubt a major contributing factor to his insomnia, he did not regret that decision in the slightest. Not only was Sarah family—and family always came first—she was also part of his team, and the success of the team was only possible if the weakest member of the team was not allowed to get even weaker. The poor kid was going to have a tough enough time adjusting to a diet of wild game.

Alma had shared part of her meal with Sarah, too, and that was also something that weighed heavily on Tim's mind.

Alma seemed fixated on Sarah, and had almost from the start. It was weird. Alma seemed like a genuinely nice person, but something about her had Tim's instincts pinging like active sonar on a submarine.

He was sure that she was lying about her age…like 99.999% sure that she was, and not just lying to the team, but to the people who ran the Survival Academy. Kevin, too. No way was that guy a teenager. Tim didn't know what sort of procedures the Academy had for screening candidates, but he imagined that some kind of background checks were performed, and that meant Alma and Kevin had taken extraordinary measures to create a false identity in order to get be a part of the same class as the Rourke kids. And the fact that they were trying to bond with the children of the President of the United States was damned suspicious.

Except he wasn't really 99.999% sure that they were lying. It was hard to tell sometimes. One boy at his school already had a mustache at fifteen. And girls were always trying to look older than they really were. Nat did sometimes, especially when she put on make-up and wore a dress instead of blue jeans and a T-shirt. Like the night of the kidnapping, when C.J. had mistaken Nat and Paula for college girls, or claimed to anyway.

Tim's instincts had been on high alert then, too, but he had ignored the warnings.

He wouldn't make that mistake again.

He had reiterated his concerns at the family meeting after dinner. This time, Nat and Paula supported him, counseling John Paul and Sarah to be cautious about trusting Alma and Kevin. The advice had not gone over well. John had steadfastly defended Kevin and reminded Tim that he wasn't the boss. Sarah had looked like she might cry.

Ugh.

One more thing to keep him awake.

A faint rustling pulled him out of the turmoil of his thoughts, though not completely. He opened his eyes and looked out past the dwindling fire, and saw Alma kneeling in front of the lean-to shelter that she shared with Sarah.

"Okay, sweetie," Alma whispered. "You get a good night's sleep, and tomorrow, we'll show these boys how tough you are."

"Thanks, Alma," Sarah said. "I love you."

Tim cringed.

"Love you, too, sweetie. Night, night."

Alma stood up and moved closer to the fire, tossing a few pieces of wood in. Tim surmised that it was the end of Sarah's hour-long shift, and the beginning of Alma's official turn, though as before, she had kept Sarah company and thus, pulled another double-shift. They were keeping the same schedule for night-watch, with Sarah taking the first shift so that she could get uninterrupted sleep. That meant Tim could get an hour of shut-eye before Alma came to wake him up for his turn.

Fat chance of that, he thought miserably.

To distract himself from his concerns, he stared up at the night sky and tried finding the North Star, just as Ma had shown them during the night-time navigation lesson. To a trained navigator, the stars were a more reliable guide than the sun, but as Ma had cautioned, "traipsing around in the wilderness at night is something you should probably avoid doing unless your life depends on it."

Polaris, the North Star, was a fixed point in the heavens around which all the other stars appeared to rotate. Of course, it wasn't the stars that were moving, but rather the earth, rotating on its axis—and Polaris was the star that appeared to be fixed above that axis. If you could find it in the night sky, you would always know which direction was north.

Polaris wasn't a very bright star—though all the stars seemed brighter out here, away from city lights—but Ma had taught them the trick to finding it. Tim easily located the Big Dipper, drew an invisible line from the two stars that formed the outside part of the trapezoid-shaped "scoop," and followed that line to the faint star in the handle of the Little Dipper. That was Polaris. That was north. When the Big Dipper wasn't visible, the middle point of the W-shaped Cassiopeia, another easy-to-spot constellation, also pointed to Polaris.

Finding north by the stars was easy, but using it to navigate was another matter.

Visibility was the biggest problem. Even with a headlamp, it was impossible to see distant terrain features, which meant staying on a true course would be next to impossible. A full moon might help some, but if it was cloudy, even the stars would be of little help.

"So what if our life does depend on it?" Tim had asked.

"Situational awareness," Ma said. "Maybe you can't see the terrain, but you can tell when you're climbing a mountain slope. The elevation changes are marked on your map. That will help you get oriented. Your ears can help, too. Listen for the sound of running water. Or highway noise."

Out here, they were far from any roads, and the little creek barely made any audible sound, even when standing in it, but there were plenty of other noises, like the persistent chirp of crickets, or the soft crunch of footsteps....

His eyes shot wide open. The footsteps could only belong to Alma, but they were growing fainter by the second, as if she was moving away from camp.

Cautiously, he lifted his head, and spotted movement, barely visible in the darkness. Alma *was* leaving the camp, but where was she going? The latrine they had dug earlier was in the opposite direction.

She was up to something, and Tim wanted to know what it was.

He slowly peeled away his sleeping bag and rolled out of the lean-to. He thought about pulling on his boots, but decided against it. He would be stealthier in his stocking feet.

His shelter mate, Randy—an okay kid, but kind of a doofus—stirred and mumbled. "Where you going?"

"Gotta pee," Tim lied.

Randy grunted and rolled over, putting his back to the fire. Tim waited a few seconds longer, then stood and crept away from the fire, heading in the same direction he had seen Alma go.

After just a few steps, he realized how impossible it would be to follow her in the darkness. He could barely make out the shape of the horizon, the ground contrasting with the starry expanse, but he could not see Alma. He stopped, listened, and thought he heard the faint sound of footsteps directly ahead. He glanced back to make sure the fire was still visible to guide him back to camp, and then continued forward.

He counted his steps, another important part of wilderness way finding, and when he had gone about fifty yards from Alpha camp, he spotted the faint glow of another fire in the distance.

Each team had been assigned a zone in which to set up their camp. The instructors had situated their camp, which also served as a general rally point, where the three zones converged, a spot roughly due south of Alpha's camp. Tim did a quick check of the stars and the position of the fire at his back.

That's southwest, he thought. *Charlie's zone.*

The sound of a voice froze him in his tracks. He couldn't make out what was being said, but it was definitely someone talking. A male voice, he realized after a few more words were said. Kevin's voice.

Kevin and Alma, meeting secretly in the night.

Tim could think of some very obvious reasons why two young people might secretly rendezvous in the middle of the night, and while survival camp didn't seem like the ideal place for a romantic encounter, he couldn't deny having entertained a few fantasies of his own in that regard…fantasies involving Devra.

It was an innocent enough explanation, yet his gut told him something else was going on. If it had been anyone else, he would have simply turned back and given them their privacy, but these two—the two who just didn't fit in, who seemed to be lying about their age, and who both had shown an unusual interest in Sarah and John… He had to know more.

He took a slow step forward, then another, straining to hear more. He could only make out a few words, but it was enough to tell him that Kevin and Alma weren't holding hands and making out under the stars.

It was a debriefing.

Tim took a couple more steps, but froze when he heard Kevin say, "…better get back."

Tim turned and hurried back toward the orange pinpoint of Alpha team's fire. It was an instinctive reaction, and it wasn't until he neared the camp that it occurred to him that he should have confronted the couple, demanded an explanation.

No, he told himself. *Not yet.*

If Kevin and Alma were up to no good, then confronting them by himself, in the middle of the night, was a very dangerous thing to do.

I've got to tell the instructors, he thought. *But what if they're in on it?*

That didn't seem possible. His own father had hand-picked Mr. Dickson to run the Academy, and probably some of the others as well. But Kevin and Alma *had* slipped through the background check, and that meant there might be someone on the staff helping them hide who they really were.

I need to know more. I need to figure out who I can trust. And I've got to do it soon, before they make their move.

He crept back to his shelter and slid into his sleeping bag. Randy was snoring, the noise loud enough to drown out the crickets. He lay there for a long time, pondering his options, feigning sleep when Alma returned.

He nearly jumped out of his skin when a hand fell upon his shoulder. It was Alma. *She knows*, he thought, panicking. "What?"

"Wake up," she said, softly. "It's your shift."

85

Chapter Thirteen - **Paula**

The echo of the shots rang in Paula's ears. Tim and Jack were dead. Natalie wasn't moving, and Paula didn't know if she was dead too, or simply unconscious.

Please God, let her be dead. Let her be safe from them.

C.J. loomed above her, fumbling with his belt, pulling down his jeans as he fell upon her, his weight pressing her to the floor, forcing the breath from her lungs in a single pathetic scream...

"Paula. It's okay."

The voice, a female voice that she knew she should recognize, pulled her out of the nightmare, but she could still feel the weight pressing down on her. She struggled to get out from under it, but even though her hands weren't tied, something was preventing her from moving.

"It's okay," the voice repeated.

Devra. It's Devra.

The realization brought her the rest of the way up to consciousness, yet there was still something pressing down on her. It wasn't very heavy, certainly not as heavy as a human body, but it was there all the same, pinning her to the ground.

By degrees, her awareness returned. It was Devra... They were at the Survival Academy... At Bravo camp...*I'm in my sleeping bag.*

"The shelter collapsed," Devra said, disgusted.

The shelter. Suddenly the weight pressing down didn't seem quite so oppressive. *That's all it is,* she thought. *My brain just ran with it.*

Her relief ebbed quickly as the import of what Devra had said finally sank in. "Collapsed?"

How was that possible? She and Devra had made the lean-to practically earthquake-proof, tying each joint several times with strips of bark, and driving the support stakes deep into the ground.

"Yeah," Devra muttered angrily. "One guess who's to blame."

Paula struggled out of the sleeping bag. The sky was still dark, but she could see that dawn was not far off. Devra was kneeling next to her, head-lamp blazing with light as she surveyed the wreckage. Around them, the others were stirring, roused by the disturbance.

"Blame?" Paula asked.

"Somebody cut through the ties."

Paula squirmed out from under the fallen canopy and switched on her own light. Sure enough, several strips of knotted bark lay scattered at the corners of the lean-to, near the upright support poles. The breaks where they had come apart certainly looked like they could have been caused de-liberately with the edge of a blade. "Who?"

"Who do you think?"

Paula's brain was still fuzzy from the rude awakening, so it took her a few more seconds to put two-and-two together.

Devra was accusing Clayton of sabotaging their shelter.

Following the evident food theft the previous day, Clayton had be-come the number-one target for scorn and abuse from his teammates. Paula had not joined in, though she certainly felt the red-haired boy de-served what he was getting. In fact, when she and Jack had approached Madison to report what was going on in their team, the student-instructor had thanked them and promised to keep an eye on the situation, which told Paula that Jack's hypothesis about the whole thing being a test was wrong, which in turn meant that Clayton probably really was a thief. For the rest of the day, the others—particularly the boys—had waged a covert campaign of harassment and mockery. The only thing that had probably spared Clayton an actual beating during the self-defense course was the fact that he had partnered with Jack, and Jack—God love him—was still professing Clayton's innocence.

Fool me once... Paula thought. "Are you sure it was him? Who was on watch duty?"

"Ha!" Devra said. "No one. Again. Clayton *forgot*—" She hooked her fingers into little air-quotes. "—to wake up his relief."

There was a muffled protest from the far side of the fire, and then Clayton was on his feet. "That's not true. No one woke me up. And I didn't do that to your shelter."

"I woke you up myself," Devra hissed. "I know you were awake."

"You did not!" Clayton's voice rose to a shout, loud enough to be heard all across the valley.

"You're a liar and a thief," Devra said, her voice as sharp as the blade of her survival knife. The intensity of the accusation surprised even Paula. "You should just drop out. Run home to mommy."

"Yeah," Dustin chimed. "Or do the whole world a favor and just kill yourself."

"Hey!" Jack jumped to his feet. "Cut it out."

"Oh, sorry," Dustin sneered. "Did I insult your girlfriend?"

Paula knew she should speak up, if for no other reason than to defend her cousin, but she hesitated. Clayton was bad news; even Jack knew it. Sure, Dustin had gone too far, but maybe they would all be better off if Clayton left.

Jack however, didn't need defending. He put his hands on his hips and met Dustin's stare. "Sounds like somebody's jealous."

Dustin's eyes went wide as the barb sank in, and then he was moving, rushing headlong at Jack.

Paula was too stunned to even gasp.

Dustin had three years and at least thirty pounds on Jack, but Jack stood his ground, right up until the last instant. Then, just before Dustin could tackle him to the ground, Jack side-stepped and hooked Dustin's foot with his own, sending the bigger boy sprawling headlong, facedown on the ground. Jack pounced after him, throwing his body across Dustin's back and wrapping his arms around Dustin's chest as the latter tried to get up, one arm coming up under Dustin's right armpit, the other coming over

Dustin's left shoulder. Jack hooked his hands together, squeezing tight, and as Dustin came up to hands and knees, wrapped both legs around Dustin's abdomen, and leaned back, pulling Dustin off balance and locking him up in the rear-mount position, just as Mr. Hickok had shown them the previous day.

Dustin evidently had not been paying attention during that class because instead of trying to break Jack's hold the way Hickok had shown them, Dustin was flailing his arms and thrashing his body, which only served to increase the pressure of Jack's arm against Dustin's carotid artery. If he did not break the hold or tap out, he would be unconscious in a matter of seconds.

Paula, still gaping in mute disbelief, caught a glimpse of movement behind her; Juan—Dustin's shelter-mate and friend—was lurching toward the two boys as they rolled on the ground. He might have intended only to break up the fight, but Paula couldn't take that chance. She leaped forward, putting herself in Juan's path, hands extended to ward him off. "Stop! Everyone just stop!"

Juan halted, more surprised than intimidated. Paula knew the pause would be short. Behind her, Dustin had ceased his thrashing, but whether it was a response to her command or because he had passed out, it was impossible to say, but she didn't dare look.

"Clayton. Go find one of the instructors. Ma or Mr. Hickok. Now. We'll let them sort this out."

Clayton just stared at her with big goggle-eyes, too petrified to move, but behind her, Dustin choked out a single word. "Wait."

Paula looked back and saw him tapping furiously against Jack's arm. Jack, after a moment's hesitation, loosened his hold enough to let Dustin speak.

"Wait," Dustin said again. "I'm sorry. I lost my temper. It's cool."

"It's not cool," Paula said. "This team is seriously messed up."

"No. Please don't. I'm on probation. Coming here was part of my plea deal. If I get kicked out, they'll send me to juvie. It won't happen again."

Paula was as stunned by this admission as she was by everything else that had happened. *Plea deal? That can't be right. That's not why my father created the Survival Academy.*

"Everyone just settle down," Devra said, her tone had lost some of its sharpness, as if she wasn't really sure what to do next, but refused to admit it. "Jack, let him go."

Jack hesitated, looking to Paula for guidance. She nodded and he relaxed his grip, allowing Dustin to pull away. The older boy got to his feet, and then, perhaps to restore some of his dignity, reached a hand out to Jack. "Sorry, man. I shouldn't have done that. Those were some pretty good moves."

Jack eyed him suspiciously. "You know what's worse than a thief? A bully."

Dustin bristled at the accusation, but did not withdraw the offer. "Got it."

Jack took the hand and let the older boy draw him to his feet.

"This is not okay," Paula said. "We're at each other's throats. Nobody trusts anyone."

"I trust everyone but him," Jenn said, pointing at Clayton.

"Fine. Maybe you're right about him. My point is that this isn't working. We need to tell Ma about this."

"Maybe I was wrong about him sabotaging our shelter," Devra said. "Maybe we just tied the corners too tight and they snapped. I shouldn't have made such a big deal about it." She pointed a finger at Clayton. "You're still a lazy, worthless piece of shit and everyone here knows it." She turned away. "Go check your snares. It's going to be a busy day. We may as well get an early start."

Paula frowned. She didn't understand why Devra was backing down. The situation was not going to magically resolve itself. If anything, it would probably get worse.

Chapter Fourteen - **Jack**

Jack breathed a sigh of relief when he saw the rabbits. Two of them, and that was only in the twitch-up snares he had set. If the rest of the team did half as well, they would not go hungry today.

Finally, something goes right for a change, he thought.

He still felt jittery, and a little nauseous, from the adrenaline of the fight—more of a tussle, really—with Dustin. He kept replaying the scene in his head, analyzing every detail and thinking about all the ways it could have gone wrong, and still might. Dustin's apology seemed sincere, but who knew how long that would last. Maybe Juan would goad him into getting some payback, or maybe the reverse of that would happen; maybe Dustin would use Juan as his proxy to insulate himself from possible expulsion from the academy.

Still, he had showed them that he wouldn't back down. Maybe that would be enough to keep them at bay. Bullies tended to avoid people who wouldn't be cowed.

Of course, the real problem wasn't Dustin, but Clayton. Jack glanced over at the red haired boy as he checked his snares twenty yards away. They were all empty of course. Clayton had given little thought to the placement of the snares, situating them in the open, where game animals could easily bypass them, which was evidently what had happened.

Clayton shrugged and headed in Jack's direction.

He wouldn't last a day in a real survival situation, Jack thought. *How did I wind up becoming his protector?*

The answer was the same now as it had been the previous day. It was the right thing to do. If Clayton was the thief, and now saboteur, that everyone seemed to think he was, then he deserved to face the consequences, possibly expulsion from the school, not mob violence. And he deserved a chance to defend himself.

When his father and John Thomas Rourke had set out on their odyssey across the nuclear wasteland, they had encountered gangs of brigands supporting would-be warlords. Men who were little better than animals—feral dogs—following the strongest alpha-male, living by the rule of might. Maybe it was human nature to revert to that kind of behavior when things fell apart. John Thomas Rourke, who could have easily risen to the top of that heap and ruled the world as king, had held himself to a higher standard.

Survival is more than just staying alive, Jack realized. *It's getting through whatever happens with your humanity intact. And that's the part nobody can teach you.*

He loosened the slip knot holding the nearest rabbit and placed the limp form on the ground so he could reset the trigger snare.

"You got one!" Clayton called out.

Jack glanced over and nodded. "Two, actually."

"You're good at this."

"Just doing it the way Ma showed us."

Clayton nodded. "Hey, listen. I want to thank you again for standing up for me."

Jack blew out a slow breath. "Yeah. Look, I don't know what's going on with you, but maybe you should talk to Ma about this. Especially if you didn't do anything."

"I didn't," Clayton said quickly. "None of it. Someone's doing this to make me look bad. I didn't take that food and I didn't sabotage anyone's shelter."

"Tell it to Ma. She's the only one who can fix this. I can't keep fighting your battles for you."

Clayton slumped. "Maybe I should just quit."

"That's up to you." Jack felt a little guilty for not offering an encouraging platitude. "Why are you even here?"

Clayton laughed but there was no humor in it. "My dad's idea. He thought I needed to toughen up."

Well, he's not wrong, Jack thought. "Have you thought about maybe trying a little harder?"

"I'm trying as hard as I can," Clayton replied, his voice pitching up into a whine.

It occurred to Jack that the boy standing before him was not the same obnoxious spoiled brat that had stood beside him during their reception to the Academy. The rough edges were gone, not merely sanded down, but pulverized, and what was left wasn't much. Jack recalled an old saying…something like "what doesn't kill you makes you stronger." That didn't seem to be working for Clayton. He wasn't getting stronger, just getting killed by degrees.

"Okay, look. If what you're doing isn't working, try something else. Try being smarter about it. Look at your snares. Why did you put them there?"

Clayton shrugged and grunted, "Dunno."

"If you had been paying attention when Ma talked about this stuff, you would have known to look for trails and burrows. High traffic areas. You want to set your snares in such a way that the animal can't avoid them."

Clayton nodded but Jack didn't know if he was getting through to the boy.

"If you start to contribute more, the others will respect you. It won't happen all at once though. You've got to work at it."

"Okay."

Jack frowned. It felt like he was beating a dead horse. "Come on. We should get back."

He headed over to the second rabbit his snare had caught and was dismayed to see that the noose had tightened behind the animal's forelegs. It was caught fast, but still alive. As they approached, it began twitching with fear.

"Uh, oh," Clayton said. "Now what?"

"It's breakfast."

94

"But it's still alive."

Jack reached out carefully and grasped the thrashing creature by the scruff of the neck. Ma had warned them that this could happen. It was important to check the snares often, not only to prevent the catch from spoiling or being taken by some other predator, but also to humanely spare the animals from suffering.

He took hold of the rabbit's ears, fully intending to break the animal's neck, but when he felt it shaking in his hands, he faltered. Hunting with snares was easy—just set them and let the trap do all the work—but this...taking a life, any life...deliberately, with his own hands, felt different somehow.

Maybe it's good that I feel this way, he decided. Taking the life of another creature, even an animal, even for the purpose of survival, was something not to be taken lightly.

Back in the real world, he never gave a second thought to the animals that lived and died so he could have cheeseburgers and pizza. It was all so neat and sanitized and distant. But that was a dangerous deception.

Life was hard, and for one creature to live, another had to die. Survival *did* mean more than just staying alive, it *did* mean keeping his humanity intact.

But that didn't mean there wouldn't be hard choices.

He twisted his hand sharply and heard the bones crack.

Chapter Fifteen - **Sarah**

"The rabbit runs out of the hole," Sarah murmured, threading the end of the rope through the smaller loop. "Around the tree, and back into the hole."

She tugged on the end to snug the knot in place, and the whole thing pulled through like when she untied her shoelaces. Exasperated, she threw the rope down. "I'm never going to get this."

"Just be patient, sweetie," Alma said.

Easy for her to say, Sarah thought. The rope she was using to practice knot-tying was stiff and bigger around than Sarah's fingers. Everything about the Survival Academy was made for bigger people.

The previous day had been a joke. The only part she had really enjoyed was the map reading and land navigation course. Everything else had been way over her head, literally, especially the self-defense class. Mr. Hickok had actually made her wrestle with one of the other kids—Thomas, a fifteen-year-old. Tim and Alma had both volunteered to work with her, but Mr. Hickok had insisted she go against someone else, someone who wouldn't go easy on her.

Mr. Hickok was mean.

Thomas had probably gone easy on her, too, but she had still failed again and again.

Alma had tried to reassure her. "Just remember what to do," she had said. "When you're older, it might come in handy."

"But what am I supposed to do now?"

Alma had given her a wry grin. "If someone tries to grab you, kick 'em in the shins as hard as you can."

Setting snares and drop-lines for fishing had been almost as bad. There was so much to remember. When she had gone out to check the snares in the morning, they had all been empty, and that was actually not such a bad thing since it meant she didn't have to cut up any furry little animals with her knife. She had hated doing that the day before. Instead, she had to watch as the others did it, and then choke down the pieces of squirrel meat that were passed to her.

I want to go home, she thought. *I hate it here.*

Alma picked up the rope and held it out to her. "Let's try it again. I'll go through it with you until you've got it down."

"Why bother?"

"Because, it's a useful skill, and once you teach your fingers how to do it, you'll never forget."

"How is it useful?" She couldn't imagine ever needing to tie a bowling knot—*what a dumb name,* she thought—back in her real life.

"Well, for starters, you've got to pass the knot tying course before you can go to the rappelling course."

"Fine. Then I won't go." Sarah couldn't think of anything she wanted to do less than slide down a rope.

"Come on, Sarah," Tim said, stepping in between her and Alma. "It'll be fun."

Alma's forehead creased in surprise at the interruption, but only for a moment. She took a step back. "That's right, sweetie. You'll love it. Here, Tim." She handed him the rope. "Why don't you help Sarah with the bowline?"

Tim snatched the rope, rather rudely, in Sarah's opinion, then turned to her. "It's easy. You just make a loop. The end goes up through the loop, around the rope and back down through the loop again. Then pull it tight." He did so, moving through the steps so quickly that, if Sarah had actually needed him to show her, she would have been lost, then just as quickly, he untied the knot and handed her the rope.

"Now you do it."

Grumbling, Sarah took the rope and gave it a twist to form the first loop.

"No, that's upside-down," Tim said, taking the rope out of her hand and reversing what she had done. He then proceeded to tie and untie the knot again before handing it to her.

Alma stood behind him, watching. She flashed a smile in Sarah's direction and nodded, mouthing something. *It's okay,* maybe.

"Just keep practicing," Tim said, handing her the rope. Then he leaned close and whispered, "Remember. Don't trust her."

Then he was gone, moving off quickly as if he was afraid to be seen spending too much time with a little girl. Alma watched her with a thoughtful expression. "Well that was certainly strange."

"He doesn't like you," Sarah said. She said it without thinking, only realizing her mistake when it was too late.

"Why is that?"

Sarah just shook her head. "I don't know."

"I'll bet he's just trying to be protective," Alma said. "We can't be mad at him for that, can we?"

She knelt down and put her hands on Sarah's shoulders. "It's okay that he doesn't trust me, sweetie. Being suspicious can actually save your life, but knowing who to trust can be just as important. Especially for you."

That was a strange thing for her to say, Sarah thought. "Me?"

"Because of who your father is," Alma said. She ruffled Sarah's hair. "I know all of this must seem very overwhelming, but someday, the things you learn here might really come in handy. Try your best and remember everything you can. Okay?"

Sarah managed to nod and then took the rope and dutifully did her best to follow the supposedly simple instructions. She kept her head down, eyes fixed on the task, so that Alma wouldn't see the fear that had blossomed behind her eyes.

Because of who your father is.

How did Alma know that?

Chapter Sixteen - **Natalie**

Ma had been right about one thing. Natalie would have killed for a plate heaped with biscuits and country gravy.

Actually, Ma was pretty much right about everything, but she had definitely been right about that.

Wilderness "cuisine" wasn't really that bad, much to Natalie's pleasant surprise. The only problem was that there wasn't much of it. The growling in her stomach reminded her of this as she sat with the rest of Charlie team at the instructors' camp, listening to a block of instruction on "wilderness first responder training," better known as "first aid"—one of three round robin sessions on the morning schedule, the others being knot tying and meat preservation, respectively. They would have to get a lot better at setting snares to make use of the latter.

Still, aside from the occasional rumble in her belly, the Survival Academy experience was starting to grow on her. She wasn't enjoying it, not by any means, but she knew that, when the hellish ordeal was finally over, she was going to like the person she would become.

If I can do this, she thought, *I can do anything.*

The realization had dawned, not surprisingly, during the self-defense class when the helplessness she had felt on the night of the kidnapping had risen up like some undead creature from a horror movie.

And she had beaten it.

I'm not helpless. I never was. I'm strong.

Whenever her father reminisced about the world that existed before the Night of the War, he tended to be self-deprecating.

I was such a nebbish, he would say, slipping into that old antiquated dialect that sometimes accompanied those trips down memory lane. *Without John Thomas Rourke, I wouldn't have lasted a day.*

Unlike Rourke, a trained intelligence operative and survival expert, Paul Rubinstein, a magazine editor, had led a sedentary life, peering at the world through thick spectacles; definitely not what anyone would call a physically imposing specimen.

Yet, she knew there was more to the story. Yes, Rourke had saved her father countless times, but not because her father had been a helpless victim. He might not have possessed the skills, not at first, but he had always possessed the *will*. It had taken the crisis of the war to bring it to the surface, but it had been there.

She was his daughter. It was in her, too.

There was nothing the Survival Academy could throw at her that she could not overcome through sheer will power.

She wondered if Paula felt the same way. There hadn't been a chance to bring it up at the family meeting the night before, and she had a feeling Paula might not feel comfortable discussing it in front of the others.

She tried to rein her musings in and focus on the instruction—first aid was definitely more interesting than tying knots—but her thoughts kept drifting to the activity that would occupy the balance of the day: climbing and rappelling.

When Ma and Mr. Dickson had mentioned this part of the instruction, she had been apprehensive. The rational part of her knew the instructors wouldn't put them in real danger, but accidents still happened. She definitely had not been looking forward to it. Now however, she was eager to face her fears, tackle them head on.

She managed to hold her own as they worked in groups, assessing and treating a variety of simulated injuries, but was relieved when they were dismissed for an early lunch break, and not just because she was famished.

As the group began to disperse, she hurried over to where Bravo team was just finishing up with the food preservation class. Natalie eyed the meat arranged on the smoking racks—simple tripods of mesquite sticks with the smaller branches whittled down to form barbs on which the meat could be hung—set up around the edge of the fire. The placement was key.

"You want to dry the meat out," Ma explained. "Do not cook it. The smoke will help preserve it, and it will add flavor."

Lean cuts from bigger animals—like deer and elk—were best, but smoking could be used to preserve small game and fish as well. Thin slices with all the fat removed—animal fat could go rancid during the smoking process, ruining the finished product—hung up to dry at the edge of a fire. Ma had scooted some of the coals out from beneath the blaze, and then dumped a handful of wet mesquite chips onto them to produce a delicious smelling smoke.

That hadn't helped Natalie's appetite any.

Evidently Bravo had managed to catch all the game that had evaded Charlie's snares. By mid-afternoon, Bravo would have enough jerky to last a couple days.

Maybe I can bum a piece from Paula, she thought as she waved to her cousin.

"Nat!" Paula came over and gave her a hug.

The display of affection wasn't out of character for Paula, but Natalie could sense that something was amiss when the embrace went on a few seconds longer than she expected. "What's wrong?"

Paula let out a slow breath. "Nothing really. Just this place. It can get to you."

Natalie understood or thought she did, but before she could probe deeper or broach the issue that had prompted her to seek out her cousin's company, someone else joined their informal meeting.

"Hey girls."

Natalie's heart did a little flutter as she turned and saw the identity of the uninvited arrival. Matthew Kestrel. He met her gaze, smiled, then inexplicably turned to Paula. "I heard you had some drama this morning."

Paula registered a mild surprise. "Wow. News travels fast."

It took Natalie, who was still riding the roller coaster of excitement, nervousness and a touch of disappointment, to parse this exchange. "Wait, what? Paula, what happened?"

Matthew nodded his head in Paula's direction. "That loser Clayton Reynolds smashed her shelter during the night."

Natalie gaped at her cousin. "That happened?"

"And then your brother decided to defend the creep," Mathew went on, now looking at Natalie, just a little judgmentally.

Paula shrugged. "There's more to it than that. We're dealing with it."

Natalie knew her cousin well enough to recognize the finality in the statement. Paula was done talking about it. Matthew however, was not.

"Clayton needs to go. He's trouble."

Natalie turned so that she was standing next to Paula, facing him. "Why do you even care?"

"A guy like that is bad news for all of us. Who knows what he might do next." He gave a little laugh. "I mean, they gave us knives, right?" It was an ominous pronouncement, but his smile never wavered. "Anyway, I just wanted to check on you. If you need anything, let me know." His gaze lingered on Natalie a few seconds longer, as if to let her know that she was included as well.

Natalie however had already moved past swooning for Matthew Kestrel. She leaned close to her cousin. "Spill it. What happened?"

Paula recounted the tale, beginning with the apparent theft of Jenn's food ration the previous day and ending with the confrontation between Dustin and Jack. Natalie was stunned at how bad things had gotten for Paula's team and it was impossible to ignore the common factor. As Matthew had said, Clayton was trouble.

"Why did he sabotage your shelter? It sounds like you and Jack were the only ones not ganging up on him."

"It might have been aimed at Devra, the girl Tim likes."

That was also news to Natalie, but she didn't doubt Paula's intuition on the matter. Paula noticed little things like that. Natalie wondered if Paula knew about her own crush on Matthew, and then decided that, of course she did, and felt a little embarrassed by it.

"Or," Paula went on, "it could be just one of those weird coincidences. Maybe it's not Clayton at all. Maybe he's just unlucky."

"It sounds like a lot more than just bad luck. And what's Jack thinking?"

"Sticking up for the underdog, I guess." Paula was silent for a moment. "I…" She faltered.

"What?"

"I've just got a bad feeling about this. Not just this. Other stuff, too. I keep thinking about…"

Natalie was pretty sure she knew what Paula kept thinking about. "Me, too. Well, we learned our lesson from that, right? Nobody's ever gonna sneak up on us again."

Paula nodded. "Be careful, Nat."

"You, too."

Chapter Seventeen - **John**

"Can you believe that guy?"

John looked up from the short length of rope he was using to practice his knots and followed Philip's gaze across the breadth of the instructor's camp to a pair of figures moving away, presumably headed back to their own encampment. He recognized Jack immediately, but it took him a moment longer to put a name to the second—the red-headed kid named Clayton. John wasn't immediately sure to which one Philip was referring.

"What about him?" he asked, cautiously.

"He's a thief. Everyone's talking about it."

John frowned. Evidently, he was the last to be included in *everyone*. He hoped Philip wasn't talking about his cousin. "Who's a thief?

"That Clayton kid. What a piece of shit."

John was a little relieved that the accusation was not directed at his cousin, but it was disturbing news nonetheless.

"I guess he was spying on the girls when they went to use the latrine, too."

"Wow. Are they gonna kick him out?"

Philip shrugged. "I don't know. I don't think anyone's told on him yet."

John nodded slowly in understanding. Like every other kid, John had been raised to believe in the importance of honesty and respect for authority. If you saw somebody misbehaving, you told an adult—a parent, teacher or policeman. And, like every other kid, John knew that if you did that, you would probably be labeled a snitch or tattletale, which was something the adults never really understood. Of course, he had not actually seen Clayton doing anything wrong, so it wasn't his place to make the report, but he wondered why Paula and Jack, who were on Clayton's team, hadn't gone to Ma or one of the other instructors.

"Huh," he said, which was about all he could say. It wasn't really any of his business anyway. He spotted Madison heading out with a thick coil of rope slung over one shoulder, and saw the opportunity to change the subject. "Are you as stoked as I am about climbing?"

"I know. I love climbing. I mean like trees and stuff."

John had done a little scrambling on back country hikes, but never anything that would involve ropes or safety equipment. Like many of the other things they had done, rock climbing and rappelling promised to be awesome but maybe kind of scary.

John was hoping for both in equal measure.

Chapter Eighteen - **Tim**

"Before you can learn to climb, you need to learn to fall." Bob Decker, the lead instructor for the rock climbing familiarization course, grinned mischievously. He reached into a large plastic tote and took out several pieces of green rope. He handed the bundle to the nearest student, who happened to be Tim's shelter-mate, Randy. "Pass those around. Everybody gets one."

As the ropes began to circulate, Decker went on. "Okay, you're probably saying, 'I already know how to do that. I was falling before I was walking.' What I really mean is that you need to learn to overcome your fear of falling. Your fear will paralyze you—"

"So will a fall," Randy muttered.

Despite the interruption, Decker gave a good natured laugh. "That's what I'm talking about. You're already afraid to fall, and that means you're afraid to climb. But falling isn't what you need to be worried about. Hitting the ground is what kills you, and if you pay attention to this block of instruction, that won't be a problem. Fear of falling, fear of heights...whatever you want to call it... It's all in your head. The only way to get it out of your head is to take the plunge."

A nervous chuckle rippled through the group. Unlike the round-robin training sessions in the morning, all three teams were receiving instruction together, and after this, they would all face that primal fear of hitting the ground. Tim guessed the class was pretty much evenly split between those who were eager for it and those who were positively petrified. The knowledge of what was coming had made it difficult for some of them to focus on the morning classes. Tim was by no means afraid to climb, but he had made an effort to stay in the moment. Pretending to splint a broken leg or being able to identify an animal by looking at photographs of paw prints and droppings might not have been very exciting, but in a real survival situation, those skills might mean the difference between life and death.

The bundle of ropes reached Tim and he peeled one off before passing it along. It was heavy duty half-inch line without any elasticity, at least ten feet long, the ends melted and wrapped in tape. The others in the group were fidgeting with theirs, coiling them, wrapping them around their waist like a belt. Sarah stared at her piece in wide-eyed disbelief, but Alma patted her on the shoulder.

Tim frowned. *What are you up to?*

He thought back to what he had seen the night before, Alma and Kevin, meeting in the darkness outside the camp. They weren't simply two strangers passing the time, socializing, flirting. He had not yet figured out what they were doing, but if it involved Sarah and John, then it was his business.

He kept flashing back to the night of the kidnapping, remembering how C.J. had lured them in, gaining their trust with a pretense of friendship. His instincts had told him something was wrong then, but he had ignored them and only by a miracle had he lived to regret it. He would not make that mistake again.

And yet, he knew this situation was different. His own father had created the Survival Academy, vetted the instructors, and established a broad range of security protocols. The students—the survivors—weren't just people who wandered in off the street.

Am I just being paranoid?

Maybe. Maybe he was being overprotective, but Sarah and John were family. It was his responsibility to look out for them, not this pair of strangers. Terry Hickok, the weapons instructor, had told them during the firearm's familiarization presentation, "Better to be judged by twelve than carried by six."

Translation: Better to be paranoid and wrong, than naïve and wrong.

"I won't lie to you and say that climbing is one hundred percent safe," Decker continued, "nothing in life is. But we don't let fear of dying keep us from living. Show of hands, how many of you had to fly to get here?"

Tim raised his hand. Everyone else did, too.

Decker nodded. "So, you spent a few hours in an aluminum tube traveling five hundred miles an hour, seven miles above the earth. After that, you got in a metal and fiberglass box and traveled down a highway at about sixty miles an hour. Planes crash. Not very often, knock on wood, but they do crash. Cars crash every day. But we don't let the possibility of what might happen paralyze us. If we did, we'd never get out our front door. But we also take steps to manage the risk. Like learning how to operate cars and planes, maintenance and inspections to make sure everything is working. Seat belts. It's the same with climbing. You train, and you make sure your equipment is working.

"Climbing is about trust. Trusting your partner, trusting your equipment, trusting yourself. The only way to learn that trust is to fall. Now let me be clear about one thing. A fall is not the same as a plane crash or a car wreck. Yesterday, when you were doing PT, Ma had you doing push-ups until your arms gave out, right? That's how we get stronger. We push ourselves to the limit, and then next time, we push a little further. When you're climbing and you come up against a tricky problem, you might fall several times before you figure out how get past it. That's how you improve."

Tim raised his hand and at a nod from Decker, said, "What if you don't have any equipment?"

"Good question. In a survival situation, you're probably not going to have a harness and a rack of gear, but if you've been paying attention these last couple days, you know that one of the items you should never be without is rope. If you've got rope, you've got all the equipment you need." He took another rope segment from the tote and held it in the middle with his left hand, allowing the ends to hang down. "All right, follow along with me. I'm going to show you how to make your own field-expedient climbing harness."

He placed the fist holding the rope against his left thigh, then reached behind his back with his right, grabbed one end, and brought it around his waist from behind. Tim did the same, crossing the ends below his navel and threading one end under the other in a half-hitch, just like tying his shoe, and then, following Decker's lead, looped it around once more.

Decker took the left end, passed it between his legs and brought it around his left thigh. "Slide it under the rope around your waist, right about where your pocket is. Wrap it around twice and then throw the end over your shoulder." He demonstrated, comically exaggerating the action. "Now repeat the process with the other side."

Tim did as instructed. As he pulled the ropes taut, he felt the fabric of his trousers bunching up against his crotch. As if sensing his discomfort, Decker said, "I know, it's like getting a wedgie from Hell. And it's about to get even worse. Take hold of the ends and then squat down to get all the slack out. Boys, you'll want to be extra careful to make sure nothing gets caught under the rope, if you know what I mean. Trust me, that's not a mistake you'll make twice."

Tim joined in the uncomfortable laughter that comment elicited, then remembered to check on Sarah's progress. With Alma's assistance, she had followed every step dutifully, but because of her slim build, her rope ends were twice as long as everyone else's.

"Good," Decker said. "Now, tie a square knot in the center and secure the loose ends to your sides with another half-hitch. Congratulations. You have just created a Swiss seat climbing harness. You'll be using this for rappelling off the tower and then later on, you'll do some actual—"

A shriek tore through the air above the group, cutting Decker off in mid-sentence. It lasted only a moment, and then died as abruptly as it had begun. A cold chill shot down Tim's spine as he realized who had been the source of the scream. He didn't know how, but he recognized the voice.

It was Madison.

Chapter Nineteen - **Paula**

Paula's first impulse was to run. A scream meant something bad had happened, and in the instant she heard it, her primal brain shuffled through the card deck of possible bad things and transported her back in time, back to the night she lived over and over again in her nightmares.

She bolted to her feet, ready to flee, but just as quickly, her rational mind caught up to the panic beast and put on the brakes.

I'm safe here. They can't get me here.

But someone had screamed. Someone, in the woods but not too far away, had cried out. Who?

She glanced around at the alarmed questioning faces of her teammates and the other students, all of whom were staring in the direction of the disturbance. Who was missing?

Paula's breath caught in her throat. Madison. She had left to go set belaying lines for the rock climbing course.

Madison had fallen. It was the only explanation.

Paula ran, but she did not flee away from the cry. Instead, she ran toward it, toward the looming sheer cliff wall beyond the tree line. She was vaguely aware of others running alongside her. She saw Tim, sprinting ahead of her and heard a rising chorus of shouts behind. She ignored everything else and focused on the path ahead. The trees thinned and then she saw, directly ahead, the supine form of the student-instructor.

Madison lay motionless, arms and legs splayed out crazily, amidst a tangle of climbing rope and colorful aluminum clips and carabineers. In her mind's eye, Paula could see the chain of events that had preceded this moment. Madison, scaling the wall, setting pitons—or whatever those devices were called—in tiny cracks in the limestone face, clipping her rope in so that if she fell, she would be safe, just like Decker had promised. But then she had fallen and the gear that was supposed to protect her had failed.

No. This isn't supposed to happen.

Paula skidded to a stop, joining the growing circle of astonished students who had, like her, come running with no clear idea of what to do once they arrived. They all stood back, as if repelled by an invisible force field, each one waiting for someone else to take the lead, or for Madison to simply get up and tell them all she was fine. But Madison wasn't moving. No one was moving.

Paula felt like screaming. *Somebody do something.*

Just a few hours ago, they had all been pretending to treat injuries in the first aid portion of the round robin training, and now, confronted with the real thing, everyone was rooted in place, caught by the inertia of letting others solve problems like this.

Somebody do something.

No. Not somebody. Me.

She lurched forward again, violating the impromptu buffer zone around the unmoving girl.

Someone behind her shouted, "Don't touch her. You might make it worse."

"She knows what she's doing," replied another voice, Natalie coming to her defense.

Do I? Paula wondered as she knelt beside Madison. She had no idea where to start.

I just went over this, she chided herself. *I've read dozens of books on emergency medicine. I'm going to be a doctor for Pete's sake.*

She did know but for some reason, when she tried to call up the memory, she drew a complete blank. Book learning and practice simulations just weren't the same thing as treating a real live patient.

What if I do something wrong? I could do more harm than good.

She stared at Madison's face, closed eyes, nostrils gently flaring as she breathed, and tried to remember what to do first.

Breathing…yes, that's good. She's breathing, so she's alive.

Checking for breathing was also one of the steps in assessing an unconscious accident victim—the ABCs of first aid they had just learned about. "A" stood for airway and there was a good reason why that was the first thing you were supposed to check, even when the patient appeared to breathing on their own. Madison might have a mouthful of blood and broken teeth, or her tongue might fall back and block the top of her windpipe and just like that, she could suffocate.

Paula reached out and laid her fingertips on the edges of Madison's jawline. If the girl had sustained a cervical injury in the fall, any movement could conceivably leave her a quadriplegic, but if her airway failed, she would die. Emergency medicine sometimes required choosing between bad options. Paralyzed was better than dead. Or at least that was what doctors told themselves. Their permanently disabled patients did not always agree.

"You're going to hurt her," someone said.

Paula did not ignore the warning but she did not let it stop her. She slowly, carefully, lifted Madison's jaw up, tilting her chin skyward. There was a soft gasp as Madison drew in a breath through her mouth. Paula checked the girl's open mouth for blood, saw none, but quickly swiped a finger between Madison's teeth, just to make sure.

Nothing.

Okay. A-B-C. The airway is stable. She's breathing. "C." Circulation.

She pressed two fingers against Madison's neck and felt a steady pulse.

Circulation. Check.

As she went through the procedures, Paula felt calmer. Her heart was no longer pounding in her chest like a jackhammer. Her breathing took on a slow rhythm, and as the primal part of her brain finally relented, she was able to access the memories of what to do next. *Check for signs of shock and bleeding. Check for broken bones. Check for spinal injuries and head trauma.*

There were no obvious lacerations or abrasions, which was a little odd considering that Madison had probably fallen from at least twenty or thirty feet up. The heavy fabric of her camp uniform had probably protected her skin, but it might also be concealing subdural injuries. Moreover, Paula knew she was only seeing half of Madison's body. To properly assess her injuries, she would have to get a look at Madison's back.

"I need some help here," she said, without looking up. "Tim. Nat. I need you to hold her head steady. We have to roll her on her side. Check her back for injuries."

"No!" It was the same voice of protest. Paula couldn't tell who it was but she wasn't about to let herself be distracted. She knew what she was doing now, knew how to minimize the risk.

"Paula, stop!"

Paula flinched as if stung. This time, the voice was different, and she did recognize the speaker. It was Ma. She looked up; meeting the woman's gaze, but did not move her hands. "I can do this. I know what to do."

Ma's expression was, as always, hard as granite but there was something in her eyes, admiration, pride even. "I know you can, hon. But let us do it."

Decker and another of the instructors were right behind her, carrying an olive drab pole litter.

Paula suddenly felt as if someone had let all the air out of her. The interruption felt like an accusation. Worse, it had taken from her the sense of purpose that had dragged her away from the dark memories of that other crisis, where she had been completely helpless, unable to do anything to save herself or her loved ones.

She sagged, embarrassed and exhausted, and offered no resistance when Tim and Natalie lifted her to her feet.

As the two instructors took her place and began their own assessment of Madison's injuries, Ma addressed the group. "We've got this under control. What I need all of you to do now is form into your teams and then move as teams back to Camp Zero. Team leaders; make sure you do a head count when you get back to camp. All activities for the rest of the day are on hold. I'll have a hot meal sent out. For now, the best thing you can do is to just sit tight."

When no one moved, she added, with her customary curtness, "Go!"

Everyone around her snapped to and began separating into teams, but Paula remained frozen in place, staring at Madison's inert form. She wanted to protest her dismissal. *I knew what I was doing. Why put us through this training if you're going to just push us aside when we try to use it?*

Ma stepped in front of her, blocking her view. "You did good, hon. Everybody else was just standing there gawking, but you did exactly what you were supposed to do. You'll make a helluva doctor someday."

Paula blinked at her. "Is she going to be okay?"

Ma pursed her lips. "Tough to say."

The naked honesty of the statement shocked Paula. She was used to adults always sugar-coating everything and making empty reassurances. Moreover, Madison did not appear to be seriously injured.

Paula tried to peer over Ma's shoulder in order to get another look at the stricken girl, but Ma shifted to prevent her. "Your team is waiting," Ma said, her voice no longer encouraging but stern, strictly business. "Get going."

The harshness of the woman's tone made Paula jump a little, but she composed herself and turned to join Jack and her other teammates for the trek back to Camp Zero.

Chapter Twenty - **Jack**

The hike back to Camp Zero was surreal. Jack was aware of the landscape around him and the rest of team, aware even of making a conscious effort to pick out terrain features and the remnants of the trail they had used when moving to the wilderness campsite, but it all seemed like something that was happening to somebody else. He felt like a spectator in his own body, completely detached from the experience. When they reached Camp Zero, he went into the team tent, dropped his ruck on the ground and sat down, still in a daze. The image of Madison, lying there, unconscious, broken, was seared into his mind's eye.

He gradually realized that Clayton was speaking to him. "This is crazy. They were going to make us do that."

"What?"

"Climbing. The rope stuff. That could have been you or me."

Jack struggled to grasp what the other boy was trying to tell him. "Are you serious?"

"She knew what she was doing, and look what happened? This place is insane. We shouldn't be doing stuff like that. It's too dangerous."

Jack was speechless. Madison's accident should have made everything else that had happened seem utterly insignificant, but somehow Clayton had found a way to make it about him.

Maybe everyone is right about this guy.

"Could you just leave me alone for a little while?" he said, trying to keep the ire out of his voice.

Clayton stared at him in apparent confusion, which rapidly gave way to hurt. "I thought you…"

He left the sentence unfinished and turned away abruptly, as if he was about to cry and didn't want Jack to see. Clayton's hurt feelings were the last thing Jack cared about at the moment. One thing he had said though stayed with Jack.

She knew what she was doing.

What had gone wrong?

He tried to take a mental step back, visualizing the scene like a detective. He considered her position on the ground at the base of the cliff, the ropes and protective gear strew randomly around her. He thought about the climbing process as Mr. Decker had described it in the class.

Climbing was dangerous, but the protection was supposed to mitigate the risk. In a fall, the climber would only drop twice the distance between them and the last piece of protective gear—twenty feet at most—before the rope caught them, or more precisely, before their belaying partner pulled in the slack and put on the brakes. But the shock of the climber's weight could conceivably pull a piton or camming device loose, doubling the fall distance—along with the amount of load on the next piton in the line. If one piece of gear failed in a fall, the odds of the next one pulling loose would be that much greater. Was that what had happened to Madison?

Jack sat up suddenly, remembering something else Decker had said.

Climbing is about trust. Trusting your partner, trusting your equipment, trusting yourself.

Climbing was not a solo endeavor. It was a partnership; one person on the wall, one person holding the belaying rope.

Who was Madison's belayer?

Not one of the other instructors; they had all been present at Decker's lecture, assisting the students with their Swiss seats when Madison's scream had sent everyone running. If not them, then who?

The obvious answer was that Madison *had* been climbing alone.

He had heard of extreme athletes who, craving the adrenaline rush of a true life-or-death challenge, climbed without any gear or ropes, but it was hard to imagine Madison choosing to be so reckless, particularly when she was supposed to be setting the example for everyone else.

Madison would be able to explain when she regained consciousness, though it seemed unlikely that he would be permitted to pose the question himself. He wondered if any of them would be told the truth, especially if Madison had been breaking camp safety rules. Maybe it would be one of Ma's teachable moments, a grim reminder of the importance of following procedures, but the question of motive would probably not be addressed.

He glanced across the tent to where Paula was sitting, similarly occupied with her thoughts, and felt an overwhelming urge to talk to her. To share his dark musings. To know that he wasn't alone in thinking such things. He rose, intending to approach his cousin, but at that moment, Ma stuck her head into the tent.

"I need everyone outside," she said, with none of her usual abrasiveness. Then, just as quickly, she was gone.

Jack exchanged a glance with Paula, and read the foreboding in her eyes. He felt it too. He waited for her near the tent entrance, and as she joined him, he heard her whisper. "I'm sure she's okay. She wasn't hurt that bad."

Jack nodded, but there was no enthusiasm in the gesture. Paula, who was studying to be a doctor, could speak with some authority, but she had only spent a few seconds assessing Madison. She didn't have x-ray vision, and couldn't know what sort of hidden injuries Madison might have sustained.

The other teams were likewise filing out of their tents and taking their place in the assembly area. Ma waved a hand in the air. "No need for a formation," she called out. "Just gather 'round me."

It was another ominous departure from the norm, and the knot of dread in Jack's gut began radiating numbing waves that left him feeling weak in the knees. It wasn't even that much of a surprise when Ma cleared her throat, and said in the same subdued voice, "I've got some bad news."

Chapter Twenty-One - **Sarah**

"Madison's injuries were more severe than any of us realized," Ma said, quietly. "She was taken to the hospital in Pecos, but never regained consciousness."

Sarah struggled to understand what Ma was trying to say. *Never? What does that mean?* She looked up at Alma and saw tears streaming down her friend's face. "What's wrong with Madison?" she whispered.

"She's not coming back, sweetie."

"Did she...die?"

Sarah was no stranger to death or to the careful way that grown-ups talked about it. Nobody liked to say "dead" or "died." They said things like "passed away" or "not coming back." Just last week, her parents had told her that Grandpa Wolf was in heaven with God, but she knew what that really meant. Now, she would add "never regained consciousness" to the list of...not lies exactly; more like a candy-coating on a bitter pill.

Alma knelt down and hugged her.

"But Madison can't be dead," Sarah whispered into Alma's shoulder. "She's too young."

"Young people can die, too sweetie," Alma said. "I wish it wasn't true, but it is."

As the low murmur of grief began to grow, Ma cleared her throat again. "This is a terrible tragedy. We take every precaution here at the Academy, but accidents will happen, to any of us, at any time. Nobody is ever immune, and the people that we love can be taken from us without warning. How we deal with it afterwards is just as important as how we prepare for it.

"John Thomas Rourke created this school for one reason: to prepare you all for a truly worst case scenario. Whether that's the collapse of civilization or a local disaster, one thing you can count on is that if you find yourself in a survival situation, some people around you have probably already met their maker. Could be your friends, even your parents. The world isn't going to let you hit the 'pause' button so you can have yourself a good cry." She paused, took a breath, and then added, "And we're not going to either."

She let that sink in for a moment. "Mr. Dickson has contacted your parents and explained the situation to them. They all agree that this is one of those teachable moments I told you about. We're not going to ignore our feelings or pretend nothing happened, but we're not going to let grief make us quit. You all came here to learn how to survive anything. Well, you're going to survive this."

There was another low murmur of conversation and then Matthew said, "You called our parents? All of them?"

Ma nodded. "Mr. Dickson made the calls."

Matthew nodded slowly as if this was a matter of great importance, then looked around at some of the other kids.

"Here's what's going to happen," Ma continued. "We're going to take the rest of the day off so you can have some time to process this. Talk to each other about what you're feeling. We've got a hot meal coming out in a bit, which I'm sure is something all of you are ready for. After that, get a good night's sleep, and tomorrow morning, we'll get back on track."

"Are we still going to have do the climbing?" someone—a boy—asked. Sarah couldn't tell who it was, but when she heard Matthew whisper, "Dumbass," she knew the questioner had to be the hated Clayton Reynolds.

Ma's expression registered mild irritation. "Being able to climb and descend a rope is a skill you may need to survive. At the risk of making light of this tragedy, completing the climbing and rappelling course is even more important now. You're all probably feeling a little extra anxious about it now. The only way to get over that is to face your fears. Get back on the horse. However, that being said, we will be conducting a thorough investigation into the incident to determine what when wrong and make sure it never happens again."

She clapped her hands together, perhaps to signal that there would be no further discussion. "That's all I have for you right now. I'll see you at dinner."

Ma turned on her heel and walked away, leaving the stunned group to decide for themselves how best to deal with their grief.

Alma's way was to continue hugging Sarah. "It's okay to be sad," she whispered.

"I know," Sarah said. She was sad, but in the same, matter-of-fact way that she felt sad when she heard about bad things happening to people far away. *Am I supposed to feel something more?*

"Sarah."

She looked up to see Tim approaching. He looked pale, as if the news of Madison's death had drained all the blood out of him. "We're having a family…" His gaze flickered to Alma for a moment then came back to her. "I need to talk to you. Privately."

She heard that too-familiar note of distrust in his voice, but nodded and pulled away from Alma in order to follow her cousin.

"I'm here if you need to talk later," Alma called after her, but Tim immediately threw a cold glance over his shoulder and took Sarah's hand.

"She won't."

Chapter Twenty-Two - **Natalie**

Natalie was still reeling from Ma's grim announcement when Paula approached and whispered in her ear. "We need to talk. Family meeting, ASAP."

She had answered with a mute nod. After such a tragedy, what better place to begin the process of grieving and healing than in the collective embrace of the family circle.

She was surprised by how hard it hit her. Madison was little more than a stranger, certainly not someone she considered a close friend. Maybe it was the fact that they were so close in age. She had overheard Sarah's whisper.

Madison can't be dead. She's too young.

The accident was a reminder that death could find any of them, anytime.

They went to the same spot where they had met at the end of the first night at Camp Zero. Natalie could not believe that it had not even been two full days. Everything was different, *she* was different, but whether the change was good or bad, she could not say.

She thought that might be the reason Paula had called for the meeting. It was not.

"Something's wrong about all this," Paula said in a grave tone.

"No kidding," Jack remarked. He seemed particularly shaken by the news of Madison's death.

Paula pushed forward. "I was the first to reach her. I assessed her. Her injuries weren't serious. Hell, I'm not even sure what her injuries were, but they absolutely were not life-threatening."

For a few seconds, no one knew what to say. Natalie finally broke the silence. "Paula, I'm not saying you don't know what you're doing, but you only had a few seconds with her. There could have been internal bleeding, or severe head trauma. I've heard stories about people walking away from car accidents and then dropping dead from internal injuries they didn't even know they had."

"Maybe," Paula replied. "But I think I'm right about this."

"What exactly are you saying? If Madison wasn't injured, then how did she die?"

"What I want to know is what she was doing out there by herself in the first place," Jack said before Paula could respond to Natalie's question. "You're never supposed to climb without a belayer."

Natalie struggled to reconcile these seemingly unrelated pieces of the puzzle. Her brother was absolutely right about the irregularity of Madison being alone at the time of the accident, a fact made all the more suspicious by the ultimate outcome. "Unless…"

"Unless what?" Paula and Jack asked, almost simultaneously.

"What if she wasn't alone?"

The others looked at her expectantly.

"What if there was someone else there," she went on. "Someone who was supposed to be on belay, but didn't catch her when she fell. Then to make sure she couldn't tell anyone what happened, he went to the hospital and made sure that she never woke up."

Paula frowned. "Nat, that's pretty far-fetched."

Natalie knew Paula was right, but the comment still rubbed her the wrong way. "You were the one who said something fishy was going on."

"So who was it?" Jack asked. "All the instructors were with us when it happened."

"It would have to be someone that wasn't camping with us. Maybe another student-instructor that we didn't know about." Natalie sighed. "Okay, I'll admit, it's a reach. It explains the 'who,' but not the 'why.'"

"I might have an idea about that," Tim said, speaking for the first time. "I agree with Paula. There's definitely something suspicious going on here.

Maybe Madison discovered what they were doing, and that's why they had to silence her."

"They?" Natalie asked. "It sounds like you've someone specific in mind."

Tim nodded. "Kevin and Alma."

Chapter Twenty-Three - **John**

"Last night," Tim explained, "I followed Alma out of our camp. She met with Kevin in secret. I couldn't hear much, but it was definitely suspicious."

The others nodded at this revelation, but John did not join in. "So what? Maybe they just wanted some time alone. It doesn't mean anything."

"I've been watching them both," Tim said. "They haven't said two words to each other. If they know each other, maybe from before they came here, they're going to great lengths to hide it."

"So?"

"Look at the facts," Natalie said. "Two people, who come here, pretending to be strangers to each other, probably lying about their age. And what's the first thing they do when they get here? Buddy up to the President's kids. And then something happens to Madison."

"You think she caught on to them?" Jack said. "Maybe she saw them last night, too? Heard something she wasn't supposed to."

John couldn't believe what he was hearing. "This is crazy. Kevin was practically standing next to me when Madison's accident happened. Alma was with us, too."

He looked to Sarah for confirmation. Her eyes were wide, similarly incredulous at the wild accusations, but she nodded. "She was with me the whole time."

"They would have to have an accomplice," Jack went on. "Someone working on the inside. Someone who could get them past the security screening process and back up their story."

"You think this might be a plot aimed at John and Sarah?" Natalie said.

John did not like the way his older cousins were talking about him as if he wasn't even there. "You guys are making a big deal out of nothing."

"I think it's a possibility we can't ignore," Tim said, answering Natalie and seeming to ignore John. "If there's even a chance that John and Sarah are being targeted, we have to do something." Then he added, "We can't ignore our instincts again."

"So what do we do?" Natalie asked. "Should we tell Ma?"

"If there is someone on the inside, it could be anyone. Even her."

"Ma wouldn't let me do first aid on Madison," Paula added gravely, as if this was a critical piece of damning evidence.

John was speechless. *First, Kevin and Alma are secretly conspiring against us. Now Ma is in on it, too. They're completely paranoid. Maybe it's because of the kidnapping.*

But what if they're right?

Madison was dead, after all, and the circumstances were mysterious. His instincts told him Tim was wrong about Kevin, and probably Alma, too, but that did not mean that Madison's death was an accident, or that they could trust everyone at the Academy.

"So who *do* we trust?" he asked.

No one had an answer. Tim broke the long silence. "We have to be ready. If we're wrong…" He shrugged. "But if we're right, an attack could come at any time."

Natalie shook her head. "That's not going to cut it. We have to go on the offensive. We need to contact our parents."

"How are we going to do that?" Jack countered. "We're cut off out here."

"We could sneak away tonight."

The suggestion was met with more uncertain silence. *We could do it,* John thought. But then Tim shook his head. "Someone would notice if all six of us disappeared. That might tip off the bad guys, and then we might be the next ones to meet with an accident. But one of us might be able to make it out if the others covered for him."

"Or her," Natalie added.

"Two of us," Paula said. "Me and Tim."

"Why you?"

"We're about to make some very serious accusations, and I don't want to do that until I'm absolutely sure we're right. We need some proof if we're going to make people believe us. If I can get to the hospital where they took her, and take a look at her chart...or her body." She paused a beat as if the very thought appalled her, but then went on. "It should still be there. I'm sure they'll want to do an autopsy. I'll be able to tell if her death was accidental, or if something happened to her on the way there."

"The hospital?" Natalie said. "In Pecos. How are you going to get there?"

"We'll hike to the Academy headquarters compound and steal a Jeep from the motorpool."

"Steal a Jeep?" Natalie shook her head in disbelief.

Paula shrugged. "My father founded this place; so technically, it's sort of like the family car. At worst, I'll get grounded for the rest of my life."

"I can think of a lot worse. But that's not what I mean. I know you know how to drive, but there's a lot more to stealing a car than that."

"Maybe not," Jack put in. "I doubt they're too concerned about security this far out in the middle of nowhere. They probably leave the keys in the vehicles. That way, when someone wants to use one, they don't have to go looking all over for them."

Paula threw a satisfied nod in Jack's direction. "I'll need Tim to help me navigate."

"What if you discover that Madison's death *was* an accident?" John asked.

"I don't think that's going to be the case, but if it is, we'll just come back, hopefully before anyone notices we're missing."

As crazy as the plan was, John had to admit that it at least allowed for the possibility that there was no diabolical conspiracy. That Madison's death, while tragic, was not a deliberate murder, and that Kevin and Alma weren't assassins waiting for a chance to strike at the First Family.

"It's settled then," Tim said. "After dinner, Paula and I will sneak away. Sarah, you'll need to cover for me. Can you do that?"

Sarah's pinched expression suggested that she was not happy about the request. "You want me to lie?"

"Just say that I'm out practicing nighttime navigation. That's the actual truth. Sort of."

Though clearly unimpressed with the rationale, Sarah nodded. "Fine."

"Okay." Tim clapped his hands together, signaling that, with the plan of action finalized, the meeting was nearly at an end. "Jack, you cover for Paula. Nat and John, you just keep an eye on Kevin. We'll leave after dinner."

John held his tongue. No one would have listened to him anyway. He still wasn't convinced that there was some conspiracy, but one way or another, after tonight, the truth would come out.

Chapter Twenty-Four - **Tim**

Supper, while simple—hot dogs and burgers, with baked beans, potato salad and fruit juice boxes—was like a gift from heaven. For Tim however, it was more than just comfort food. He was storing up energy for the long night ahead. After everyone was fed, he went back for more, stuffing his pockets with juice boxes, which he hoped would provide a quick energy boost during the five mile hike back to the Academy compound.

Five miles. That was how far it was on the map anyway. He and Paula ought to be able to cover that distance in less than two hours, provided they kept a steady pace, with no rest stops, and didn't get lost or deviate too much from the mostly straight line course he had plotted. That, even more than the physical exertion, would be the tricky part.

It looked straightforward enough on the map. There was a saddle pass through the mountain ridge, the same pass they had driven through on their way to Camp Zero. If he kept Polaris on his right, more or less at the two o'clock position, while they ascended the mountain slope, they would find the pass. The terrain itself would guide them in the dark, provided of course that he got them in the ballpark.

As the satiated group dispersed, returning to their respective tents, Tim caught Paula's eye and held up his hand with all his fingers extended. *Five minutes.*

She returned a nod and then, as they had discussed, passed the message along to Jack and Natalie. Tim found Sarah, not surprisingly walking with Alma, and managed to give her a surreptitious signal as well. Her evident lack of enthusiasm for their plan concerned him but he knew any further attempt to convince her would be futile and probably jeopardize their mission.

Next, he sought out Matthew Kestrel. Even though he had not interacted with Tim that much, preferring the company of the older boys on the team, Matthew had shown himself to be both a natural leader and an able strategist. Tim had considered sharing his suspicions with Matthew, but ultimately rejected the idea, fearing that Matthew might try to take control of the situation and torpedo their planned excursion.

Better, he decided, *to keep it in the family.*

He found Matthew, as expected, sitting in the Alpha team tent, surrounded by the older boys. They were talking about Madison's accident, speculating about what might have happened as if they might, with the gift of 20/20 hindsight, undo what had been done. Matthew met his gaze as he approached.

"Hey, grab a spot," Matthew said.

"Thanks, but I think I'm going to get some air. I thought I might take a little night hike, practice my celestial navigation skills."

"Cool. That's a good idea. We should all go."

Tim's heart skipped a beat. "No. Umm, I mean. Sure, you can. But me and Paula already made our plans. Three's a crowd and any more than that? I mean, what's the point, right?"

"Gotcha," Matthew said. "Well, don't get lost out there."

"If I do, I guess I'll get to practice my survival skills a little." He managed a laugh, which Matthew echoed. "Anyway, don't worry about us. We could be gone a while."

Matthew nodded but there was a knowing gleam in his eye, as if could see right through Tim's subterfuge. "Good luck."

"Thanks." Tim hurried away, stopping only long enough to shoulder his rucksack. While the added weight would almost certainly slow him down on the hike, the gear inside might prove lifesaving if they did get lost, or if weather conditions changed unexpectedly. Then, without further delay, he exited the tent and circled around to the opposite end, away from the fire, where he found Paula already waiting.

"Ready?" she asked.

Tim suddenly felt very unready, but he nodded. "Let's do this."

Before they took a single step however, he turned his gaze heavenward and began looking for the Big Dipper. He located the two stars that formed the end of the bowl of the constellation, followed them to the slightly dimmer North Star, and then made a quarter turn to the left. "That way."

They started off at a determined pace, which seemed more prudent than trying to sneak away. That way, if anyone spotted them, they could easily fall back on their "night hike" cover story. Evidently, no one did notice their departure, and in a matter of just a few minutes, the only visible sign of the camp was the faint orange glow of the fire. Then that too winked out.

It took a few minutes for their eyes to adjust to the darkness, but soon, they were able to make out the silhouette of the mountain ridge ahead of them, and differentiate between the dark green of vegetation and the lighter-colored rocky soil. Harder to make out however, was the uneven surface beneath their feet, and for nearly fifteen minutes, they groped their way forward blindly, hands outstretched in front of them to avoid colliding with trees as they took tentative steps forward, probing the terrain with their boot soles to avoid tripping or spraining an ankle on a loose rock.

"This is going to take all night," Paula finally said. "We need light."

"They might see it," Tim cautioned.

"It's a chance we have to take. But I think we're far enough away from camp that no one will see a red light."

A red lensed flashlight, they had learned during that first night navigation course, was the preferred choice for use at night in the wilderness because red light—the longest wave-length, shortest frequency on the spectrum of visible light—did not rapidly deplete the protein responsible for night-vision. If they used white light, and then for some reason had to turn their lights off, it would take up to forty-five minutes for the photoreceptors in their eyes to build up sufficient amounts of the night vision protein, rendering them effectively blind during that period. Even now, they were still feeling the effects of light exposure from being in camp.

For the same reason, red light was harder to see, especially at longer distances, particularly to people whose eyes were not adjusted to the darkness. As long as they kept their lights pointed away from the camp, and no one was actively looking for them, they would probably go unnoticed.

Tim switched on the red LED in his headlamp, showing what lay directly ahead, though beyond about thirty feet, the red light revealed little. He did a quick check to confirm their bearings, and then they were off again, moving at a considerably faster pace. His hopes that they might be able to make up for lost time were soon dashed however when they reached the base of the mountain ridge and came to a dead stop.

After nearly an hour of hearing nothing but the rhythmic crunch-crunch of his footsteps, Tim found the silence both awe-inspiring and a little unnerving. The sky above had never seemed quite so big, and he had never felt quite so insignificant—a mere speck of dust in the endless universe.

I wish I could just stay right here for a while, he thought, but then dismissed the notion. They were racing against the clock and every second of delay threatened their chances of success.

He consulted the map, studying the contour lines that indicated the changing elevation of the mountain range. Closely spaced contours indicated a very steep ascent, virtually impassable even under ideal conditions, but they would also give them something to look for as they traversed the slope. The contours were spaced widest along the approach to the saddle and the pass that would afford them the easiest route, but in the dark, it was difficult to guess which direction they needed to go to reach it.

Tim found Polaris again, and oriented himself directly toward it for a moment. Although he could not see very far along the ridge, the slope and the angle at which it deviated from north, gave him a rough idea of where they were on the map.

He recalled one other thing Ma had mentioned about the difference between true north—the axis around which the earth turned—and magnetic or compass north. True north was the same no matter where you went on earth, but magnetic north not only changed depending on where you were, but was constantly drifting. Every map included the declination—the adjustment in degrees required to compensate for the difference—but it was also important to check the date on the map, since the location of the earth's magnetic north pole might change as much as twenty-five miles per year. Fortunately, all maps were oriented to true north, so there was no need for Tim to perform additional calculations.

"The pass should be about a quarter of a mile south of here," he said. "If it's not, and the pass is north of us, we'll eventually run into a sheer cliff. Then we'll just have to backtrack."

"And we'll have wasted another half an hour," Paula said.

Tim could only shrug. "At least we sort of know where we are."

They started out again, following the terrain and staying off the loose rocks on the hillside. Five minutes later, Tim's prowess as a navigator was confirmed when they spotted the parallel lines of the Jeep trail. Tim let out a whoop of joy and started jogging along the meandering track.

Paula was less sanguine. "Now for the hard part."

Chapter Twenty-Five - **Paula**

The ascent was grueling, and as the minutes ticked away, Paula realized how foolhardy they had been to think they could, in the short span of one night, sneak out and return unnoticed. It had been nearly two hours since they set out from Camp Zero, and they weren't even through the pass yet. If they could not find a way to make up some time, they would be lucky to make it as far as the Academy headquarters before dawn.

This was a mistake, she thought. *Why did we think this was a good idea?*

Her feet were on fire. She could feel blisters rising on the soles of her feet, as if her very skin was boiling over from the friction. Her calves ached and her shins felt like someone was squeezing them in a vise clamp.

She revealed none of this to Tim, however. She was not about to let herself appear weak in front of her younger brother. He was probably suffering just as much as she was, and voicing her misery might send them both spiraling into unrecoverable defeatism.

We're doing this for a reason, she told herself. *We aren't wrong. The danger is real.*

The danger, or at least the possibility of it, *was* real. She kept reciting the litany of…not facts exactly, but suspicious developments, as a way to keep her mind occupied.

I saw what I saw when I was assessing Madison's injuries. And now Madison is dead.

Tim saw what he saw when he followed Alma to her late night rendezvous with Kevin. Both of them are lying about who they are. And both of them are trying to get close to John and Sarah.

We aren't wrong. The danger is real.

The mantra kept her moving when she didn't think she had anything left to give. She had to keep going, for Madison. For John and Sarah. For all of them.

Their parents had sent them to the Survival Academy so that they would be ready to face just such a situation. Failure was not an option.

When they crested the pass, she almost broke into sobs. Far off in the distance—though if the map was correct, it wasn't actually that far at all—she could see the lighted buildings of the Survival Academy compound.

"Almost there," Tim said. He was hoarse, breathless, but there was no mistaking the satisfaction in his voice. "It's all downhill from here. Well, at least until we come back."

"I think..." She faltered, took a sip from her water bottle. "I don't think we need to worry about trying to make it back. One way or another, we're calling home. If we're wrong, we admit what we did and accept the consequences, but if we're right, and I know we're right, we can ride back in a police car."

"We aren't wrong," Tim said.

Paula smiled, wondering if he had been tuned into her thoughts during the arduous ascent. *Maybe I was saying it out loud.*

Downhill felt easier, though that was probably as much due to the fact that they could at last see their destination as it was the fact that gravity was now on their side. The Jeep trail was easily distinguishable, even in the dark, so they switched off their red lights and picked up the pace.

The compound was quiet. The building exteriors were well-lit, but most of the windows were dark. "That's odd," Paula murmured as they drew near.

"What's odd?"

"I would have thought with the accident, this place would still be hopping. It looks like there's just a skeleton crew here."

"That's good for us. It'll make it easier to borrow one of those Jeeps." He pointed to a row of nearly identical vehicles lined up to one side of the administration buildings.

The close proximity of this intermediate goal, and the end to the long and arduous hike, should have buoyed Paula's spirits, but instead the sight of the Jeeps opened up a new batch of anxieties.

Back at Camp Zero, the thought of stealing—or as Tim had said, borrowing—a Jeep and driving it to the nearby town of Pecos, had seemed pretty straightforward. Now however, it seemed like an impossible task. She had driven a car before, though always closely monitored by either one of her parents or a driving instructor. Judging by their feedback, she was nowhere near experienced enough to test for her license. And she had no experience whatsoever with *borrowing* a vehicle.

Tim crept to the nearest Jeep and tried the handle. The door opened and the interior light flashed on.

"Shhh!" Paula whispered, though in fact, Tim hadn't made a sound. "Get in. Quick. Someone will see the light."

She darted to the other side, opened the door and realized only then that she wouldn't be able to get in without first dropping her rucksack. She did so, shoving it in the back seat, and Tim followed suit. It was only after they were both seated with all the doors closed, returning them to relative darkness that Paula realized she was sitting in the passenger's seat.

"Looks like I'm driving," Tim remarked.

"Very funny. Are the keys in it?"

Tim groped the steering column for a moment. "Not in the ignition. Check the glove compartment."

As Paula did that—it was empty save for the service manual—Tim flipped down the sun visor. Something fell from it, but Tim caught the object as it dropped. "Got 'em. Jack was right."

She stared at the key protruding from Tim's fist, then held out an open hand to take it from him. There was no turning back now.

They switched sides and a few seconds later, Paula found herself ensconced behind the steering wheel. After one final check to make sure that nobody had noticed them, she slotted the key into the ignition and gave it a twist.

The engine turned over right away, but she inadvertently held the key in the 'start' position a few seconds too long, unleashing a strident grinding sound that broke the stillness. At the same instant, the seat-belt warning began pinging and the dashboard lights came on. Paula jerked her hand away from the key as if it had become red hot and the engine immediately settled into a quiet purring idle.

She cringed. "Do you think anyone heard that?"

Tim returned a helpless shrug. "Nothing we can do it about it. Just go."

She put her seatbelt on to silence the incessant trilling, then found the gearshift lever and fought with it a moment before remembering to depress the brake pedal first. A dull red glow flashed behind them as the brake lights came on. The gearshift lever finally relented and she moved it to the "R" position, which caused the red light to change to a brighter white light.

Paula muttered a curse under her breath. Evidently, it was impossible to be sneaky when *borrowing* a vehicle.

Backing up was the part of driving she hated most. Everything was backward. If you turned the steering wheel one way, the front end of the car swung the other. The trick, or so she had been told, was to avoid making any turns until the last possible moment.

She let her foot off the brake and the Jeep immediately began rolling backwards. Panicking, she stomped the brake pedal again, and the vehicle lurched to a complete stop, throwing her back into the seat.

"Calm down," Tim said. "You're doing fine. Just take it slow."

"Not helpful," she said, gritting her teeth and easing the pressure off the brake pedal. The Jeep crept back a few more feet, and when she thought she was clear, she turned the wheel cautiously to the left. She was pleasantly surprised when the Jeep went exactly where she intended it to.

She brought the vehicle to a much gentler halt, and moved the gear-shift to the "D" position. The back-up lights went out and when she slipped her foot off the brake pedal, so did the bright red light, returning them to darkness. With an equally light touch on the gas pedal, she began rolling forward.

Slow and smooth, she told herself, echoing one of her father's old mantras.

"Slow is smooth, and smooth is fast," John Thomas Rourke would often say, and she knew what he meant. Rushing led to mistakes and mistakes meant starting over.

Once they were on the road, she increased the pressure on the pedal, watching the speedometer needle creep up to thirty miles per hour, then forty, and feeling the acceleration in her bones.

I'm doing it, she thought. *I'm driving!*

And, she added after a moment's consideration, *I just stole my first car.*

Chapter Twenty-Six - **Jack**

Despite the hearty meal and the absence of any organized activities on the schedule, no one seemed ready to retire for the night. The evening dragged on, with everyone stuck in a grief induced holding pattern. Jack was acutely aware of this fact as he endured Clayton's presence at the fireside.

"It's too bad Madison got killed," he told Jack. "I kind of thought she was pretty."

Jack stared back in disbelief. "Whereas if she had been ugly, it would be okay?"

"Well, no. I didn't mean that. I just… I meant she was pretty and it's too bad she's not around anymore."

Jack wanted to tell the other boy to get lost. Actually, he wanted to deck him. His hands had unconsciously curled into fists. But letting Clayton run his mouth provided a welcome distraction from the matter that was really weighing on Jack's thoughts.

Paula and Tim had been gone for nearly two hours. If things were going according to plan, they were probably well on their way to Pecos, and hopefully, to learning the truth. And if things weren't going as planned?

The worst part was not knowing.

He was pretty sure that his cousins hadn't been caught or their unauthorized sojourn discovered by the staff. If that had happened, he and the others would probably have already been hauled in front of Ma or Mr. Dickson to explain their actions. But there were plenty of other things that might have gone wrong. Tim and Paula might have gotten lost in the dark, or been injured or attacked by a mountain lion or a bear or a pack of coyotes.

Suffering Clayton's inappropriate attempts at conversation was not exactly preferable to worrying about his cousins, but it did at least keep his mind occupied.

"I'm surprised no one has blamed me for it," Clayton went on. "They blame me for everything else."

Somehow, this comment seemed even more offensive to Jack. Madison was dead. Whatever indignities Clayton had endured paled into insignificance alongside that.

"Can we not talk about it," Jack said, fighting to keep his anger in check.

Clayton gave a little shrug. "I guess." The ensuing pause did not last long. "I don't want to climb. It's dangerous. In fact, I don't even want to be here anymore."

Jack felt like screaming, *Then quit. Do us all a favor and go home.* But he didn't. If Paula and Tim were right and something bad was happening, none of Clayton's concerns would matter. The Survival Academy was already finished. By morning, they would probably all be on their way back home.

He gradually became aware that Devra was standing above him, looking down at him... no, she was staring at Clayton, studying him the way a cat might contemplate its prey from a distance. When she realized that Jack had noticed, she turned her attention to him. "Where's Paula?"

Jack's heart skipped a beat. It was the first time anyone had acknowledged his cousin's absence. "She went for a night hike," he said, trying—to his ears, unsuccessfully—to sound nonchalant. "With Tim," he added. "I don't know when they'll be back, but she said not to wait up."

He thought Devra, as Bravo team leader, might be angry that she had not been consulted before the unauthorized outing, but the other girl just nodded slowly.

"Interesting," she said. Her gaze returned to Clayton for a moment, and then she walked away without further comment.

"She just took off?" Clayton asked.

"It's no big deal," Jack lied.

"I'm surprised you didn't go with her."

I wish I had, Jack thought.

Chapter Twenty-Seven - **Sarah**

"How are you doing, sweetie?"

"I'm okay," Sarah mumbled, trying to raise her eyes to meet Alma's questioning gaze. She knew that if she didn't Alma might get suspicious. She managed a moment of eye contact and a smile, then looked away again.

"It's tough losing someone," Alma went on, putting an arm around Sarah and giving her a hug.

Sarah flinched involuntarily. Not because she was afraid of Alma, though if Tim was right, Alma was a bad person, plotting something terrible, and her attempts to act like a caring friend were just a horrible lie designed to get Sarah to lower her defenses. Her reaction had nothing to do with that. She recoiled because she felt guilty. Guilty for keeping secrets from her friend, guilty for almost believing the worst.

They'll see, she thought. *Tim and Paula will find out they were all wrong, and everything will be okay.*

"Sweetie, what's wrong? Are you sad about Madison?"

Sarah shook her head without thinking, but then seized on the opportunity. "I guess so."

"Is it something else? You can tell me, you know." When Sarah did not respond, Alma went on. "I know your cousin doesn't like me very much, but he's just looking out for you."

The comment caught Sarah off guard and she sucked in a breath. "But what if he—" She caught herself.

"What if he what?" Alma asked.

Sarah felt like crying. She hated this, hated having to lie to her friend and pretend nothing was wrong.

"Where is he, anyway?" Alma said. "I haven't seen him for a while."

Sarah bit her lip. She knew what she was supposed to do. Tim's words echoed in her brain.

You'll need to cover for me. Just say that I'm out practicing nighttime navigation. That's the actual truth. Sort of.

Sort of?

"Alma, how can you tell good people from bad people?"

"That's a tough one, sweetie. A lot of times it's obvious by the things they do, but some bad people are very good at hiding what they are."

The words sent a chill down Sarah's spine. "Then how can you know who to trust?"

"You just have to go with your instincts." She spoke the words slowly, trailing off at the end. Then, without warning, she took Sarah's shoulders and turned her so that they were face to face, and when she spoke, there was nothing friendly or comforting in her tone. "Sarah, where's Tim?"

"He…ah…" Sarah couldn't seem to draw enough breath to get the words out. "Went for a hike. Night navigation practice."

Alma continued to stare into her eyes. "Sarah, it's very important that you tell me the truth. Where is Tim?"

Sarah took several breaths before answering. "He went for a hike," she said, slowly, deliberately. "To practice nighttime navigation."

Without letting go of Sarah, Alma raised her head and looked around the campsite, searching faces. "Paula," she whispered. Her eyes came back to Sarah. "Paula and Tim are missing. Where are they, Sarah? What are they doing? You have to tell me. It's serious."

"I did tell you." Sarah's voice rose an octave.

"You're hiding something." She paused, took a breath, and then tried to bring back some of her earlier empathy. "Sarah, what's going on? Do your cousins think that I'm a bad person? Is that what this is about?"

Sarah couldn't help herself. She nodded.

"I'm not a bad person, Sarah. You have to believe me. Do you?"

Sarah wanted to. She nodded.

"I'm here to keep you safe," Alma said. "Now, you have to tell me everything."

And Sarah did.

Chapter Twenty-Eight - **Natalie**

When she saw Alma grab Sarah's shoulders and start interrogating the young girl, Natalie knew that all their suspicions had been correct. There were still a lot of pieces missing from the puzzle, but the abrupt change in Alma's demeanor was all the proof she needed.

Is this it? Are they going to make their move now?

She rose and started across the camp toward the pair. She had no idea what she would do when she got there, but she couldn't stand by and watch any longer.

Someone stepped in front of her and she barely had time to stop. It was Matthew. "Hey, Natalie. How's it going?"

"Sorry. Can't talk right now." She shifted left to go around him but he sidestepped to block her again.

"Is everything okay?"

She felt like screaming at him, or maybe at the universe for its lousy timing. *Why now?* She tried again to maneuver around him but he did not relent. Instead, he put out a hand, not quite touching her.

"Natalie, I can help."

That stopped her. "Help? What are you talking about?"

"There's something going on, right? That's why your cousins ran away?"

"They didn't…" She looked him in the eye, wondering if he might be just the ally she needed to confront Alma. "How much do you know?"

He shook his head. "Not much. Just that Tim and Paula snuck off and the rest of you are trying to cover for them. I figure there's got to be a good reason for that, and that it's probably somehow related to what happened to Madison. Are they going for help?"

"Something like that." She looked past him, and saw Alma take hold of Sarah's arm, and set out for the last tent in the row—Charlie team's tent.

Kevin's tent, she thought. "I have to go."

"Let me help. Just tell me what's going on."

Natalie was torn between the urgency of the situation and the uncertainty of her suspicions. Could she trust Matthew? Would he believe her, or would he interfere, perhaps insisting that she take the matter to someone in authority?

"We don't think Madison's death was an accident," she said, speaking slowly and choosing her words carefully. "And we think Kevin and Alma are lying about who they really are."

"Kevin and Alma," Matthew said, nodding. "What makes you think that?"

His tone was almost patronizing. *He doesn't believe me.* She considered pushing past him, rushing to intercept Alma before she could warn Kevin. "They're definitely lying about their age. And they've been meeting in secret at night."

Matthew's eyebrows furrowed. "That's all you've got?"

"If you don't believe me, then get out of my way."

"I believe you," he said, a little too quickly. "I'm not sure how you get from there to Madison being murdered though. Why not tell Ma, or one of the other instructors?"

"Because they might be in on it. We don't know who to trust. That's why Paula and Tim left."

"Okay, so what's your plan?"

"There's no time for a plan," she said, growing exasperated.

"Natalie, listen to me. I believe you. And I can help, but we need to be smart about this." He offered his hand again.

Behind him, Alma had vanished into the Charlie team tent, taking Sarah with her. Kevin was inside that tent and probably John as well. But Matthew was right. She had no plan, and without a plan, there was no hope of stopping…whatever it was she was trying to stop.

She took his hand. "Okay. Smart. How do we do that?"

146

"We're going to get reinforcements." He offered a smile that was probably meant to be reassuring, but there was a dangerous gleam in his eyes.

"Reinforcements?"

"You came here with family," he said. "So did I."

Something about the way he said it made Natalie think he wasn't just talking about his brother, and the fact that he too was keeping secrets left her feeling even more vulnerable.

Chapter Twenty-Nine - **John**

"Kevin!"

John looked up from his cards as Alma threw back the flap and stuck her head inside the Charlie team tent. The suddenness of her appearance triggered an immediate and wholly irrational guilty response in him and he quickly pressed the playing cards to his chest as if to hide them.

Technically, he wasn't doing anything wrong. Philip had been teaching him how to play blackjack as a way to pass the time and keep from thinking about the earlier tragedy, but while they weren't actually gambling for real money, he still felt like he had been caught with his hand in the cookie jar. Alma however, did not even look his way.

"Kevin," she repeated. "We need to talk."

Kevin, who had been laying on his sleeping bag on the other side of the tent, jumped to his feet. His normally easy going expression had been replaced by a look that was equal parts irritation and concern. "What the hell are you thinking?" he asked through clenched teeth.

"It doesn't matter now. We're blown. It's time to hit the panic button."

Alma stepped through past the opening into the tent, and John realized that she was not alone. Sarah was with her, her tiny hand clutched in Alma's fist.

John gaped at his sister in disbelief. Alma was not exactly dragging her, and Sarah wasn't struggling to get free, but there was a look of terror on Sarah's face, as if *she* was the one who had gotten caught doing something wrong. John thought about what Tim had said earlier, how Kevin and Alma couldn't be trusted. He had not wanted to believe it, but what else could explain this?

Kevin dropped his voice low. "Jeez, Alma." He looked around furtively at the curious faces of the other students then gestured to the entrance. "Outside."

"It's too late for that. We've lost containment. Two of them snuck off."

John let out an involuntary gasp. Alma knew that Tim and Paula were gone. Had Sarah let something slip, or had the woman figured it out on her own? Either way, a storm of trouble was about to descend on the Rourke clan. He looked around the tent, searching frantically for Natalie, but she was nowhere to be found.

"What's going on?" Philip asked in a low voice that only Jack could hear.

John had to take several quick breaths before he could manage his own whispered reply. "My cousin thinks those two are up to something."

"Who? Kevin and Alma?"

John nodded. "He saw them talking last night. They're…" He didn't know what else to say. Despite Tim's bad feeling, there was no evidence to indicate that the older students posed any sort of threat. The truth was, he genuinely liked Kevin, who treated him as an equal rather than dismissing him as a little kid, the way Tim and Jack and other older boys sometimes did. "I don't know."

Philip blinked at him.

"We need to hit the panic button," Alma repeated. "Lock this place down until we can account for them."

Kevin seemed to consider this request for a moment. For the first time since the intrusion, he turned and stared directly at John. The look lasted only a moment, but it made John want to crawl into his sleeping bag and hide.

"The principals are safe," Kevin said after returning his attention to Alma. "Let's not overreact. The others just ran away, right?"

"*Just* ran away?" Alma echoed, incredulous. "They're in the wind."

Kevin raised his hands in a placating gesture. "The principals are our primary concern. The staff can take care of the others. Have you told them?"

"No. I came directly to you."

"Okay. Damage control. Tell Sandy." He turned away from her. "Everyone. Outside for an accountability formation."

John's heart dropped a few more inches. There would be no hiding the absence of Tim and Paula now. Still, something about Kevin's reaction nagged at him. His actions weren't what John would expect from someone who was planning to cause trouble. A burglar didn't call the cops when he discovered the door to the house he planned to rob was wide open. He turned to share this observation with Philip, but the other boy was already gone.

Crap!

John joined the line of bewildered students filing past Kevin and Alma on their way out of the tent. He could not meet the gaze of either but he did steal a glance at his younger sister. Sarah was staring dejectedly at the ground.

As he moved out into the dimly lit assembly area, he heard Kevin shouting, repeating the command for a general muster loud enough for everyone in the camp to hear. Ma and one of the other instructors sitting near the fire pit jumped to their feet in obvious alarm, but neither of them did anything to contradict Kevin.

What's going on? Why are they letting him act like he's the boss?

"Sandy," Kevin said, striding toward the head instructor. "We need a headcount. I think a couple kids have gone AWOL."

Ma went instantly pale but she recovered and then bellowed at the top of her lung, "You heard the man. Accountability formation, now. Assemble by teams."

John felt like he was walking in a dream. Nothing about the camp seemed familiar now. He stared at the cluster of his fellow teammates and had to look twice to recognize any of them. He spotted Natalie, along with Matthew Kestrel, moving in from the edge of the camp. Philip appeared, as if materializing out of thin air, and ran to intercept his brother. Natalie, whose expression told John that she was thinking the same thing he was, didn't seem to notice.

Seeing his cousin gave John his first measure of relief. *Okay. Nat's here. She can explain.*

He moved over to the Charlie team formation and took his place. Most of his teammates were already there since they had been the first to receive the order, but even though Alpha and Bravo teams were still emerging from their respective tents, the absence of Tim and Paula was glaringly apparent. Even more conspicuous, Kevin and Alma did not take their place with the other students, but remained in front of the group, standing alongside Ma and the other instructors. Alma continued to hold Sarah's hand.

Ma waited until the last of the stragglers were in place before speaking. "We're missing two." She seemed to be staring right at Natalie. "Tim and Paula Rourke. Where are they?"

Natalie stood her ground, defiant. "They're trying to find out the truth about what happened to Madison." She stabbed an accusatory finger toward Kevin. "And who those two really are."

"Who they *really* are," Ma replied, her tone even more abrupt than usual, "is your teammates." She paused and then, with a visible effort, managed to dial back her ire. "What happened to Madison was a terrible accident. That's all there is to it."

"Bullshit!" Natalie retorted.

John gasped. Profanity wasn't a big deal—everyone said a four-letter word now and then—but most kids knew better than to swear in front of an adult.

Natalie wasn't finished though. "Something is going on here and you're either too blind to see it, or you're in on it."

Dead silence followed the accusation. John felt a tingling sensation in his extremities, as if the air was filled with electricity.

Alma stepped forward, one hand extended as if to calm a frightened animal. "You're right, Natalie. We've been keeping a secret from you."

"Alma!" Kevin's warning was as sharp as it was immediate.

"We can't do our job if they don't trust us," Alma said, though she kept looking at Natalie. "The truth then. Kevin and I are here to protect John and Sarah. You know why, Natalie, but it's probably best if we don't talk about it out in the open."

Of course, John thought, and immediately felt some of the tension ebb away. Kevin and Alma were Secret Service agents. He and Sarah had been told that they wouldn't have a protection detail but evidently their father, the President of the United States, had changed his mind.

Now it all makes sense.

Natalie however did not back down. "Prove it."

This time, Alma did look back to Kevin. He frowned but shrugged. "Why not? It can't possibly make this any worse." He dug into his pocket and brought out a slim leather wallet which he flipped open to reveal a gold shield with a five-point round-tip star at the center, along with accompanying government issued identification. John recognized the Secret Service badge immediately, but he did not need to see it to have his doubts wiped away. He knew intuitively that Kevin was telling the truth.

"Satisfied?" Kevin asked.

Natalie, evidently, was not. "You could have saved us all a lot of trouble by just being straight with us."

"We had our orders," Alma said. She looked down at Sarah. "This is the way your parents wanted it. You're here to learn to be self-sufficient. To work without a net. Now you know the truth. We can't put that genie back in the bottle, but maybe now we can focus on doing what we came here for."

"This still doesn't explain the things that have been happening here," Natalie said, persistent. "Madison's death? Paula says there's no way she could have died from that fall. And what about all the other things that have been happening?"

"That's enough." Ma raised her hands, her sharp tone returning with a vengeance. "In all my time as an instructor here, we've never had to deal with a situation like this. I'm going to call Mr. Dickson and recommend that we cancel the course. As soon as we round up our strays, you're all going home."

The harsh announcement hit John like a slap. Ma's reaction was completely unfair. It wasn't his fault that Alma and Kevin had lied about who they were, wasn't his fault that Tim and Paula had snuck off. If the adults had just had been truthful, none of this would have happened. There was no reason to punish everyone.

Ma appeared ready to make good on her threat. She unclipped a walkie-talkie from her belt, but as she raised it there was a flash of movement from somewhere off to John's right, and then Ma staggered back.

John's brain struggled to process what he had just seen. A tree limb seemed to have sprouted from Ma's chest... No, it was a crude spear. But why was it—?

A scream went up and then the camp erupted into chaos. The other students scattered, crashing into one another in full panic mode. A few ran toward Ma and the others who had been standing at the front of the formation. John recognized Philip and Matthew, and the girl Tim liked— Devra Merlin. All three were brandishing their camp issued knives. Before John could even begin to wonder why, Matthew drove his blade at Kevin's throat.

The Secret Service agent threw up a hand to block the thrust and all John saw after that was a splash of red.

Blood.

Matthew had just stabbed Kevin.

Devra slashed her blade at Alma, just as the woman thrust Sarah behind her protectively. There was another gush of dark blood.

Matthew and Devra. Philip. Knives. *What?*

Philip was charging another of the instructors, a man half again as tall as he. There was not a trace of hesitation in his stride.

Philip, what are you doing? John's mouth worked, trying to form the question, but no sound came out.

Natalie leapt into motion as well, racing into the fray, but instead of attacking anyone, she ducked under the reach of Devra's knife and, without slowing, scooped Sarah into her arms. John heard her voice above the screams.

"Jack. John. Run!"

The sound of his name was like a word in a foreign language amidst the inexplicable pandemonium, but it shook John out of his paralysis. He jolted forward, pivoting away from the scene of carnage and focusing on Natalie's retreating form. She was heading for the woods, following a pack of other students. As he sprinted after her, he caught a glimpse of the formation area. Bob Decker and another of the academy staff were surrounded by a knot of knife-wielding students; Philip, Matthew and Devra had been joined by three others—Tom Sayers, Ryan Stern, and Holly Raffin. He saw the unmoving bodies—Ma, Alma, Kevin—and blood. So much blood.

What the hell is going on?

He looked away and kept running, plunging into the darkening woods chasing after Natalie. He wondered if he would find safety there, or anywhere.

Chapter Thirty - **Tim**

The drive seemed to take forever, longer even than the shuttle bus ride from the airport in El Paso to the Academy, which was nearly twice the distance. It was an illusion of course, confirmed every time Tim checked his watch. Time seemed to be crawling by.

They were, he had to concede, making good time. Paula was growing more confident with each passing mile, pushing the Jeep faster. They had been on the road for over an hour. The last road sign they had passed indicated that Pecos was still about twenty miles away. The nearly empty highway and the mostly featureless flat Texas prairie beyond the windows, offered little to occupy his mind, which in turn allowed his anxieties to run wild. Had anyone discovered their absence yet? Had the authorities been alerted? If it had not already happened, it surely would eventually. They were racing against a countdown clock with no way of knowing how much time was left to them.

He kept checking their rear and examining every car that passed by, looking for the tell-tale flashing lights of a police cruiser that would signal the end to their desperate search for answers.

"Settle down," Paula said, without looking over at him. "We're going to make it."

"Do you think they've discovered that we're gone yet?"

"They have or they haven't," she replied, her voice strangely calm. "Worrying about it won't change a thing."

"When they do, they'll probably call the police. Maybe we should ditch the Jeep and find another car."

"Right. We'll just steal the next unlocked car with the keys in the visor."

Tim let out a growl of frustration. She was right, but that didn't mean he had to like it.

"If we get arrested, we'll tell the police what we know. Even if they don't believe us, they'll still have to check it out, or at the very least, let us call home. Mom and Dad *will* take us seriously, especially when we tell them that there might be a threat to John and Sarah. The Secret Service will swoop down in helicopters. That might not be such a bad thing."

"So maybe we should just find a phone and call them ourselves."

"Believe me, I'm thinking about it. But I think we should stick to the plan, learn as much as we can before we make that call. Besides, if we're wrong, keeping this a secret is still our best option."

Tim couldn't argue with that, even though he was sure that they weren't wrong.

Pecos was a small, sleepy town, and finding the hospital posed no great difficulty. They needed only follow the distinctive blue signs marked with a white "H" but as they approached their destination, Tim's heart sank. The signs may have said "County Hospital" but the single-story building with the nearly empty parking lot looked more like an urgent care clinic.

"You've got to be kidding me," Paula said. "That's the hospital? There's no way they would have brought a trauma victim here."

"In an emergency, beggars can't be choosers," Tim replied, even though he shared his sister's skepticism. "It's not much, but it is the closest place."

"A hospital this small isn't equipped to make serious interventions," Paula went on, though she seemed to be thinking out loud. "The most they would do is triage and stabilize for transport, probably by helicopter."

Tim recalled Ma's ominous announcement. "Ma distinctly said they took her to Pecos. Maybe there's another hospital in town?"

"Not likely. Pecos is barely big enough to support this."

"So what do we do?"

Paula tapped her hands on the steering wheel. "Let's go see if there's anyone around. Maybe they can at least tell us if Madison came through here and where she went."

"And if they can't?"

"I don't know." She looked over at him and gave a helpless shrug. "I guess we'll figure something out."

Chapter Thirty-One - **Paula**

The waiting room of the county hospital was about exactly what Paula expected it to be, a dismal little room with molded plastic chairs, magazines that were practically pre-war relics, and a sliding glass window to separate the receptionist from those seeking medical attention. Fortunately, there was somebody sitting on the other side of the glass. Evidently, the hospital—such as it was—was staffed around the clock.

Tim was lingering outside, partly to keep a lookout but mostly because two teenagers wearing dirty military-style uniforms and showing up in the middle of the night was conspicuous enough to attract the wrong kind of attention. Even one was pushing it.

She took a deep breath, made eye contact with the middle-aged woman sitting at the counter, and started forward, mentally rehearsing what she would say one last time.

"Can I help you, miss?"

Paula managed a tight smile. "I sure hope so. I came as fast as I could."

The woman blinked, waiting for her to elaborate.

"My sister is here. Madison. There was an accident. I heard they brought her here." The words came out in an almost incoherent jumble. "I'm sorry. It all happened so suddenly."

The woman's forehead creased like a frown. "You're from that survivalist camp, aren't you?"

The statement came as a surprise, but not as much as the off-hand way in which the woman said it. Paula's heart began racing. "That's right," she said, making an effort to speak slowly. "There was an accident on the course. I came as fast as I could."

She knew she was repeating herself, filling up the silence because she didn't know what else to say.

"Strange. I didn't hear about that." The woman seemed genuinely perplexed.

Paula felt her hopes of learning the truth slipping through her fingers. "They said they were bringing her here."

"I doubt that. We mostly deal with runny noses here. But I'll look real quick." She swiveled in her chair to face her computer terminal. "What did you say her name was?"

"Madison."

"Last name?"

Paula silently cursed herself for an idiot. She had no idea what Madison's last name was. "Umm, it's ahh…" She swallowed. "I don't know if she uses my dad's last name or my mom's. They're divorced and I…ahhh…" She shrugged.

The woman frowned but then began tapping the keyboard. "Well, we probably didn't see very many people named Madison today…In fact, we didn't see any. Sorry miss, but your sister didn't come here."

"Where else would they have taken her?"

"Well, there's county memorial up the road a ways, but if her injuries were serious, they probably would have sent her by air to Dallas. That's what we usually do." The woman must have seen the desperation on Paula's face and decided to take pity on her. "I am sorry, honey. Tell you what; let me call the emergency services dispatch operator. If anyone responded to a call out at your camp, they'll be able to tell me where they took her."

Paula's despair turned to panic. If the authorities were looking for her and Tim, calling the dispatcher would bring the police down on them. But what other options were there? "Okay," she finally said.

The woman nodded and then picked up a telephone handset. Paula listened carefully to the one-sided conversation, watching the woman's body language for any hint of suspicion. "Hey Darlene, it's Mona…Fine.

Listen, did you log any calls to that survivalist place out in Big Bend?" She glanced at Paula and smiled.

Why did she do that? Does she know?

"No? Nothing at all?" Another pause. "Can you do me a favor and check the transport logs? We're looking for a trauma patient transfer by air or ground…Oh, nothing serious. Just a little case of wires getting crossed… No transports at all? Okay, thanks for checking. Talk to you later."

The woman returned the phone to its cradle, looked at Paula and shrugged. "I don't know what to tell you honey. Your sister's not in our system."

"What does that mean?"

"Honestly, I don't know. If she was taken by a privately owned vehicle to another hospital, the dispatcher wouldn't have a record of that, but if she was hurt bad, it would be foolish not to call an ambulance."

"If she…ummm… died… where would they take her?"

"Oh, honey. I promise you, if something like that had happened, Darlene would have told me. Don't you worry. Maybe she wasn't hurt as bad as you heard. Have you tried calling her?"

Paula shook her head and turned away, half-stumbling toward the exit.

Tim was waiting just outside. "Well?"

Paula didn't know what to say. "Not here."

"Another hospital?"

"She's not at another hospital. She's not anywhere."

"What do you mean? Ma said—"

Paula cut him off. "Ma lied. Or someone lied to her. Madison was never brought to this hospital or any other. I don't think she ever left the Academy."

Tim's eyes moved back and forth as he struggled to process this. "No, of course not. This makes more sense. They couldn't risk an official investigation."

"They," Paula echoed. "We still don't even know who *they* are."

"So what do we do now?"

"We go back. That's where the answers are."

Chapter Thirty-Two - **Jack**

The darkness held little promise of refuge, but to remain in Camp Zero was a guaranteed death sentence. Jack tried to put the carnage out of his mind, but it was impossible to separate what he had witnessed from the urgency of the moment. It was not the victims he saw in his mind's eye—Kevin, Alma, Ma Tempest, the other instructors—but the perpetrators. His fellow students.

A bunch of kids.

They had been so worried about Kevin and Alma, who had indeed been lying about their age in order to maintain their cover and keep an eye on John and Sarah, while the real danger had been lurking all around them.

A bunch of kids. Damn.

He could see them all in his mind's eye.

Devra and Holly, so covered in the blood of their victims, it was impossible to tell them apart.

Matthew and Ryan, the older boys, always taking the lead in their respective teams. One of them had taken the lead in ramming a spear into Ma's chest.

Thomas, who looked like he was about the same age as Jack. A stone cold killer.

Philip…

Philip was the same age as John. Twelve years old.

Philip, with a gleeful smile on his face as he slashed one of the instructors with his knife.

What in God's name is going on?

Nat had fled into the darkness with Sarah, and John had followed. Some of the other students had gone after them. In that moment, Jack had made the decision to run the other way. It had made sense at the time. Splitting up would make it harder for the killers—

Killers. They're just kids.

—to track them all down, but now he wondered if he had made a potentially fatal mistake, sacrificing the only advantage they actually had, strength in numbers.

In the confusion, he had managed to bring what was left of Bravo team along with him. Clayton was alternately panting and whining, struggling to keep up. The others, none of whom had much respect for Jack, were talking to each other in a low conspiratorial whisper, trying to make sense of the massacre in Camp Zero, and wondering whether they were next on the hit list.

That was something Jack was worried about, too.

When he and the rest of the Rourke kids had held their family meeting, they had been so certain of both the nature of the threat and the perpetrators, but now that had been turned on its head. In fact, the revelation that Kevin and Alma were Secret Service agents meant that everything he and Tim and Paula and Nat had worked out was completely wrong. No conspiracy. No plot to kill Sarah and John.

No reason at all for six of his fellow students to suddenly go on a homicidal rampage.

"Where are… we going?" Clayton asked, the question divided equally between two breaths.

It was the one question Jack hadn't considered. He glanced up and after a few seconds of searching, found the North Star. It was on his left. They were heading east.

"We'll head for the wilderness camp."

"Then what?" asked Jenn. "That's the first place they'll look."

"We don't even know that they are looking for us," someone else said. Jack wasn't sure whom. Dustin, maybe. "This is crazy."

The boy was right about that. Without knowing what had motivated the attack, it was impossible to determine the safest course. *Assume the worst,* he thought. *Until we know differently, assume that they're hunting us.*

He glanced back, searching the darkness for confirmation, but his light revealed nothing beyond about thirty yards.

The lights!

"Everybody. Lights off, now."

"What?" Jenn shot back. "We'll break our necks."

"Do it. If they're after us, our lights are a dead giveaway. We'll take it slow, at least until our eyes adjust."

There were a few murmurs of complaint, more of assent, and one by one, the headlamps went out, plunging them into darkness.

"Everybody stop for a second," he said. "Just listen."

"For what?"

"Shhhh!" Jack closed his eyes and cupped his hands over his ears, trying to catch any noise that might indicate pursuit, but the only thing he heard was the pounding of his own heart and Clayton's ragged breathing nearby.

"I don't hear anyone," he said after a moment, "but that doesn't mean they aren't there. We need to keep moving. And we should be careful not to leave a trail."

We were supposed to get a class on that, he thought. *Guess I'll have to fake it.*

"We'll walk single file. Step carefully. Avoid trampling any plants or kicking rocks." When no one challenged him, he added, "And get your knives out. We panicked before, but if they come for us, we fight, understand?"

"Bring 'em on," someone—definitely Dustin—snarled.

Jack admired the fierce attitude, but he couldn't help but think that if Kevin and Alma, Service Agents, highly-trained in hand-to-hand combat, had been overwhelmed, cut down in a heartbeat, what chance did any of them have?

Chapter Thirty-Three - **Sarah**

Passed away. Gone to heaven to be with God. Never regained consciousness. Dead.

Alma was dead.

What does that even mean?

It meant that Sarah would never see her again. A week ago, she didn't even know Alma. Now, Alma was gone forever from her life, just like Grandpa Wolf.

Sarah's head understood this, but her heart couldn't quite make sense of it. Maybe that was why she didn't really feel scared.

Natalie was holding her hand, squeezing it tightly as if afraid that, if she let go, Sarah might be caught away in the wind, never to return. Sarah didn't try to pull free, even though her hand was starting to hurt and she was having trouble keeping up with her older cousin.

"Stop," someone called out. It was an older girl about the same age as Natalie but taller. Sarah didn't know her name. "What are we doing?"

Sarah wasn't sure how many of the others had followed Natalie. They were guided by the illumination of a single headlamp, and that was hooded and pointing forward to avoid giving away their location.

"We're staying alive," Natalie said, not looking back.

"What's going on?" asked someone else. "Why is this happening?"

Sarah had wondered about that, too. Her cousins had been convinced that Alma and Kevin were plotting something, but they were gone now, killed by Matthew and Thomas and some of the other kids. Why?

"Natalie," she whispered. "Why did they do it?"

"I don't know," Natalie admitted. "It doesn't make any sense."

"Was it because Alma was protecting me?"

Natalie's stride faltered, just for a second, but it was as clear an answer as anything she might have said.

"That's why, isn't it?" Sarah pressed. "Everything was fine until Kevin showed them his badge."

"It sure looked that way."

"Kevin was one of the good guys," John said, his voice full of anger and bitterness. "You told us not to trust him."

"I know John," Natalie said. "We were wrong."

"You were wrong and now he's dead."

"Stop it, John!" Sarah shouted, surprising even herself. "Natalie was looking out for us. None of this is her fault. If they had just told us who they were, none of this would have happened."

John did not respond. He knew it was true.

She looked back the way they had come. There was a flicker of orange in the darkness, the light from the fire at Camp Zero. "They're going to come after us now, aren't they?"

"They might. We'll head for the woods. We can hide there."

"For how long?" asked someone else.

"For as long as we have to," Sarah said. "Natalie is trying to save us. Don't you see that?"

Natalie's grip on her hand relaxed a little, and then she gave a quick squeeze of gratitude.

They reached the trees a few minutes later. Natalie called for everyone to stay close and pushed deeper into the trees at a walking pace. Sarah immediately felt a chill from the cool night air and knew that it would only get colder as the night wore on. Worse, they had only the clothes they were wearing to keep them warm. Their sleeping bags and anything else that might have kept the chill at bay were back at Camp Zero.

Natalie stopped abruptly. "Bring it in everyone. Huddle around me."

Sarah felt bodies pressing against her and was grateful for the warmth. In the glow of Natalie's light, she saw the faces of their group. She immediately recognized her teammates Randy, Dan and Luke. The tall girl from Natalie's team was there, along with another boy, but she didn't know their names. John and Natalie were there, of course, but there was no sign of Jack. She wondered if he had made it out, if any of the others had made it out.

"All right, listen up," Natalie said. "We have to keep our heads on straight if we want to get out of this alive. I know you've got questions. Believe me, so do I. But right now, we have to prioritize. Survival comes first. That's what we came here to learn about. Now it's time to use what we know.

"First, we need lookouts." Her eyes darted around the group. "Heather. Gary. Can you handle that?"

The tall girl and the other boy from Charlie team both nodded.

"Your only job is to keep an eye out for trouble. Move out fifty yards or so. Keep your lights off. Whistle if you see anything. While you're at it, collect moss, bark, grass…anything you can stuff in your clothes to provide some insulation. Everyone needs to do that. While you keep watch, the rest of us will put up a shelter. We can't risk a fire but a closed shelter with something between us and the ground and our body heat should be enough to get us through the night. It will also give us some concealment.

"Randy, Luke, you guys find branches for the frame. The rest of us will gather foliage to cover the sides and floor. We'll build it right here. You'll need to use your lights, but keep them covered as much as possible. If you hear a whistle, put your light out, draw your knife and get your back against a tree so nobody can sneak up on you. Once you're set, stay put. Don't move. Don't. Move. Anybody moving after that is probably one of them. If they get close… well, do what you have to do.

"We'll need a signal for all clear, just in case it's a false alarm. Let's say three quick whistles, but only the person who gives the warning can sound the all clear." She paused a moment. "Okay, everyone has a job. Let's get to work."

As the huddle dispersed, Natalie took Sarah's hand again. "Stay close to me. You too, John. Keeping you safe is *my* first priority. Understand?"

"I understand," John replied, with none of his earlier bitterness.

"Me too," Sarah said, nodding in the darkness. "And I'm glad you're here with us."

"Believe me kiddo, right now I'd rather be anywhere but here. Family's gotta stick together, right?"

"Do you think Jack is okay?"

"I'm sure he's fine. I saw him heading east with some of the other kids." She gave Sarah's hand a reassuring squeeze. "We're gonna get through this. All of us."

Chapter Thirty-Four - **Natalie**

The words felt like a lie, a promise she couldn't keep.

She would try. She would give her life to make sure that nothing happened to Sarah and John, but there were six of them—the killers—and only one of her. And that wasn't the worst of it.

You came here with family, Matthew had told her. *So did I.*

She had been completely fooled, taken in by his good looks and charm. And it wasn't just Matthew. Three of her teammates had joined the murderous rampage. Yet even with the gift of perfect hindsight, she could not see the warning signs that surely must have been there.

I fell for it. Again. And this time, people died.

The worst part was that none if it made any sense at all. She tried to heed her own advice, focus on the immediate problem of survival, but the unanswered questions were as relentless and inescapable as a black hole.

You came here with family. So did I.

Family?

Matthew and Philip were brothers, but as far as she knew, there was no relationship between the others. Devra and Holly might have looked like sisters, but they were from different cities.

That's what they told you but they were lying, weren't they?

A lie like that meant a much bigger conspiracy. The massacre had not been some random unprovoked act of violence. Matthew and his "family" weren't just vicious killers. They had been trained, the way spies were trained. Taught how to blend in, manipulate people, gain the trust of others in order to get closer to their targets.

They're just kids. Philip is John's age. Who would do that to a child?

The possible answers to that question left her feeling even more helpless, and made her promise to protect her cousins seem even emptier.

"I'm cold," Sarah whispered.

"Rub your hands together and then hug your chest like this." She demonstrated, warming her hands with friction before crossing her arms over her chest and tucking her hands under her biceps. The respite from the chill was brief but welcome. "Come on. We need to find some insulation."

There was not much moss on the trees, but a few handfuls of dry grass stuffed into their uniform blouses were sufficient to create an extra layer between their skin and the fabric. It did not bring immediate relief from the increasingly bitter cold, but Natalie knew that as their body heat warmed the air trapped in that layer, it would keep hypothermia at bay while they searched for branches with foliage. Nearby, the headlamps of the others seemed to float like fireflies in the darkness, bobbing up and down as they knelt to pick up material for the shelter.

A piercing whistle cut through the air. It took Natalie a second to register the sound, but John and Sarah reacted instantly, clicking off their headlamps.

"Nat," John whispered. "Your light."

The message finally hit her brain, triggering a dump of adrenaline into her nervous system.

They found us!

She looked left, then right, spotted a nearby tree and propelled her cousins toward it. In the same motion, she drew her knife, and then flicked off her own headlamp, plunging her world into total darkness.

She took two big steps in the direction of the tree, then another more cautious step, one hand out to avoid any low hanging branches. One more half-step and she felt the rough bark on her outstretched fingertips. She pivoted, crouched down and softly whispered, "Shhhhhh."

The echoes of the whistle had long since died away, leaving them in near total silence. Even the insects had gone quiet. Natalie cocked her head sideways, straining to catch the sound of footsteps on the forest floor, the crackle of boots treading on dry vegetation. She heard only the rush of blood in her ears and the rapid boom-boom-boom of her heartbeat.

Breathe, she told herself, inhaling as deeply as she could, holding it for a count of five before slowly letting it out again.

Remarkably, it worked. Her pulse slowed and the panicked jumble of thoughts in her head began to clear.

A twig snapped, as loud as a gunshot in the stillness. She tilted her head toward it, trying to gauge the distance. Twenty yards? Ten?

Closer?

There was a faint rustling sound, so soft that it might have simply been her imagination, but she knew it wasn't. It was the sound of fabric bending and crumpling, the sound of boot soles slowly settling onto the ground then lifting off again, one stealthy step at a time, getting louder, louder, louder with each passing second.

God, she thought. *This is really happening.*

Her fingers tightened on the hilt of the knife. She stared into the empty darkness from which the sound was coming, straining to catch a glimpse of the hunter relentlessly advancing toward her.

Does he see me?

In her lecture about red light and night vision, Ma had talked about how long it took for a person's eyes to get used to seeing in the dark after the lights went out, as much as forty-five minutes. Less than half that much time had elapsed since they fled Camp Zero, which meant the killers' eyes weren't fully adjusted, but unlike Natalie and her group, they had not relied on headlamps to light their way.

Another whisper of movement, closer still.

He does see me. He's going to attack.

Ma had said something else, too. Something about the structure of the human eye. Natalie hadn't paid close attention to the technical detail—that was Paula's area of expertise—but she remembered something about rods and cones, two different types of light receptors in the eye. One type—

rods, maybe—were very sensitive to even trace amounts of light but couldn't differentiate color. Animals like cats and dogs could see better in the dark because they had a lot more rods than humans, but for the same reason, they were probably color blind. She also recalled that in the human eye, the sensitive photoreceptors were at the outer edge of the eye, which meant that in the dark, peripheral vision was better than looking straight forward.

She took another breath, turning her head back and forth, and saw him, a silhouette like a living shadow, looming right in front of her.

Two instinctive impulses competed for supremacy in her brain.

Don't move. If you move, he'll see you and kill you.

He already sees you. He's going to kill you if you don't kill him first.

He's a killer. I can't beat him.

If you don't fight, you're dead already. And then he'll kill Sarah and John and it will be your fault.

No. I won't let that happen.

Then fight!

The killer still had the advantage. He could see her, while she would be striking blindly, but there was a way to level the playing field, and maybe even turn the odds in her favor.

As she raised the knife in her right hand, she reached up with her left and turned on her headlamp.

Chapter Thirty-Five - **John**

The flash of light surprised John, but not nearly as much as what it revealed. Philip was standing almost face-to-face with Natalie, one hand thrown up reflexively to shade his eyes from the brilliance. Even more astonishing was what Natalie did next. With a shriek of primal fury, she leapt forward and slashed at Philip with her knife.

Philip threw up one arm to ward off the attack and John saw a flash of red as Natalie's blade sliced open Philip's sleeve and the skin beneath. Philip let out a yelp of pain and scrambled back several steps, but even as he retreated, his demeanor changed. He crouched low in a fighting posture that reminded John of a gladiator in a movie. The fear and pain melted from his face, revealing stony determination.

He's going to kill Natalie.

"Philip. Don't."

The protest tumbled out unbidden, some vestige of childish naiveté momentarily bubbling to the surface like a pocket of swamp gas, and had about as much effect. Philip lunged at Natalie, swiping the blade back and forth through the air so fast that all John could see were blurry trails of light reflecting off the blade.

Natalie took a step back and bumped into the tree trunk, giving Philip all the time he needed to close the remaining distance.

"No!" The shriek, even more blood-curdling than Natalie's war cry, came from Sarah as she launched herself at Philip. Her attack was so fast, so unexpected, that Philip did not have time to block or dodge. Sarah kicked him in the shins, hard enough to make him howl. He stumbled, giving Natalie the time she needed to throw herself to the side, while Philip crashed into the tree. The collision stunned him and he staggered back, the knife falling from his grasp.

John seized the opportunity and rushed his former friend, tackling him the ground. He landed atop Philip with sufficient force to drive the wind out of him, but even as they crashed down, he remembered grappling with Philip the previous day during the self-defense class. He could almost hear Mr. Hickok shouting advice.

"Get him in the dominant position. You're on top. Go for the front mount."

Unfortunately, Philip had received the same instruction, and John had a feeling that hadn't been the other boy's first lesson in hand-to-hand combat.

John pushed up, trying to straddle Philip's chest, but the other boy was bucking under him like a wild mustang. Something hard—a knee, maybe— slammed into his back and launched him headlong, and just like that, Philip was free and John was face down on the forest floor.

John rolled over, sat up, remembering the rest of the lesson as Philip lunged at him.

"If you get knocked on your butt, you need to get back up. Unfortunately, while you're flailing around like a turtle on his back, you're not going to be able to do much to defend yourself. So I'm going to teach you how to stand up in a fight."

The moves came back to him. He planted his right hand on the ground behind him, extended his right leg out, and jammed his foot at Philip's face. He made only glancing contact as Philip twisted away, but it was enough to give him a chance to bring his left leg in, foot planted firmly on the ground. Then, using his back hand to lift his buttocks up, he brought his right leg back, underneath him and came up in a ready stance, just like Mr. Hickok had showed them.

Philip, evidently recognizing what John was trying to do, sprang back to his feet with considerably more finesse, but instead of trying to close with John, he retreated to the base of the tree and knelt down quickly. Although his eyes never left John, when he stood up again, his knife was once again in his right hand, and without a moment's hesitation, he charged straight at John.

John fumbled for his own knife, still sheathed on his belt, even though he knew there was no way he would be able to draw it in time.

Suddenly, Philip dropped like a sack of potatoes, crashing senseless to the ground. Behind him stood Natalie, still gripping her knife after slamming its pommel into the base of Philip's skull.

Philip was out cold.

John was trembling from the rush of adrenaline in his system. They had beaten Philip, but it had taken all three of them to do it, and even then, it had been a close thing. If not for Sarah's bold intervention, Philip would have cut Natalie down and then gone on to carve the rest of them up.

Natalie looked up suddenly, hearing something, and then John heard it too.

Footsteps.

Someone was moving toward them.

John didn't know if it was one of their group rushing in to offer belated assistance, or one of Philip's confederates, so he got his knife out and then flipped the switch to activate his headlamp. Darkness wouldn't help them now.

Natalie turned in the direction of the sound, and their combined flashlight beams revealed Thomas, one of the boys from Alpha team.

One of the killers.

He was moving in a low crouch, not quite running, but walking very fast. In his right hand, he held a long tree branch, the end carved to a sharp spear point.

When he got within ten yards of them, he raised the makeshift javelin and cocked his arm back, ready to throw. The point seemed to be aimed right at John.

"Get away from him," Thomas hissed.

John took an involuntary step away from Philip, but Natalie knelt down beside the fallen boy and thrust the tip of her blade against Philip's neck. "You take one more step, and I'll cut his throat. Swear to God."

Thomas froze, but only for a second. "I don't think you've got it in you," he said, and then took another deliberate step forward.

Natalie's arm tightened and John thought he could see a bead of ruby red blood appear on the point. "I mean it," Natalie threatened. "You're killing him."

"Then do it." Thomas took another step. "Kill him, if you've really got it in you. And then there won't be anything to stop me to from gutting you like a fish."

"You can try," Natalie snarled back.

Her ferocity galvanized John into action. He brandished his blade and moved closer to his cousin. Sarah did the same, the survival knife looking like a short sword in her little hand.

Thomas laughed. "Ooooh, three of you. Scary."

"Four of us." A light flashed on in the woods to Thomas's left and a figure emerged from the shadows. With the headlamp blazing, John couldn't make out a face, but he recognized the voice. It was Heather.

More lights began to wink on all around them, and in a matter of seconds, the entire group that had left with Natalie emerged from hiding, knives at the ready.

Thomas did not appear to be the least bit intimidated by their defiance, but he halted his advance and turned slowly, looking at each member of the group in turn. "Eight of you," he remarked. "Is that everyone, or are there still some cowards pissing their pants behind the trees?"

"We're not afraid of you," Gary shouted, though the tremor in his voice suggested otherwise.

Thomas turned another slow circle, staring at them all as if looking for some sign of weakness. His utter lack of fear made John wonder if he had brought along reinforcements of his own—where were the others? Matthew, Devra, Holly and Ryan? Had this been a bold gambit to draw them all into the open so that the others could swoop in and finish them off?

To John's utter astonishment, Thomas lowered his makeshift javelin and brought his gaze back to Natalie. "If he dies, I'll come back and kill every one of you."

As soon as the threat was made, Thomas spun around and broke into a run, passing through the gap between Heather and Gary before any of them could even think about trying to stop him.

John watched him disappear then turned to Natalie. "What just happened?"

Natalie shook her head. "I'm not sure."

"Maybe he's going to get the others."

"Maybe." She looked down at Philip's motionless form. "Maybe he can tell us."

Chapter Thirty-Six - **Tim**

"Do you think they know?" Tim asked as they rolled toward the Academy's parking lot.

Paula shook her head uncertainly. "If they do, we'll have to be very careful about who to trust. If not, we do what we came here to do. Either way, we're going to get some answers."

Nevertheless, she slowed the Jeep, turned off the lights, and coasted the rest of the way in. She eased the vehicle to a stop, and shut off the engine. Tim expected to see people rushing out to confront them, but that did not happen. Their arrival, and perhaps their departure also, had evidently gone completely unnoticed.

They removed their rucksacks, leaving the Jeep almost exactly as when they had found it, save for a nearly empty gas tank, and crept to the edge of the nearest building. They waited and watched for a few minutes, and when they were certain that no one was looking, advanced into the courtyard where they had been greeted upon arrival just a few days before, and where they had assembled before leaving for Camp Zero. Tim mentally reviewed the layout of the facility, identifying the mess hall and the barracks, the armory and their immediate goal, the administration building on the far side of the yard. There were lights burning in some of the offices, but all the windows on the east end were dark. Paula pointed a finger in that direction and Tim nodded.

There was an exit door on the east facing wall, a door without a doorknob. Tim knelt before it and slipped the blade of his knife in between the door and the strike plate. It took a few minutes, but he was able to work the latch bolt back and open the door. The hall beyond was dark and empty.

During the long drive back from Pecos, they had held despair at bay by alternately speculating on the true nature of the conspiracy they faced—

an ultimately pointless effort since they simply didn't have enough information to go on—and pondering how best to learn the truth. Examining Madison's body now seemed even more imperative than ever, but there was no guarantee that they would find it at the Academy. It was just as likely that the real killers had disposed of her remains in the vast wilderness, where they would never be found. Still, they would have to search every corner of the compound, just to be sure. While they were at it, they would keep eyes and ears open, looking for anything that might hint at the identity of the conspirators.

If none of that yielded results, they would use one of the telephones to call their parents and bring in the cavalry.

The first room they came to appeared to be a storeroom, with boxes of supplies, files, and mothballed equipment. No Madison. No evidence. They moved on to the next office which was a desk and computer workstation, but not much else. There was no indication that the office had ever been used. Door by door, they cleared the eastern half of the building. Some of the offices had personal touches that offered clues to the identity of the occupants. The framed prints of rock climbers probably belonged to Mr. Decker, and the Detonics pistol calendar was almost certainly in Mr. Hickok's office, but the rooms were mostly utilitarian. Tim tried accessing a computer in one of the rooms, but couldn't get past the password screen.

When they reached the hallway leading back to the entry foyer, they were confronted with a choice. Break off the search and look elsewhere, or try to eavesdrop on one of the occupied offices. The latter choice carried great risk, but also the greatest likelihood of learning something useful. One of those offices might well belong to the mastermind of the conspiracy.

While Paula watched their back, making sure that their escape route was clear, Tim crept forward to the first door, which was marked with a simple placard that read "OPERATIONS," and pressed his ear against it.

He could hear bits of conversation from inside. Mr. Dickson's deep baritone was easily recognizable and while he couldn't make out every word, it was clear that he was upset about something. The other voice, softer, higher-pitched, was harder to make out. Tim thought it might belong to a woman, but definitely not Ma. He listened for a few seconds then risked opening the door a crack.

The female voice immediately became audible. "—Zero, this is Base, come in. Ma, do you copy?" There was a pause, then, "Still nothing."

The voice was familiar but Tim couldn't put a face or name to it. In addition to the instructors, he had seen several people in support roles working at the headquarters, young men and women, probably advanced students working as interns. The young woman who was clearly trying to raise Ma on a radio was probably from that group.

"I'm going to head out there," Mr. Dickson said. "I'll take a fresh walkie along. I'm sure it's just a dead battery or something."

"Both radios?" countered the young woman. "What are the odds of that?"

"That's why I'm going out there. Just to be sure. Keep trying to raise them."

Tim sensed that Mr. Dickson was about to leave the room so he quickly retreated down the hallway, motioning for Paula to join him in one of the empty offices. Sure enough, a moment later they heard the sound of footsteps in the hallway.

"Well?" Paula whispered and the footsteps faded. "Did you find out anything?"

"I'm not sure. They can't raise anyone on the radio. Mr. Dickson is heading out to investigate."

Paula's forehead creased in alarm. "I'll bet they've figured out that we're not there. Do you think he's in on it?"

"I couldn't tell. There's someone else working the radio. He told her to keep trying to make contact. Maybe we can find out some more."

Paula nodded and then they both crept back to the door which was now standing wide open. The voice of the radio operator was audible, even in the hallway.

"Camp Zero, do you read? This is Base, over."

"Who is that?" Paula whispered. "I know that voice."

Tim shook his head. "Me too, but I can't place it."

Standing outside the door, all they could see was a wall lined with bookshelves and the corner of the desk where the woman sat. Tim eased forward a step, but all he could see of the woman aside from the tan camp uniform was the back of her head. Her short-cropped auburn hair was maddeningly familiar, but it wasn't until he heard Paula gasp that he finally figured out who it was.

"Madison?"

The young woman whirled around in alarm, and Tim saw that it was indeed Madison, very much alive and well. "What are you doing here?" she asked, trying to sound authoritative but unable to completely hide her guilt at having been caught in a lie.

"You're supposed to be dead," Tim blurted.

Paula took a defiant step forward. "I knew it. I knew you weren't really injured." She turned to Tim. "She faked it. That's why no one in Pecos knew anything about this. It was all an act. She's obviously a part of whatever is going on." Then, she drew her knife and started forward.

Tim was almost more stunned by his sister's sudden aggression than by Madison's return to the land of the living. "Paula, what are you doing?"

"Wait!" Madison protested, throwing both hands up. "I can explain."

"That's the idea," Paula said, not slowing.

"It's part of the course," Madison said quickly, the words rushing out in the time it took Paula to cross half the distance. "A simulation to teach the students how to deal with loss in a survival environment."

Simulation? Tim struggled to make sense of what he was hearing, but coming on the heels of this latest discovery, that was a tall order. *Madison is still alive. She isn't dead, so she wasn't murdered and there isn't a cover-up. And we were completely wrong about everything.*

"What about Kevin and Alma?" he blurted. "Are they in on it?"

Madison's eyebrows came together in a furrow of confusion. "Kevin and—"

"Nice try," Paula said. She raised the knife almost to eye level, holding it in an overhand grip, the point reaching out menacingly in Madison's direction. "But I'm not buying it."

"Stop right there!" barked a deep voice from behind Tim. He whirled around to find Mr. Dickson standing in the doorway, his right hand resting on the butt of the pistol holstered at his hip. "Paula, you need to step back and put that knife down, right now."

Tim reflexively retreated a step, then winced as he recalled Mr. Hickok's advice from their self-defense course.

"Run away from a knife, but toward a gun. You can keep a knife from hurting you just by staying out of the other person's reach, but a bullet can run faster than you can, so if someone is pointing a gun at you and you think they'll pull the trigger no matter what, rush them. It's a lot harder to hit a moving target, especially one that's moving right toward you. Maybe you'll get shot, but it's the best chance you've got of taking the bastard down—pardon my language."

Tim's unintentional retreat meant he would have to cover that much more ground if he was to have any chance of overpowering Mr. Dickson.

The big man seemed to read Tim's thoughts, but instead of seizing the advantage and drawing his weapon, he brought both his hands up in a pleading gesture. "Stop. For God's sake, everybody just take a step back. Paula, please. Put the knife down."

"Not until somebody explains what's going on," Paula insisted. Her voice was unusually calm, controlled. Tim glanced back and saw that his sister had circled around Madison and was now using the young woman like a human shield. The edge of Paula's blade was poised across Madison's throat.

"I told you," Madison said, speaking slowly. "I faked my death as part of the course."

"It's true," Dickson put in. "Our curriculum has one purpose: getting you kids ready to face a worst case scenario. We can teach you all the bushcraft in the world, but all that is gonna go right out of your head when your best friend or your brother or your sister dies in your arms. The only way to really get you ready for something like that is to make you live through a simulated tragedy. That's all this is."

"That's crazy," Tim managed to say. "When my dad finds out about this—"

"Son, it was your father's idea. All the parents are fully briefed on this part of the curriculum."

"I don't believe you," Paula said.

Dickson shook his head in consternation. "Every class reacts a little different to it, but I've never had students take it upon themselves to play Sherlock Holmes." He sighed. "I suppose I should have expected this from Rourke's kids. Would it help if I called your father? Let him explain it to you? If I know John, he'll be proud of you for taking the initiative."

"What about Kevin and Alma?" Tim asked. "Are they in on this, too?"

"What makes you ask that, son?"

"For starters, they're lying about how old they are. And meeting in secret after dark. And trying to get close to John and Sarah."

"I see nothing gets past you." The corners of Dickson's mouth twitched up in a smile. "Kevin and Alma *are* staying close to your cousins. That's their job. They're with the Presidential Protection Detail. Secret Service. Undercover, of course."

"Secret Service?" It was another staggering revelation, but it made complete sense.

"It's hard to teach youngsters to be self-reliant if they know they've got a bodyguard looking out for them, but the Director of the Secret Service insisted that they have round the clock protection, so they found two agents who they thought could pass for teenagers... obviously, they were wrong about that. But I have copies of their personnel file. Would that convince you?"

Tim glanced back at Paula. "It makes sense. I think he's telling the truth."

Paula's eyes darted from Tim to Dickson and back again. He could almost read her thoughts. *If we're wrong about this....*

Paula however was still not ready to yield. "What's going on at Camp Zero? Why can't you reach them?"

Dickson's smile slipped. "That's a very good question. They're overdue for a check-in. I don't suppose you kids have anything to do with that? Did you sabotage the radios before you left?"

"Of course not," Tim replied, though he wondered if Natalie and Jack might have taken it upon themselves to do just that.

"Hmmm. Well, I'd really like to get out there and check on them if it's okay with you. I'll do whatever it takes to make you believe me, but I'd like to get moving as soon as possible. And I would really appreciate it if you moved that blade away from my daughter's throat."

"Daughter?" Tim looked back again, and immediately saw the family resemblance. *I guess that got past me*, he thought.

Paula lowered the blade a few inches and seemed about ready to release Madison, but before she could, a loud bang sounded from somewhere outside the building. Tim recognized it immediately as the report of a gun.

Dickson cocked his head sideways, just as two more shots were fired. "That's coming from the armory." He then turned his gaze back to Tim and Paula, his hand dropping once more to the butt of his pistol. "Stay here. Maddie, you keep them safe."

"Wait!" Paula shouted, but Dickson was already gone. She let go of Madison and moved around to look her in the eye. "What's going on? Who's shooting?"

Madison just shook her head. "I have no idea."

Chapter Thirty-Seven - **Paula**

Seeing Madison—alive and completely uninjured—was like finding a hidden image in a picture puzzle. Once seen, it was impossible to look at the picture and not see it. It all made sense now. Why Madison had not appeared to have suffered any physical trauma, why Ma had been so insistent on making Paula stop her assessment. The explanation she and Tim had been given however was not quite so obvious.

Maybe it was part of an elaborate mind game, devised to toughen them all up, teach them how to cope with grief and carry on. It was cruel, but it would not be the last time any of the students would have to face tragedy. But what if that explanation was just a lie meant to conceal a darker purpose?

Paula wanted to believe, because if it was true, then the ordeal was over and all her suspicions could be laid to rest. Yes, they had all overreacted and that thought was a little embarrassing, but given the circumstances, they could hardly be accused of paranoia. They probably wouldn't even get in trouble over sneaking away from Camp Zero and "borrowing" the Jeep.

But she had been fooled before. Fooled by C.J. on the night of the kidnapping. Fooled by Clayton, the thief and troublemaker who had protested his innocence, while plotting his next act of destructiveness. Even this charade with Madison's accident had fooled her at first. Could she trust her judgment now?

And who's shooting?

Tim took a step toward the door.

"Don't," Madison warned. "You heard my father. Stay here until he gives the all clear."

More shots, and not all of them sounded the same. There was a distinctive difference in the loudness and pitch. *Two different kinds of guns*, she thought.

"That's my father's pistol," Madison exclaimed.

Paula stared at the empty door for a moment and then reached a decision. *I will not be fooled again.*

"Paula. Don't."

She paid no heed to Madison's plea, but it was not as easy to ignore Tim's questioning look. "We need to know what's going on again. Maybe this is another one of their sick mind-games."

She did not actually believe that, but the alternative explanations were too frightening to consider.

"It's not," Madison insisted. "Whatever's going on out there is bad. We need to get down, find a place to hide."

Paula shot a glance back at her. "If something bad is happening, we have to do something. Find weapons of our own."

"Those shots were coming from the armory. That's where all the weapons are."

"All of them?" Tim asked. "I'll bet your dad keeps a gun or two in his office."

"Just the .45, and he's got that with him." Even as she said it, she cocked her head sideways, listening, and her expression went tight with concern. Following the earlier exchange of gunfire, an ominous silence had set in.

"We can't stay here," Paula said. "We can try to sneak around the armory, go in the back door." She didn't know if the armory *had* a back door, but she felt a real need to get moving. "At the very least, maybe we can get a look at what's going on out there."

Madison was clearly torn between her sense of responsibility to carry out her father's instructions, and the desire to do exactly what Paula was suggesting. She took a breath. "Okay, we can do that, but you've got to follow my lead. Your safety is my responsibility."

"No it's not," Tim said quickly. "Survival is an individual responsibility. You told us that, remember?"

"I suppose I did." She pursed her lips, as if contemplating whether or not to push the issue. "Follow me."

She stopped at the door, edged out into the open, and then advanced down the hallway to the exit door at the west end of the building, with Paula and Tim right behind her. As they lined up behind her, preparing to leave the building as discreetly as they could, there was a burst of gunfire—multiple shots, possibly from the same weapon, fired in rapid succession. There was a brief pause, and then another burst.

"That's not coming from the armory," Madison said. "They're moving."

"Where are they?" Tim asked.

"Not sure." She coaxed the door open a few inches, then a few more. There was another burst, definitely coming from somewhere to the south, in the reception courtyard or somewhere beyond it. Madison advanced to the corner of the building, peeked around the corner, then waved for Paula and Tim to join her.

"Those shots were coming from the parking lot," she whispered. "And I think I heard a Jeep drive away."

They waited a few more seconds but when no more shots were fired, broke from cover and crossed the courtyard toward the armory building. The front door stood ajar, and as they neared it, Paula could smell the distinctive sulfurous odor of recently discharged firearms. Madison paused a few steps from the door and motioned for them to crouch down, then cupped a hand to her mouth and shouted, "Hello in the armory?"

"Maddie!" a faint voice—Dickson's—croaked. "Help."

Madison rushed in. Paula followed, but was stopped in her tracks by the carnage inside.

There was blood everywhere. Splattered and streaked on the floor and walls. It took her a moment to realize that most of it was concentrated around two motionless figures wearing the camp uniform. Dickson lay just a few feet inside, a semi-automatic pistol still within reach. He had rolled onto his side and had his hands pressed to a spot on his chest, but seemed unable to stanch the flow of blood from a wound there. From where she stood, Paula could see a second wound in his back, a few inches from his left armpit. His breathing was wet and ragged.

Madison was kneeling next to him, but seemed too stunned to do anything to help. Paula felt a similar paralysis taking hold of her and forced herself to keep going. Dickson was still alive, but if someone didn't help him, he wouldn't be for long.

I guess "someone" is me.

She knelt beside Madison and gripped the young woman's hand. "I've got this. Go check the others."

Madison looked back at her, confused at first, then grateful. She nodded.

"Tim," Paula said. "Give her a hand. Then find me some first aid supplies."

She returned her attention to Dickson, and tried to remember what she was supposed to do.

A-B-Cs…No, that's not right. He's not unconscious and I already know what the injury is. Gunshot wound, through and through. He's bleeding out.

Stop the bleeding. Apply pressure to the wound.

She used her knife to carefully cut away Dickson's blood soaked uniform blouse and the T-shirt underneath to lay bare the wound, a ragged hole in the man's back too filled with blood for her to see what lay beneath. Paula knew this was probably the exit wound, where the bullet, deformed by the initial impact had erupted outward, tearing away a sizeable chunk of flesh in the process. In contrast, the wound on the front of his chest looked tiny, as if someone had stabbed him with a nail or ice pick. There was some bruising around the site but surprisingly little blood. There was no indication of bubbling around either wound, which she took as a hopeful sign; by some miracle, the bullet had not pierced his chest cavity.

Working quickly, she sliced Dickson's T-shirt into several long strips which she tied together. She balled up the rest of the fabric and pressed it firmly over the wound, using the strips to hold it in place, threading it under his arm, around his chest and over his right shoulder, and then cinching it tightly to put pressure on the wound. Dickson, who was still clinging to consciousness, grunted a little but did not fight her.

"You're going to be okay, Mr. Dickson," she said, as much to calm herself as her patient. She didn't know if that was true, but decided there was nothing to be gained by acting with anything less than total certainty.

She was so focused on what she was doing that she didn't even notice Tim and Madison returning until Tim held out an armful of medical supplies. "Will this help?"

She looked up. "The others?"

Tim swallowed down the bulge of emotion in his throat and shook his head.

They're dead? The realization stunned Paula, but she shook it off. *I guess this was what they were trying to teach us by faking Madison's death,* she thought. *When something bad happens, you have to push through and keep going.*

She tore open the wrapping on several gauze sponges and placed them directly on top of her makeshift bandage, which was already partially soaked through with blood. Short of suturing the wound herself—something Paula definitely didn't think she could do—adding more pressure to the wound seemed to be the only way to keep him alive until a surgeon could repair the damage.

"Madison. You need to call emergency services. Get a rescue helicopter out here."

Madison stared at her for a moment, eyes wide with a deer-in-the-headlights look, but then she nodded and moved off to find a telephone.

Paula checked the bandages. There was so much cloth over the wound, it was hard to say whether she had slowed the bleeding, but Dickson's skin was pale, and that wasn't a good sign. "He's lost a lot of blood," she told

Tim, keeping her voice low so that Madison wouldn't hear. "We need to get his volume up. Was there an IV starter kit with the first aid supplies?"

"I'll check."

As Tim bounded away, Paula saw Dickson's hand move, his fingers curling in a beckoning gesture. Realizing that he wanted to tell her something, she leaned down and put her ear next to his mouth.

"Kids," he whispered.

Paula thought she understood. "The kids back at Camp Zero? You're worried about them."

A faint headshake." Did… this."

Paula had been so focused on treating Dickson's injuries that she had given no thought to who had caused them. "Are you saying that kids did this?"

"Matt," he whispered. "Ryan."

An electric charge shot through Paula's extremities. Matt? Was Dickson identifying Matthew Kestrel, her teammate, and Ryan Stern from Charlie team as the shooters?

Camp Zero wasn't answering their radio.

"Oh, God." She stood up too fast, felt the blood leave her head and dropped back to her knees to keep from fainting. Tim was there a moment later, steadying her. She looked up at him. "We have to get back to Camp Zero."

Tim stared at her for a moment then nodded. "We can take one of the Jeeps."

Dickson managed a weak nod. "Take… guns."

"Guns?" Paula echoed. That was what Matthew and Ryan had come here for.

"I'll go see what I can dig up," Tim said. He held something out to Paula, a plastic bag full of clear liquid with a length of clear tubing wrapped around it several times.

Paula stared at the IV kit and then looked down at Dickson. No matter what was happening at Camp Zero, she had a patient right here who needed her. She took a deep breath and began unwinding the tubing.

Madison returned just as Paula was tying a rubber tourniquet around Dickson's biceps. "They won't send a medical helicopter until the police clear the scene," she said, bitterly. "It could be morning before help gets here."

Paula located a vein in the hollow of Dickson's elbow, swabbed the surrounding area with an alcohol soaked pad, and brought the uncapped needle catheter close to the vein.

"Have you ever done that before?" Madison asked.

"No," Paula admitted. "I've read about it, but this will be my first try."

"Well, you're doing fine. Just be careful not to punch all the way through. Watch for a flash of blood in the tube."

"Maybe you should do it."

"You're almost done. Just poke it through…"

Paula felt the needle break through and then saw the flash of blood Madison had described.

"Good. Now advance the catheter."

Paula slid the thin tube through the hollow needle and into the vein, and then taped it in place before withdrawing the needle. Madison handed her the tube, which was already connected to the bag of saline solution, and she attached it to the end of the catheter and opened the valve, then removed the tourniquet, releasing a steady flow of fluid to Dickson's depleted circulatory system.

"Good job," Madison said. She hugged Paula. "Thank you."

Paula let out the breath she had been holding. "I can drive him out. You and Tim need to go to Camp Zero."

Dickson tapped her arm. "I'll be…okay. Go. Camp."

"Will these work?" Tim shouted, stepping out from the gun locker in the rear of the building. He was holding three rifles and had a satchel slung over one shoulder. "AR-15s."

"Those will work," Madison said. "Make sure you get ammo and magazines."

He patted the satchel.

"Take… radio," Dickson said. "Be careful."

Paula didn't like the idea of leaving Dickson behind, but he appeared to be stable and she had already done about everything she could for him. And there might be people at Camp Zero who needed help a lot more than he did. They made him as comfortable as they could, then headed out.

A grim discovery awaited them in the parking lot. Before taking two of the Jeeps, the killers—Matthew and Ryan, if Dickson was correct—had shot up the radiators on the remaining vehicles. Madison however was quick to point out an alternative.

"We can take the quad bikes—all-terrain vehicles. We've got a bunch of them in the garage."

Before they could turn away though, Paula spotted lights moving in the distance. A vehicle, or possibly more than one, was negotiating the trail up the mountainside.

"It's them," she said, feeling a chill that had nothing to do with the cold night air. "Ryan and Matthew. They came here for weapons, but now they're going back to Camp Zero."

"Why?" Madison asked.

"Unfinished business. We need to get moving."

Despite the fact that the killers had a head start, Paula clung to a sliver-thin ray of hope. If they were going back, it meant that someone was still alive at Camp Zero.

But for how much longer?

Chapter Thirty-Eight - **Jack**

"We're lost," Jenn complained, not for the first time, and as before, the others shushed her. They weren't lost. Being lost would have required a destination, a physical objective, and right now their only goal was to move away from Camp Zero, away from the killers whom Jack felt certain were still stalking them.

Initially, the rest of the group had supported Jack's decision to simply run, but as the hours wore on and the night chill deepened, the seeds of dissent took root. Dustin argued that they should stop and set an ambush. Juan seconded this idea, and added a twist.

"We should set traps like the guy in that story. The one where this dude hunts other dudes."

Jack was familiar with the reference, the timeless classic *The Most Dangerous Game* by Richard Connell, in which a big game hunter becomes the prey for another hunter, and despite being armed only with a knife, manages to outwit and ultimately kill his opponent. It was a story that had survived the War not only in its original form, but in dozens of adaptations.

Turning the tables on the six young killers, their former teammates, was tempting, but Jack was obliged to dissuade the others from making the attempt. Without knowing how much of a lead they had on their pursuers, they might very well be caught before their preparations were complete. Moreover, judging by their ferocity and efficiency with which the six had eliminated the adults at Camp Zero, Jack doubted his group would last long in a fight. Better, he advised, to keep moving, at least until daybreak when they would be able to see what they were doing. The others had agreed, reluctantly, but Jack knew it was a temporary capitulation.

As time passed, their ability to see in the dark improved and soon they were moving at about a normal walking pace, which was evidently a little too fast for Clayton, who struggled to keep up and probably would have been left behind had Jack not doubled back to urge him on.

"We should just leave him," Jenn said. "He's slowing us all down."

"Maybe you should," Clayton shot back, his tone more defeated than petulant. "Just leave me out here to die."

"Cut it out," Jack admonished in a loud whisper, a tacit reminder for them both to keep their voices down. "We're still a team, and that means we stick together."

"Why?" Jenn retorted. "If he can't keep up, he's putting us all at risk. Staying with him will get us all killed. It's simple math."

Jack couldn't believe what he was hearing. Jenn was suggesting they sacrifice Clayton to save themselves. "Enough people have died tonight," he said.

Dustin spoke up. "Jack, I know he's your friend, but Jenn might be right about this."

Jack felt like screaming, *He's not my friend! I don't like him any more than you do, but he's your teammate.* Instead, he shook his head in the darkness. "I'm not leaving anyone behind."

The grunted reply told Jack that Dustin did not share that position and that if Jack could not cajole Clayton into keeping up, they might both be left behind.

"What's that?" Juan mumbled.

Jack had no idea what Juan was referring to, but he could see well enough to know that they had all stopped. He could also see that the horizon, where the night sky disappeared into the darker landscape, was now high above their heads.

"Mountains, maybe," Dustin answered.

"We've reached the other side of the valley," Jack said. "We must have overshot the wilderness campsite. I wonder how we missed the creek."

"Great," snarled Jenn, sarcastically.

"Actually, it is," Jack said quickly. "It means we're making better time than we thought. It also means we'll have the high ground by morning if we keep going."

Yet, something about the situation made Jack uneasy. A few minutes later, he realized what it was when they reached the base of a cliff.

"This is where Madison fell," Dustin said, stating what Jack had already realized. A nervous hush fell over the group as they stood on the ill-omened spot, contemplating what to do next.

Jack finally broke the silence. "We need to climb it."

Clayton, despite being out of breath from the long forced march, was quick to reply. "You want to climb this in the dark? No way. I wouldn't even try it in broad daylight."

"In case you forgot," Dustin shot back, "we're trying to get away from a bunch of murderers."

"We can do it," Jack said, with more confidence than he felt. "We'll have to use our lights but we can do it. Even if they see us, we'll make the top before they can get here, and then we'll have the high ground."

"It's a sheer cliff," Clayton persisted. "We'll be saving them the trouble of killing us."

Jack's answer was to click on his headlamp, illuminating the rock face and revealing a craggy rock face studded with protrusions and riddled with cracks. He tilted his head back, shining the light up to the top and saw more of the same. "This is doable," he said. "I've seen playground equip-ment that's harder to climb."

"I'll bet Madison would disagree with you," Clayton grumbled.

"Shut up," Jenn said sharply.

The apparent ease of the route did seem to conflict with the tragic outcome of Madison's earlier attempt, but if that fall was no accident, then there was no reason to believe the route itself was unsafe.

Jack gripped one of the outcroppings and put his weight on it to see if it would crumble. It did not. "We just have to take it slow. Three points of contact at all times, just like Mr. Decker said. It'll be like climbing a ladder."

"Without ropes?" Juan asked, skeptical.

"Ropes are just there to save you if you fall," Dustin countered. "I don't plan on falling."

More lights came on and then Dustin moved forward and, with just a momentary hesitation, placed his hands on the wall and began climbing. Somebody drew in a sharp anxious breath, but Dustin didn't back down. In a matter of seconds, he reached the halfway point, and kept going, never slowing, never looking down.

As he neared the top, Jack felt an uncomfortable burning sensation in his chest and realized he had been holding his breath. He let it out and sucked in fresh air, just as Dustin heaved himself up and over the edge, and disappeared from view. A moment later, his light beamed down on them as he stuck his head out into space.

"Piece of cake," he called out, sounding a little winded. "Just don't look down."

Juan swaggered forward and mounted the wall with even more assertiveness, and in less than two minutes, Dustin was pulling him up and over the edge.

Dylan, the quietest member of the team, went next, but his ascent was not as smooth as the older boys. When he was only about ten feet up, he froze. "No. I can't. Get me down."

"You can do it," Jack called up. "It's just like a big ladder. You can climb a ladder, right?"

Dylan didn't budge. "I can't. My arms are too tired. I'll fall."

Jack hooded his light and glanced back out across the valley, wondering if the killers had seen their lights. Were they, even now, closing in for the kill?

"Dylan, listen to me. Do you have good footholds?"

"Yeah."

"Okay, what you need to do now is get a good grip with your left hand...and then let go with your right."

"I can't let go."

"You can," Jack assured him. "Let go with your right hand and shake it out for a few seconds. Then switch and do the same with the left."

After a few more seconds of hesitation, Dylan succeeded in relaxing his grip as Jack had urged. This small victory seemed to bolster his confidence, and after about thirty more seconds of resting one arm, then the other, he resumed his climb. He was considerably slower than Dustin and Juan, pausing twice more for rest breaks, but he made the rest of the climb without freezing up.

Jenn turned to Clayton. "Your turn."

Clayton shook his head. "Nope. I'm not doing it."

"We have to," Jack urged. "You saw how easy it is."

Jenn shook her head in disgust. "He's not gonna do it. You should just leave him behind." Then, without further comment, she started up the wall, moving with surprising ease.

"See?" Jack said to Clayton, pointing up at her. "If she can do it, you can too."

It was, evidently, the wrong thing to say. "She's right," Clayton said. "You should just leave me."

"I'm not going to leave you," Jack replied, gritting his teeth in frustration. "But you need to suck it up and climb that wall."

Clayton shook his head and then, to Jack's dismay, turned and plopped down on the ground and hugged his knees to his chest, curling into a defensive ball like a frightened hedgehog.

"Clayton..."

"Forget about him," Dustin shouted. "He's dead weight. Don't get yourself killed for him."

Jack looked up at the row of headlamps blazing from the top of the cliff. Every one of them belonged to someone who had overcome the innate fear of falling and simply done what had to be done. They had all taken responsibility for their own survival, even Jenn. If Clayton wasn't going to do the same, maybe he deserved to be left behind.

It was clear that no amount of prodding or taunting would get Clayton up the cliff. Even if, by some miracle, he could be convinced to approach the wall, he would almost certainly balk or freeze. Nevertheless, Jack couldn't bring himself to abandon the other boy. "Damn it, Clayton. You're going to get us both killed."

He cupped a hand over his mouth and shouted up to the others. "You guys go on ahead. We'll find another way up."

"We're not going to wait for you," Dustin called back. "If you're smart you'll just leave him, Jack. If not, you guys are on your own."

Then one by one, the lights vanished, leaving Clayton and Jack alone at the bottom of the cliff.

Chapter Thirty-Nine - **Sarah**

The slap sounded as loud as a gunshot, and Sarah jumped a little, not only startled by the noise, but also shocked by the anger behind the blow.

"Wake up," Natalie snarled, striking Philip's face again.

The boy's head snapped to the side with the impact, but then his eyelids began to flutter.

"Why did you kill those people?" Natalie said.

Philip mumbled something. It sounded like "starring."

Natalie must have heard something different. "Starlings? What does that mean?"

Sarah didn't recognize that word at all.

"Starlings are birds," John said.

The comment seemed to rouse Philip from his daze, but as he became fully conscious, he closed his mouth and stared up at Natalie defiantly.

"Good," Natalie said. "You're awake. Your buddy Thomas took off. I guess he doesn't care what happens to you."

Philip's jaw moved but he kept his silence.

Natalie slapped him again. Sarah winced as if she had been the one struck. This was a side of Natalie she had never seen before and it scared her. She had to remind herself that Philip was a killer. She had seen him kill one of the instructors at Camp Zero. One of his friends had killed Alma.

"Why did you kill them?" Natalie said. "Are you going to kill us all? Is that the plan?" When Philip didn't answer, Natalie grabbed hold of his arm—the arm she had wounded earlier—and squeezed, digging her fingernails into the cut. Philip tensed, his face contorting in agony. "If you're planning to kill us, then maybe we should kill you right now."

Sarah sucked in her breath. *Killing him like this would be murder, wouldn't it?* She hoped Natalie was just bluffing.

"Go ahead," Philip snarled, breaking his silence. "Kill me, and you're all dead."

"So? That was your plan all along, wasn't it?"

"You don't matter."

Natalie relaxed her grip. "We don't matter? Why not?"

Philip now raised his head to look at the rest of the group who stood around him in a tight circle. "Let me go, and maybe I'll forget about this."

"Why don't we matter?" Natalie asked again. "You killed the others. Why? Did they matter?"

"They were in the way."

Natalie squeezed his wound again. "In the way of what?"

"You need to let me go," Philip said through clenched teeth.

"That's not going to happen. You're a murderer. If you answer my questions, I might just keep you alive until the police get here."

Philip gave a snort of derision, unmoved by the threat.

Natalie changed gears. "Why did you mention starlings?"

"I didn't. You misheard."

"No, I don't think so. Is that some kind of code word?"

Philip's silence seemed to confirm this, so Natalie pressed on. "You're Starlings, aren't you? That's what you call yourself. You and Matthew and Devra."

Philip's left eye twitched and then, to Sarah's astonishment, he spoke. "Starlings are mimics. They learn the songs of other birds so they can blend in, hide in plain sight. Just like us."

"Only you're not birds. You're assassins." Natalie paused as if saying it aloud had unlocked the mystery. "You're assassins," she repeated. "Children trained to be assassins. Is Philip your real name, or did you kill the real Philip and take his place?"

Sarah was horrified by the suggestion, and even more by the fact that Philip did not refute it. *How many people have they killed?*

"So, you and your Starlings killed a bunch of kids who were on their way to the Survival Academy, and then took their place so you could get closer to your target."

"You've got it all figured out," Philip replied, sarcastically.

"So who do you work for? A foreign government? Neo-Nazis? The mob? Who trains kids to be killers?"

Despite his obvious pain, Philip threw his head back and laughed. "Just what do you think it is they do here?"

"That's not the same thing," Natalie said. "We're learning how to survive, not how to be assassins."

"Whatever lets you sleep at night," Philip said, still chuckling. "The strong kill the weak to stay strong. That's what survival is. That's the law of nature."

Sarah was horrified, and not just because of Philip's callous attitude toward life and death. There was a sliver of truth in what he said. Everything they had learned at the Survival Academy could be boiled down to a single rule: Do whatever it takes to survive.

And that was what Natalie was doing. Threatening Philip, hurting him, in order to learn more about the Starlings and the threat they posed, which in turn just might help them all stay alive.

But if you have to become a monster in order to survive, what's the point?

Natalie drew back suddenly and, for a moment, Sarah thought her cousin was thinking the same thing she was, but then Natalie grabbed Philip's arm again. "Who's the target? Sarah and John? Is that why you killed Alma and Kevin? Eliminate their bodyguards so you can get a clear shot at them?"

Philip grimaced, blinked, but said nothing.

Natalie let go. "No, you were even more surprised than the rest of us when Kevin pulled that badge. You didn't even know the President's kids were here."

"Surprise," Philip sneered. "The world doesn't revolve around you and your family."

He dropped his voice to a sullen mumble. "The plan was working perfectly. Nobody would have gotten hurt. Nobody would even know what was happening. But then suddenly we've got two undercover cops and Ma is threatening to shut the course down. We had to improvise."

"Nobody hurt?" Natalie said, then nodded. "Not an assassination. A kidnapping."

"We were going to make it look like he just ran away."

"Who?" Natalie pressed.

Philip narrowed his gaze. "You should let me go. No one else has to die. We don't care about any of you. We just want Clayton."

Chapter Forty - **Natalie**

"Clayton?" Natalie echoed. *Clayton the trouble-maker. Clayton the thief.* Although she had not had any direct interactions with the heavy-set red-headed boy, she had heard the gossip. How he had sabotaged Paula's shelter, and stolen food.

And who had been spreading that gossip?

"*A guy like that is bad news for all of us,*" Matthew had told her. "*Who knows what he might do next. I mean, they gave us knives, right?*"

Matthew Kestrel, who had hurled a spear into Ma's chest and driven his knife through Kevin's throat.

"Why him?"

Philip's willingness to share evaporated. "What difference does it make? I'm offering you your life. All of you. Just let me go."

Natalie dug her fingernails into Philip's wound again, harder this time, as if she might squeeze into him the helplessness she felt—the weakness that had plagued her ever since the kidnapping. Philip grimaced, a whimper of pain slipping past his clenched teeth.

"Why him?" she repeated.

"His father," Philip gasped. "Pressure."

She didn't know who Clayton's father was or why the Starlings wanted to pressure him, but she could make an educated guess. Clayton's father was probably an influential public figure or maybe a politician, who had decided to send his son to the Survival Academy for much the same reason the Rourke children were there. If the Starlings succeeded in abducting the boy, they would have leverage to influence policy or extort favor in order to further their agenda.

Their objective had never been to kill Clayton, or anyone else, but the revelation that there were undercover federal agents at the Academy had forced them to improvise. In the confusion following the massacre at

Camp Zero, they had lost track of their target, which in turn had compelled them to split up and track the escaping survivors. Philip and Thomas had come after Natalie's group, and when they had realized Clayton wasn't with them, Thomas had chosen to break contact, abandoning Philip, not because the odds were against him, but so he could relay the message to the other Starlings.

Natalie had heard other rumors concerning Clayton. She knew that Jack had formed an unlikely friendship with the boy, defending him against the incessant accusations and persecution, even getting into a fight with one of their teammates. Jack and Clayton were almost certainly traveling together with the rest of the survivors, and they had no idea what was coming for them.

She let go of Philip. "We have to help Jack."

"We don't even know where he is," Luke said.

"We can backtrack to Camp Zero. If we have to, we can follow Thomas to the others."

"They're killers," Heather said.

"That's right. And they're hunting my brother." That was reason enough for Natalie, but she knew a more persuasive argument would be needed to convince Heather and the others to join her. "You're right. They've had more training than us, and they're not afraid of us. But we've had some training, too."

"One lesson," Heather shot back. "Unarmed self-defense. They've got knives and spears."

"We've got knives, too." Heather did not respond to this, but Natalie could tell she had failed to convince the other girl. "All right. It doesn't matter. I'll go alone if I have to."

"I'm coming with you," John said.

Natalie shook her head. "No. You and Sarah are staying here."

"You just said—"

"You're the President's kids," Natalie said. "I'm not about to put you in danger."

There were other reasons, better reasons for not bringing her cousins along, foremost being their age, but she wasn't about to use that argument against them. She also wasn't about to put any more of her family members in harm's way, but that was something she would not admit in front of the others.

"That's not fair," John protested. "My dad would want me to help."

"Your dad would want you to protect your sister," Natalie said. "That's the most important thing you can do right now."

"I want to go, too," Sarah chimed in.

"No. You're staying here. That's final."

"Wait, the President's kids?" Randy said. "As in *the President?*"

"Try to catch up, Randy," someone muttered.

Natalie ignored him. She stood up. "I have to get moving. Get in the shelter. Stay warm and stay out of sight until help arrives."

"I'll come," Heather said in a quiet voice.

Gary stepped forward. "Me, too."

One by one the others all signaled their willingness, though somewhat more reluctantly, probably motivated more by peer pressure than anything else. Randy was the last to speak, so Natalie figured he was the least willing.

"Randy, I want you to stay behind and keep an eye on John and Sarah."

She could see the relief in his eyes, but to his credit, he tried to act disappointed. "Are you sure? Maybe someone else should stay?"

"They're the President's children," she assured him. "Keeping them safe is a very big responsibility."

Randy gave a solemn nod, then pointed to the still glowering Philip. "What about him?"

Slit his throat, Natalie wanted to say. But there were too many reasons why that wasn't an option, not the least of which was that he was only a child, the same age as John. Natalie didn't know how the boy had been transformed into a psychopath, or if that programming could be undone. That would be a decision for courts and psychiatrists. "Tie him up. Hands and feet. Use his bootlaces. And gag him. When he heard this, Philip tried to pull away, forcing Natalie and the others to pin him down while Randy began stripping his bootlaces.

"You're all dead," Philip raged. "After we get Clayton, we'll come back and gut every one of you."

Natalie used her knife to cut a strip of cloth from Philip's uniform blouse, and jammed it into his mouth, silencing the tirade. "I'll knock you out again if you keep struggling," she said.

The threat worked, but Philip remained rigid and uncooperative as Randy looped the heavy-duty string around his ankles and cinched them tight. When that was done, they rolled him over and forcibly crossed his wrists behind his back, eliciting a howl of pain, and tied them together as well. Natalie checked all the knots, verifying that they would not slip, and then stood up.

"Cover him up, too," she advised Randy. "And then get into the shelter. Take care of them." She stressed the last part, and waited for an acknowledging nod before turning to the others. "Let's get going. We've got a lot of ground to cover."

They regarded her with naked trepidation, but none of them balked. Natalie wondered if soldiers looked that way before going into battle. In a way, that was exactly what they were now. There was no guarantee that any of them would survive what was coming.

But still they went.

Chapter Forty-One - **John**

As they piled tree branches atop Philip to camouflage him, John had to fight the urge to kick the boy. He was angry. He couldn't remember ever having been so angry at anyone, not even the Neo-Nazis who had killed his step-grandfather. Philip hadn't just attacked them; he had betrayed John personally, pretending to be a friend in order to hide the crime he and the other Starlings were planning.

He wished Natalie had done more than just cut Philip's arm and knock him out. And he wished he could have gone along with his older cousin to kill the rest of the Starlings instead of being left behind like he was little kid who needed protecting. But Sarah *was* a little kid who needed protecting, and that was his job, too.

"That should be good enough," Randy said. "Now, let's go finish the shelter and warm up. I'll start a fire."

"I don't think Nat would like that," Sarah said. "She told us to hide. The Starlings might see a fire."

Randy gave her an irritated frown. "If there's anyone out there to see a fire, they've probably already seen our lights."

"But they might come back," Sarah persisted. "We shouldn't do it."

"The smell of smoke might also attract attention," John added.

Randy threw up his hands. "Fine. If you guys want to freeze your asses off, we won't build a fire. But I don't want to hear any complaints."

John suspected the only complaints would come from Randy himself, but he didn't say it out loud.

They followed him back to the partially-built shelter and quickly finished weaving in the roof of leaves and branches to shut out at least some of the chill. When they were done, they switched off their headlamps and crawled inside, sitting back to back to share their body heat.

John immediately felt a little warmer, but after so much activity, sitting still was harder than he thought it would be. He hugged his knees to his chest and tried not to think about how far off the morning was.

"Do you think Jack's okay?" Sarah whispered.

"I'm sure he's fine," John said, not because he was sure, but because it was a better answer than "I don't know."

"Shhh," Randy said, with more than a little sarcasm. "The Starlings might hear us, and that would make Natalie mad."

"Don't be such a jerk," John shot back.

Randy made a dismissive snorting sound in the darkness and then asked, "Is your dad really the President?"

"Yep," Sarah said, proudly.

"My dad says your dad is the worst President ever. He says he's ruining everything."

John felt Sarah slump a little and had to fight the urge to respond in kind. Instead, he said, "Well, you can tell him that when he gives you a medal for protecting us."

"Whoa," Randy said. "Do you think he'd do that? Give me a medal?"

John rolled his eyes.

"That would be sweet," Randy went on; his earlier inflammatory comment already a distant memory.

A loud crack, like a tree limb splitting, silenced his musings, and a moment later, John was flattened by a crush of loose foliage as the shelter collapsed upon them. The impact left him disoriented, the struggle to right himself only served to further entangle him in the makeshift web. Sarah let out a squeal of alarm and Randy swore, thrashing to get free, which had the effect of dumping even more branches onto John.

A light flashed on and John could see the silhouette of Randy, standing up amid the wreckage, kicking his way free of the pole frame with little regard for how this would affect the other two people trapped beneath it.

Something moved in the shadows behind him, striking with the suddenness of a rattlesnake's bite, and the light went flying, but in the brief instant before it did, John could see Randy's face contorting, blood erupting from mouth and nose, as a rock, bigger than both his fists put together, slammed into the side of his head. John also saw the face of the person holding the rock.

Philip! No!

The light went out, plunging the world into what seemed like total darkness. John didn't see Randy crumple to the ground, practically on top of him, but he heard the crunch. With a heave, John burst free of the shelter and rolled away from the sagging form of Randy. He reached up for his headlamp, but his hand encountered only hair. *Must have lost it when the shelter fell on me,* he thought, reaching instead for his knife.

"You should have just let me go," Philip said from out of the darkness. "Now I'm going to have to kill you."

John whirled, trying to orient himself toward the disembodied voice, and slashed the air in front of him, just in case.

"Here's a little tip," Philip went on. "When you take a prisoner, you should search them thoroughly. You know, for little things like hidden razor blades. Won't do you much good now, though. You know, when we found out who you were, we thought about taking you, too."

The voice was closer and off to John's left. He shifted position and sliced the air again.

"But since your dad isn't going to be President much longer, we decided it wasn't worth the bother."

"What—?" John bit off the question. Philip was trying to distract him, keep him off balance. He had to focus.

"That's right. The dominos are all lined up. They're already falling. Just like in Germany."

Germany? The brutal attack that had taken the life of John's grandfather had been carried out by Neo-Nazis. Were the Starlings part of that same global conspiracy?

Was his father next on the list?

"Not that you'll live to see it," Philip went on. "But maybe I'll keep you alive long enough to watch what I do to your little sister."

He's trying to make me mad, John told himself. *Trying to distract me.*

Ignore the words; focus on the sound of his voice. Where is he?

Over the thrum of his own beating heart, he could just make out a soft crunch-crunch of footsteps, getting closer.

He spun around completely, slashing back and forth with his blade, striking only air, and then something hit him, hard enough to knock him off his feet. He slammed into the ground, the wind knocked out of him, the knife falling from nerveless fingers. He flailed his arms frantically, trying to ward off the next attack, but a moment later, a blow struck the side of his head, the impact flashing like lightning through his skull. Then, something punched into his chest and suddenly his whole body felt like it was on fire.

A horrible shrieking noise filled the night, and through the haze of pain, John realized the sound was coming from him. His left arm felt like it was made of molten lead, no longer connected to the rest of him, and when he tried to move, the pain drove him to the edge of consciousness.

Philip had stabbed him, probably with his own discarded knife, driving the blade into his pectoral muscle, just below his left shoulder. The wound throbbed, the flesh seeming to swell up around the metal. It felt like the blade had gone clear through him, nailing him to the ground.

There was another flash, but this one was different because this time, he could actually see by its light. He glimpsed Philip's outline, looming above him, one hand still wrapped around the hilt of the knife that jutted from John's chest.

The light wasn't a mirage induced by nerve pain. It was real.

Sarah?

Run. Run as fast as you can and don't look back.

He tried to shout, but the words never left his brain.

Philip started to turn toward the source of the light then he threw up his hands to ward off Sarah's attack.

John knew there wasn't much his little sister could do against the trained killer. He would easily overpower her, and then, as he had promised, kill her while John's own life drained away.

"No!" The cry slipped through John's clenched teeth. He reached out with his right hand, but the knife—or maybe it was the pain—held him transfixed where he lay.

The knife….

He reached across his chest, took hold of the hilt in a backhand grip, and heaved himself to a sitting position. The effort sent an electric surge of pain through him, bringing him to the very edge of consciousness, but the sudden movement caused the blade to slip free. He felt a measure of instantaneous relief as the offending piece of metal left his body, but that was not the reason he had pulled the knife out.

With the last of his strength, he hammered forward with his fist, driving the knife into the side of Philip's neck. The boy cried out, twisting away from the blade, and just before the darkness claimed him, John felt something warm splash onto his face.

Chapter Forty-Two - **Tim**

Before leaving the Academy compound, they returned to the armory to update Dickson, and check on him one last time before heading out. They found him, not only conscious, but attempting to crawl to the nearest telephone. When Madison told him about the Jeeps and the fact that Matthew and Ryan appeared to be on their way back to Camp Zero, he grunted, "Better take NODs."

"NODs?" Tim asked. "What's that?"

"Something that might give us a fighting chance," Madison said. She darted back into the weapon's locker and returned with three small plastic cases, which she handed to Tim and Paula. Tim opened the clamps on his and immediately recognized the device, which looked a little like a pair of mini-binoculars nestled inside. "Night vision goggles."

"We call them NODs. Night optical devices," Madison explained. "They're for the instructors. So they can monitor students during the field exercise. This way, we can keep our lights off so they won't see us coming. I'll warn you, they'll take a little getting used to."

Tim took his out and saw that it was actually a monocular—with just one eyepiece. Madison showed them how to put in batteries and attach a head strap mounting system which was more complicated than Tim would have suspected.

Once they had all donned the devices, Madison led them outside and gave a quick lesson in how to use them as they made their way to the garage. Tim immediately noticed that the NODs played tricks with his depth perception, making the ground seem closer than it was. "I'm going to have to learn how to walk all over again," he said.

"Don't worry," Madison told him, pointing to a row of all-terrain vehicles—quad-bikes—parked inside the garage. "We won't be doing that much walking."

After another hasty lesson in how to operate the quad-bikes, they headed out. Madison set a slow pace at first until Tim and Paula had the hang of shifting gears up and down as dictated by the terrain. Tim caught on quickly—it was a little like playing a video-game while riding a bicycle, only he didn't have to pedal. Wearing the NODs was a surreal experience, and the strangest part was how bright the sky looked. Night vision devices functioned by amplifying available light, which meant that stars which were too dim to be seen with the naked eye, blazed like fireflies.

Under better circumstances, it would have been one of the most awesome experiences of his life but the distant headlights of the stolen Jeeps moving up the mountainside—enhanced to near searchlight intensity by the NODs—were a constant reminder that this was no joyride. And when those lights disappeared behind the mountain, it was a warning for them to hurry.

The nimble quad-bikes charged up the trail, which had seemed dangerously narrow when riding in a Jeep. Tim reckoned they were making good time, but when they reached the summit of the pass, he saw the headlights moving across the valley floor, and knew that they had not closed the gap nearly enough.

They were only halfway down the mountainside when the lights stopped moving, and a few seconds later, went out.

"That's Camp Zero," Madison called out.

As they rolled onward, Tim kept expecting to hear the report of rifle fire, which would have been audible even over the persistent burr of the ATV engines. The absence of it was even more ominous.

When they reached the valley floor, Madison signaled for them to stop. "We'll go on foot from here," she said. "It will take longer, but we can't risk the noise."

"Every second we waste—"

"She's right," Paula cut in. "There hasn't been any shooting. Maybe the plan was to take hostages. Sneaking in is the only way to make sure they don't start killing people."

They moved forward in a line, walking quickly but taking short steps to minimize the sound of their footsteps. As they neared their destination, the glow of the fire became visible in the night vision display, but remained too dim to see with his unaided eye. There were no other lights in the camp.

Madison signaled another halt. "It's too quiet in there," she whispered. "They must be in the tents. I'm going to circle around, approach from the backside. You two cover me."

"Cover you?" Paula asked.

"If you see someone, start shooting. Aim high. You haven't zeroed these weapons and I'm guessing you've never fired a rifle using NODs, so the odds of hitting what you're aiming at are pretty much nil at this distance. And since we don't know where the hostages are, there's a chance you could hit one of them with a stray bullet."

Tim recalled what Mr. Hickok had said about the importance of zeroing a weapon—adjusting the sights to the individual shooter—before taking it into the field. At point blank range, it wasn't that much of an issue, but at distances greater than fifty yards, seemingly minor variations in a shooter's natural sight picture could mean the difference between a hit and a miss. The only way to compensate was to shoot several rounds under controlled circumstances, and then adjust the weapon sights up or down, right or left, to make sure that the bullet went exactly where the sights were pointing.

"Then why shoot at all?" Paula said.

"To let me know there's trouble. And to keep the bad guys busy."

"You only need one of us to do that," Tim said. "Let me go with you."

Madison gave him an appraising glance. With her night vision monocular in place, she looked like a cyborg, half-human, half-machine. "All right, but don't take a shot unless you're sure you can hit what you're shooting at."

Tim gave a solemn nod. The enormity of what they doing, of what they would have to do when they reached Camp Zero, finally sank in. They were going to have to kill Matthew and Ryan.

The rifle in his hands suddenly felt very heavy.

Chapter Forty-Three - **Paula**

Paula stared down the length of the barrel of her AR-15, watching the embers of the fire for any sign of movement in the camp. Though she hadn't said it aloud, she was secretly relieved that Madison had set her in an overwatch position. As far back as she could remember, she had dreamed of being a doctor, saving lives. She didn't know if she had it in her to take one. But she also knew that, sometimes it was necessary to take a life in order to save another. Matthew and Ryan were killers. They had already killed at least two people, and would kill a lot more if given the chance. Her cousins might be next on their list of victims. Killing them was the only way to ensure the survival of her loved ones.

That, she realized, was the lesson Mr. Hickok had been trying to teach them. Being ready to fight, to kill if necessary, didn't make you blood-thirsty, but hesitation—not being ready, not knowing how to protect your-self—could have fatal consequences. She hadn't been ready on the night of the kidnapping, and she didn't feel much readier now.

Something moved near one of the tents and she swung the rifle toward it, careful to keep her finger away from the trigger. It was just Madison and Tim, moving stealthily toward the tents after having skirted around the camp to approach from the rear. She tilted the barrel up, pointing it at the distant mountains, but kept her eye on the camp, ready to fire at the first sign of a threat.

The seconds ticked by with agonizing slowness. A minute passed. Two. Then Madison stepped out into the open, her weapon no longer at the ready. She waved her hand in the air and then made a beckoning gesture.

Paula's heart sank. If Camp Zero was deserted then the killers were still at large, and the fate of the others remained uncertain. Nevertheless, she started forward, crossing the distance to the edge of the camp at a jog. Her anxiety deepened when she saw Tim and Madison shuffling around the assembly area like sleepwalkers, bending down every few steps to look at something on the ground. She knew, even before she got there, what they were doing. She broke into a run, not stopping until she reached the first body.

She knew, even before she knelt to check for a pulse, that the unmoving form wasn't merely unconscious. The body looked more like a discarded mannequin than a human being. The skin was unnervingly cool to the touch, and when she reached for the carotid artery, she saw the open gash, covered in dark blood, stark against the green-tinted skin.

It was Mr. Decker, the climbing instructor. His throat had been cut.

"He's dead," Tim said from behind her, his voice a hoarse whisper. "They're all dead."

He was right about Decker, but Paula was not going to simply accept that he was right about the others. She stood, started toward the next closest body. The spill of dark hair around the victim's head unmistakably identified it as Alma.

Dead.

The initial shock of the discovery was wearing off. Paula moved to the next body like a machine, numb to the horror. She imagined this must be how first responders felt when arriving at a mass casualty incident, unplugged from the grim reality of so much carnage, seeing the bodies merely as a logistical challenge.

Check for a pulse, move on.

Kevin. Dead.

Hickok…There was something different about the grizzled weapons instructor. His skin was cool, but she could sense that there was still life in him. She felt for a pulse.

"He's still alive," she shouted, her voice breaking with emotion. The discovery galvanized her. Before, she had been facing only the prospect of violence and death, but now there was a very different goal on her horizon.

Tim and Madison rushed over to her, and working together, they rolled him over and exposed his injuries. His head was misshapen, the right side of his face bruised and swollen from a blunt impact, and there was long gash across his chest still oozing blood. He had been clubbed and slashed with a knife.

"This didn't just happen," Madison said, her voice oddly detached.

As a member of the Academy teaching staff and the daughter of its chief of operations, Madison was probably very close to the other people who worked there, and was surely devastated by the loss of so many of her friends, but somehow, she had compartmentalized her emotions, locked them away in order to deal with the immediate crisis. Paula envied her ability to do that.

"What do you mean?"

"This probably happened a couple hours ago. Before Matt and Ryan went to retrieve the weapons." Madison glanced around the camp as if seeing it for the first time. "Where are the rest?"

"You're right," Tim said. "There's only…seven…eight bodies here. Everybody else must have taken off."

"Taken off?" Paula echoed. Then it hit her. "They're still alive. Nat and Jack and the kids."

"They aren't here," Tim said, his tone guarded but hopeful.

"That's why Matt and Ryan came back here," Madison said. "They're hunting the ones that got away."

Paula looked up sharply. *Hunting?* "You have to go after them."

Madison looked back uncertainly then glanced down at Hickok.

"I'll take care of him," Paula promised. "You need to go and save the others."

"She's right," Tim said. "Paula knows what she's doing. She saved your dad."

Madison frowned but then nodded slowly. "There are medical supplies in the instructors' tent. Get Mr. Hickok in there. I'll go see if I can pick up their trail."

As Madison moved off, Paula did a quick head-to-toe assessment to make sure it was safe to move Hickok. A head blow hard enough to render him unconscious for hours might very well have caused a spinal cord injury, which might result in paralysis or even death if they moved him wrong. The only way to know for sure was with an X-ray, which was why paramedics usually immobilized accident victims with a backboard or c-spine collar before attempting to move them, but since that wasn't an option, she would have to make do. There were a couple of obvious signs that might indicate such an injury. She gently probed the back of his neck. The skin was cool, but everything felt normal. There was no swelling or crackling of displaced cerebrospinal fluid. She moved one hand down and felt his crotch.

"Umm, Paula…?"

"I'm checking for priapism," she said, probing the area, feeling nothing.

"Priapism."

"An unexplained erection is one indication of spinal trauma. In men, anyway." She managed a wan smile. "It's okay. I'm going to be a doctor."

He returned the smile. "Does he…?"

"No, but it's not a perfectly reliable indicator, so let's be extra careful when we move him. We'll do a two-man seat carry. Reach under him and grab my hands."

She slipped her left arm under Hickok's shoulders, angling her biceps to hold his head in place, then slid her right hand under his knees. Tim mirrored her and they joined hands underneath the stricken man, lifting him together.

When they had made him comfortable in the tent, Paula headed back out. "We need to check the others. If he made it, maybe someone else did, too."

Paula didn't know the name of the next man they came to, one of the Academy support staff who had come out with the dinner delivery and stayed. The young man was alive, but unconscious and struggling to breathe. He had been stabbed in the chest and Paula suspected that his chest cavity was filling up with blood. He probably needed a chest tube to relieve the pressure, but knowing that and knowing how to do it were two very different things.

It was, she realized, a triage situation.

In a mass casualty event—and that was exactly what this was—with just one medical responder with limited training, it was critical to separate the victims into categories based on the urgency of their need before attempting treatment of anyone. Paula didn't know all the categories, but understood the underlying principle.

Sometimes, you couldn't save everyone.

"Let's check the others," she told Tim.

"He's in pretty bad shape."

"I know. I don't think I can save him, but there might be someone else out here that I can save. We have to focus on the people who still have a chance. I'll do what I can for him, but only after we check the others."

The next body they came to was cold and pale. Paula checked for a pulse, then moved on without looking to see if it was someone she knew. The last person they checked, a woman lying on her back with a short wooden spear protruding from her chest, was recognizable even from several feet away.

"It's Ma," Tim said in a small voice. "How did they do it? How did they get the drop on all the instructors?"

Paula had been wondering that as well. Hickok and Ma were both trained survival instructors, and Kevin and Alma were government agents, but somehow two teen-aged boys had overwhelmed them and others using just blades and pointed stakes. The question went out of her head when she saw Ma's mouth move.

"Tim, she's alive." Paula bent down and checked for a pulse, just in case what she had seen was some kind of post-mortem nerve twitch. "She's alive," Paula repeated. "Pulse is faint, but steady."

Tim reached out for the spear, but Paula hastily stopped him. "Don't touch it. If you remove it, she could bleed out. They can take it out at the hospital. Right now, let's just get her to the tent so I can start an I.V."

They lifted Ma using the same two-man seat carry as before and deposited her beside Hickok then returned to the other injured man. For a few seconds, Paula thought he was already dead, but then he twitched and drew another hitching breath. "Let's get him to the tent. I don't know if I can help him, but at least we can make him comfortable."

Madison returned as they were transporting the man. "Jeremy," she said, her voice catching in her throat. "Is he…?"

So that's his name, Paula thought. "It doesn't look good," she admitted, "but he's hanging on."

Madison nodded and held back the tent flap for them. "I found a couple of trails leading out of here. It wasn't hard. They trampled the ground like a herd of elk."

"Two trails?" Tim asked.

"Two groups. One headed west, one headed east."

"Can you tell which way Matthew and Ryan went?"

"I'm not that good. But if I had to bet money, I'd say east. We didn't pass anyone coming in, so the trail to the west might be something else."

"You've got to go after them," Paula said.

"We will," Madison promised. "But you've got to think about your own safety. Keep an ear out. If you hear anything, get down and stay ready. This will sound cliché, but wait until you see the whites of their eyes to shoot."

"Because I might miss?"

"Because it might be someone you don't want to shoot."

Paula nodded. "Understood."

As Tim and Madison headed out, Paula went to work. She started intravenous drips on all three patients, and then began wound care.

She found a pair of shears in the first aid kit and used them to cut away Ma's uniform and expose the swollen flesh around the spear shaft. The area was discolored but there wasn't as much blood as she expected. About all Paula could do was clean the wound and pack it with sterile bandages, and then cover Ma with a sleeping bag to keep her warm.

She did the same for Hickok, and then, almost reluctantly turned her attention to her most critically wounded patient. She couldn't believe he was still alive. "Well, Jeremy," she muttered, "if you want to stay alive this badly, I guess I should at least try to help."

She cut away his shirt to reveal the chest wound. It wasn't bleeding that bad on the outside, but she knew that every ragged breath he took was pulling more blood and probably some air into his chest cavity. She covered the wound with a water proof bandage, which would keep him from drawing in any more air, but he would still need a chest tube to drain the fluid from around his lungs.

Paula had read about the operation—the technical name for it was thoracotomy—and knew that it was actually pretty simple. All she had to do was make a small incision in his side, between the ribs, and then insert a tube into the pleural space. If she messed up, it would kill him, but if she didn't try, he would probably die anyway.

The medical kit actually contained a sealed thoracotomy tray, which contained scalpels, suture kits, needles of various size, tubing, bandages and other implements that Paula couldn't even name.

As she swabbed his chest with an alcohol pad, she probed his ribs, trying to locate the best spot to make her incision. She marked the spot with a forefinger, and then without stopping to think about what she was doing, made the cut. Blood oozed from the incision, but she had seen so much of it in the last few hours, she barely noticed. She mopped it away with a gauze sponge and then without even stopping to think about it, pushed the tube through the intercostal muscle between the ribs.

There was a loud pop as she penetrated through to the pleural cavity and then an aerosol spray of blood erupted from the tube.

It took her a few seconds to figure out how to attach the one-way valve to prevent the tube from drawing more air into the chest cavity, but once she did, the change was swift. Jeremy's breathing became less labored.

"I'll be damned," she whispered, leaning back. "I did it."

She checked her watch and saw that more than half an hour had passed since Tim and Madison's departure. She had been so focused on what she was doing that time itself had ceased to have any meaning.

Half an hour, she thought, and wondered if Tim and Madison had caught up to the two boys who had murdered the instructors and thrown Camp Zero into total chaos. She wondered if, in her state of single-minded focus, she would have heard the sound of gunfire in the distance.

As if to underscore this lack of awareness, she heard a strange noise, a scraping sound, coming from outside the tent.

Madison's earlier advice came back in a rush. She dropped to one knee, picked up her rifle and aimed it at the tent flap. The scraping sound continued, increasing in volume as the source drew ever closer to the camp. Madison had also told her to wait until she could see the whites of her target's eyes. If she stayed where she was, that wouldn't happen until the approaching intruder was actually in the tent with her.

That sounded like a very bad idea.

I've got NODs, she told herself. *I'll see them before they see me.*

She took a deep breath and then started forward.

Chapter Forty-Four - **Jack**

After a while, the persistent rhythmic crunch of their footsteps took on a hypnotic quality, blurring Jack's perception of time. He was a machine, putting one foot ahead of the next. They had headed south—Why south? Why not?—skirting along the bottom of the slope, initially hoping to find a place to make their ascent and rejoin the others, but after a while, Jack had stopped looking. The slope was too steep and the soil too loose, and the further they went, the less important making the climb seemed. Besides, the rest of the team had made their intentions pretty clear. There would be no one waiting for them up there.

He stopped when he heard a loud thud behind him, turned and listened for a moment. "Clayton?"

The other boy mumbled something incoherent, and Jack knew the sound had been Clayton hitting the ground. Had he tripped? Or simply dropped in his tracks, overcome by exhaustion and despair?

Jack's eyes had adjusted to the darkness well enough to make out Clayton's shape. He hiked back and knelt beside him. "Are you okay?"

"No. I don't want to walk anymore. Go on without me."

"We have to keep moving," Jack insisted. "At least until dawn."

Clayton's answer was a childish negative grunt. In Jack's mind's eye, the other boy was sitting, arms folded defiantly over his chest, lower lip protruding in a pout. Even though it was purely the product of his own imagination, the image made Jack seethe.

"Damn it, Clayton, people are getting killed. Get off your ass and keep moving."

"No."

"Fine. If you won't walk, I'll drag you." Jack reached out and grabbed a handful of Clayton's uniform. His fingers locked on, vise-tight, and then he hauled Clayton off the ground. Clayton didn't fight back, but stayed in a defensive ball, refusing to stand. Jack did not let this stop him. He began walking, dragging Clayton along behind him across the rough ground.

The friction quickly broke down Clayton's defenses. "Stop!" he shrieked, thrashing and kicking in a futile attempt to break Jack's grip. The harder he fought, the more fiercely Jack held on.

"Either you shut up," Jack threatened, "or I'll shut you up. I'm not letting you get me killed." *And I'm not letting you get you killed*, he thought. *Even though it would make this a lot easier.*

Clayton pulled hard again, using the leverage to get his feet under him. Suddenly, it was Jack on the ground, with Clayton atop of him, pummeling Jack furiously with his fists. Most of the blows were glancing and ineffectual, but he got a few good hits in before Jack shoved him off, more surprised than angry. He could just make out the boy's silhouette against the night sky, but it was the sound of shuffling feet that alerted him to the impending charge. He sidestepped and wrapped his arms around Clayton, tackling him to the ground.

"Let me go," Clayton shouted. "Let me—"

Jack clamped a hand over Clayton's mouth, hard enough that he could feel the other boy's teeth against his palm. "Shut. Up."

As Clayton struggled under him, and then, to Jack's surprise, he felt Clayton curl up beneath him, exactly the way Mr. Hickok shown them, during the self-defense course. *He was paying attention after all.*

"Are you mad?" Jack hissed into his ear. "You wanna hurt me?"

Clayton growled like a rabid dog.

"Good," Jack said. "Use it. Get off your ass and keep going."

The struggle stopped but Jack could feel the boy heaving under him, panting to catch his breath.

"You're stronger than you think," Jack whispered. "You let yourself believe that you're weak. That it's okay to just quit or give up whenever things get tough. Well it's not. When things get tough, you've got to get tougher."

There was a faint tremor beneath him. Jack thought Clayton was sobbing, but then realized the boy was nodding. "Okay," Clayton mumbled into his palm.

Jack rolled off him then found his hand and lifted him to his feet. "You okay?"

"I don't know."

"That was pretty crazy. I'm gonna have to start calling you Wild Man."

Clayton laughed softly. "Sorry."

"It's all right. Sometimes getting mad helps. The trick is knowing how to make it work for you."

"Great speech, Jack." The shout from out of the darkness, dumped a cold jolt of adrenaline into Jack's circulatory system. He recognized the voice instantly.

"Devra," he whispered. He drew his knife and thrust Clayton behind him.

"Very motivational," she went on. "You could be one of the instructors here."

She seemed to be right in front of him, maybe twenty feet away. *But she's not alone,* he reminded himself. She was trying to distract him so that the others could flank them. He reached up and flipped on his headlamp.

Devra was just about where he expected her to be, one hand raised to shade her eyes from the unexpected brilliance of his light. The other hand was curled around the pistol grip of an AR-15. The weapon was held with casual indifference, the barrel pointed at the ground, but the very fact of its presence was enough to make the skin all over Jack's body go tight.

How did she get a gun?

"You, too," he said, trying to sound nonchalant. He glanced left and right, but saw no sign of her accomplices. If they were there, they were staying hidden. "Tracking us in the dark. Pretty impressive."

"I have exceptional night vision," she replied. "We all do."

The strange comment seemed to confirm that she was not alone. Without turning his head, he whispered, "Get ready to run."

"She's got a gun," Clayton whispered back.

No shit, Jack thought, but then it hit him. *She has a gun, and she could have taken us out anytime she wanted to. So why didn't she?*

"Nobody else has to die," Devra said. "We're here for Clayton—"

"Clayton?" Jack asked, at the same instant Clayton said, "Me?"

Why do they want him?

"We're not going to hurt you," she went on. "You're no good to us dead. And we don't need to hurt you, Jack. Just walk away."

Clayton was the target? Jack struggled to make sense of this.

"All the stuff he got blamed for," Jack said slowly. "That was your doing wasn't, it? You got everyone to turn on him and drive him away. That was your plan. Get everyone to bully him and then when he disappeared, everyone would just assume he ran away and say good-riddance."

Devra laughed. "It wasn't hard. He was already a lazy piece of shit."

It had never been about John and Sarah. He and his cousins had gotten everything wrong. They had let their suspicions turn them against the people who could have actually done something to protect them all. If they had just gone to one of the instructors, all the people that had been killed might still be alive.

And Clayton would have disappeared one night and everyone would have just assumed he ran away.

"Why me?" Clayton asked. "What did I ever do?"

"You aren't important," Devra said. "But your father is."

"My father?"

"Your father designs and builds directed-energy weapons. We want him working for us."

"Who's we?" Jack asked.

"That's not important, Jack. And right now, the less you know, the longer you'll live. Just walk away. I promise, we're not going to hurt him."

"You did all this...Infiltrated the Academy, set him up to be the scape-goat for every bad thing that happened, just so you could kidnap him?" Jack almost laughed aloud. All this time, he had been trying to keep Clayton alive, when he was the one person the murderers absolutely did not want to kill.

And if I step away from him, what's to stop them from killing me?

Not a damn thing.

Jack took a step closer to Clayton and brandished his knife. "No, I don't think I'm going to do that."

"Jack, it's okay," Clayton said. "I'll go with them. I don't want anyone else to get hurt."

Of all the times, he picks now to think of someone other than himself. "If you go with them, they won't hesitate to kill everyone here, just to get rid of the witnesses. And if they get their hands on the next generation of energy weapons, a lot more innocent people will die. So, I'm sorry, but I can't let you do that."

Devra's expression hardened. She raised her rifle, aimed it at Jack. "You might want to rethink that."

Clayton stepped in front of Jack. "No. Jack's right. I'd rather die than go with you."

The barrel jerked to the side and then a tongue of orange fire leapt from the end. The report was almost deafening at such close range, and Jack flinched as the supersonic projectile creased the air beside his head, but he stood his ground. So did Clayton.

Devra lowered the rifle. "All right. I guess we're going to have to do this the hard way."

Chapter Forty-Five - **Sarah**

"John?" Sarah reached out to her brother, touched his shoulder intending to shake him gently, but then snatched her hand away as if she had been shocked. His uniform was soaked in blood.

"John, are you—"

Alive?

"—awake?"

There was no response. She thought she could see his chest moving, rising and falling just a little. Still breathing. Still alive, but if he didn't get medical treatment soon, he might not be for much longer.

"Randy! Help!" She crawled over to where the older boy lay, unmoving, but her pleas died in her throat when she got a look at him.

Randy's head was cracked open like an egg. She bent close, listening for breath sounds but heard nothing. She felt his wrist to see if there was a pulse. If there was, she couldn't feel it.

Randy wasn't going to be able to help her or anyone else ever again.

"I don't know what to do," she whimpered, but then another voice whispered. *Yes you do.*

It sounded a lot like Alma, but Sarah knew that it wasn't her because Alma—

Passed away. Went to heaven to be with God. Never regained consciousness.

—was dead and Sarah didn't believe in ghosts, so it had to be just her imagination.

I'm too little, she told the voice without speaking aloud. *I can't do it by myself.*

You have to. There isn't anyone else. John will die if you don't do something.

She bit her lip, wondering what to do first. Paula would know what to do, just like she had when Madison fell, but Paula wasn't here.

Sarah crawled back over to her brother again. There was so much blood, too much for the single tear in his uniform where Philip had stabbed him.

It's Philip's blood, she realized, and felt a glimmer of hope. Maybe John's injuries weren't as bad as she thought.

She loosened his uniform blouse, pulling it back to expose the wound. John groaned and twitched a little when she moved him, but she took that as a good sign. "You're going to be okay," she told him.

There was a two-inch-long cut in John's T-shirt and the area around it was stained red. She gripped the fabric in her fingers and pulled, tearing it open to reveal the ugly gash in her brother's body. As she stared at the wound, she started to remember what she had been told in the first-aid course, but without any medical supplies, what could she do?

I'll bet there's first-aid kit at Camp Zero, she thought. *For all the good that does me.*

She wasn't sure how far away Camp Zero was, or if she could find it in the dark, or if she could find this spot again once she had the supplies. But she couldn't just stay here and watch her brother die.

I need to get him to Camp Zero. He can't walk and I can't carry him. What else can I do?

As she looked around for inspiration, her headlamp revealed the wreckage of the shelter. Although most of the covering branches had been knocked loose, the study framework of poles lashed together with strips of bark remained intact. It reminded Sarah of a mattress.

Or a stretcher.

Sarah knew there was another name for what she was thinking of, but it was a strange word and she couldn't remember it. Unlike a stretcher which had wheels, this was something that could be pulled along like a sled. John was a lot heavier than she was, but not as heavy as an adult, and she wouldn't even have to lift him up that high. She might be able to drag him at least part of the way back to Camp Zero.

"John. I'm going to move you onto this…this sled, and pull you to Camp Zero."

No reply.

She dragged the…what was the word? *It's like 'travel'… travel-sled?* That wasn't it, but it was close enough. She got it next to John and then tried dragging him up onto it. It was harder than she expected, and even though she tried to be careful, a moan of pain slipped past his lips.

"Oh, John. I'm so sorry."

Once she got his upper body onto it, the rest was easy. She grabbed his belt and pulled his hips and legs onto the sled. Then, without pausing to catch her breath, she grabbed hold of the corners closest to his head, and started dragging. It was heavier than she expected and the rough ground didn't make it any easier, but with some trial and error, she discovered a better way to grip the sled and that helped.

She made it to the edge of the woods before stopping for a rest break. Once clear of the trees, she could see most of the valley, silhouetted against the night sky. She dug out her map and picked out the symbol for Camp Zero. Although she couldn't be precisely sure of her location, she could make an educated guess based on the outline of the peaks on either side of the valley, and if she was right about where she thought she was, then all she needed to do was head due east for a mile or so to reach Camp Zero.

"Easy," she muttered, lifting the sled again.

She had not forgotten about the Starlings. If they came back to check on Philip, or just happened to spot her as she trudged across the benighted landscape, she would be in big trouble but she couldn't let her fears paralyze her. The risk would have been the same if she had simply stayed put. Perhaps even worse.

She pulled the sled until she couldn't pull anymore. When that happened, she stopped and rested for a few minutes, then tried again. The interval between the breaks grew shorter, as did the distance she was able to travel, but she did not give up.

"Almost there," she said aloud, more to motivate herself than reassure John.

And then, like a miracle rising out of the wilderness, she found the road.

Calling it a road was a bit of an exaggeration. It was really just a pair of parallel grooves, compacted by the repeated passage of vehicle tires, but there was no mistaking what it was, even in the darkness.

For a moment, she felt profound disappointment. Crossing the road meant that she had misjudged her location relative to Camp Zero. Then she remembered that the road would take her there.

It was as if her batteries had been recharged. The smooth compacted earth offered considerably less resistance than the open terrain, but it was the knowledge that she was not lost and that the end lay just ahead which kept her moving.

When she finally spotted the tents and a pair of parked Jeeps, she started crying, but the tears of relief quickly became something else, a stew of emotions. This horrible night wasn't over, not by a long shot. She still had to figure out how to treat John's injuries. The Starlings were still out there. And even though she couldn't see them in the darkness, she knew that the bodies of the slain—*Alma!*—were all around her.

She fell to her knees, the tears flowing freely, sobs racking her little body. The inner voice which had compelled her to make the long journey to Camp Zero was still speaking to her, urging her to keep going, to never give up, but it all felt so impossible....

"Sarah?"

She started, leapt to her feet, knife in hand. *That wasn't my imagination.*

"Oh, my God, Sarah. It is you."

"Paula?" she whispered. She could just make out a shape moving toward her.

"I'm here." Paula reached her, hugged her tight. "I'm here. It's okay."

"John," she gasped through her sobs. "He's hurt."

Paula pulled away and knelt beside the sled. Sarah couldn't see what her cousin was doing, but a moment later she spoke. "He'll be fine. I'll take care of him. Where are the others?"

The story spilled out of Sarah in a rush. She didn't know if she was making any sense and, after a few seconds, Paula hugged her again. "You're safe now."

Safe, Sarah thought. *But what about the others?*

Chapter Forty-Six - **Natalie**

Natalie realized, only after leaving the woods behind, that she had no idea how she was going to be able to track Thomas, much less find Jack and his group. They had received only basic instruction in how to look for animal tracks, and in the darkness, even obvious trail signs might go unnoticed.

She decided their best course of action was to return to Camp Zero—if they could find it—and then hopefully figure out which direction the others had gone.

If. Hopefully.

She tried not to dwell on all the ways it could go wrong. The prospect of what might happen if or when they caught up to the Starlings was even more ominous, but she had to do something.

When they spotted headlights coming down from the mountain pass, she felt a glimmer of hope but tried to rein it in. There was no way to know if the vehicles were bringing help or more Starlings. She warned everyone to stay down, and watched as the vehicles moved across the valley floor. It looked at first like the vehicles were headed right toward them, but as they drew near, it became apparent that they were merely following the road back to Camp Zero, which lay just a few hundred yards from where Natalie and her group were concealed. When the lights passed them, Natalie gave the signal to resume the trek, but warned the others to stay low and quiet.

Her caution was well-advised. When the vehicles stopped, she heard the sound of familiar voices. Thomas. Ryan. Matthew.

"You left him?" Matthew said, ire raising his volume loud enough for Natalie to hear. She held her breath anxiously.

"He can take care of himself," Thomas said, defensively. "We have a job to do."

"If anything happens to him…"

The rest was lost to her as their voices became more subdued and then diminished to nothing. It took her a moment to realize that the Starlings had left Camp Zero. They were going after Clayton.

"What do we do?" Heather whispered.

"We follow them," Natalie said. What else could they do?

Following the Starlings in the darkness was easier said than done. The killers moved with unnatural stealth, like nocturnal predators, but from time to time, she caught the sound of voices drifting on the breeze and adjusted course.

We're going to have to get a lot closer, she thought. *We're going to have to fight them.*

More voices came from just ahead, Devra or Holly—it was hard enough to tell them apart when she could actually see them—or more likely both, rendezvousing with the others.

"They split up. Some of them went up the cliff. The others headed south."

"How long?"

"Fifteen minutes, tops."

"Our boy is terrified of climbing. We go south. The others don't matter."

"I'm sure you're right but—"

"I am right. Let's finish this."

As the Starlings moved off again, Heather drew close to Natalie. "There's five of them. It took all of us just to beat two of them. What are we going to do against five?"

This fact had not escaped Natalie. She didn't have a good answer. "They don't know we're here. That gives us an advantage. The element of surprise."

"If we can sneak up on them," Gary said, his tone betraying just how impossible he believed that was.

Natalie sensed that she was about to lose them. "Look, I have to do this. I can't do it alone, but I can't make you go with me. I get it. This is scary stuff. If you want to back out—"

She felt a hand on her arm. "Nat, it is scary. We're with you. But you've got to make us believe that we've got a chance."

How can I do that when I don't even believe it?

She took a deep breath, trying to analyze the situation like a math problem on a test. Five of them versus five Starlings. Once they made their move, the element of surprise would be gone and it would be simply a test of skill and that certainly favored the enemy. Was there some variable that would tip the odds in their favor?

"They're completely focused on grabbing Clayton," Natalie said, a plan finally coming together in her head. "When they catch him, we'll make our move. They'll be distracted. We hit them hard before they know what's happening; take out two or three of them."

Take out.

Kill.

Could she do that? Could the others?

"If you don't think you can do that then you need to speak up right now. Last chance."

They all chose to stay with her.

With each step forward, the gravity of the choices she had made compounded. She wanted to beg the universe for more time, pray for divine intervention or some alternative to what they were about to do, but wishful thinking was the deadliest sort of self-deception.

A strange noise, like two animals fighting, reached her from out of the darkness. Then one of the animals spoke, and it had Jack's voice.

"Are you mad? You wanna hurt me?"

Natalie curled her finger around the hilt of her knife. If Jack was close, then the Starlings were even closer, watching him, waiting to make their move. There was not a doubt in her mind that Jack was talking to Clayton, trying to cajole him into moving, unaware that the time for running was past.

But where were the Starlings?

Another voice spoke from out of the darkness. Devra, taunting Jack, trying to get him to surrender Clayton without further bloodshed. Natalie didn't think they would honor such a promise and evidently Jack felt the same way.

Jack's headlamp flashed on, shining on Devra, but as Natalie's eyes got used to the brightness, she could make out some of the other Starlings, hiding behind trees and shrubs, arrayed in a half-circle around Jack and Clayton. They were totally focused on what was happening in front of them.

Then she saw something else. The Starlings had guns.

How did they get those?

It didn't matter. She leaned close to Heather. "Go left. Take Gary and Luke with you. I'll take Dan and go right. Start at the ends and work toward he center."

"How do we...?" Heather made a stabbing motion with her knife. *How exactly do we kill them?*

That was something that hadn't come up in any of their classes. Should they stab? Slash? In movies with swordfights, people dropped like flies whenever the hero so much as brushed them with a blade, but she had a feeling it wasn't going to be that easy.

She thought about how she had managed to subdue Philip.

"Use the pommel," she whispered. "Club them in the back of the head as hard as you can. That might not knock them out, but it will stun them long enough for you to cut their throats."

Did I just say that?

She remembered thinking how paranoid Mr. Hickok had sounded when telling them his rules for a gunfight. Now she understood. This wasn't a game. To survive the next few minutes, they would all have to unlock the cage that contained a savage brutal part of themselves that most people kept locked away.

"Don't hold back," she whispered. "Because if you don't kill them, they *will* kill you. You've seen what they can do. Remember Mr. Hickok's rules. Always win."

Heather crept away with Gary and Luke. Natalie tapped Dan on the arm and motioned for him to follow. They backtracked a ways, staying low and swinging wide to avoid prematurely alerting the Starlings. She had been right about how intently they were focused on Clayton. The Starlings had developed a serious—hopefully fatal—case of tunnel vision.

She crawled forward on hands and knees, moving with excruciating care to avoid making any sound. Directly ahead of her, one of the Starlings crouched behind a bush, his rifle and his gaze fixed on the source of the light in the clearing beyond. He was just twenty feet away…ten feet….

The noise of a gunshot startled her, but the report drowned out any inadvertent noises she might have made. Nothing else seemed to have changed. Jack's light was still shining.

A warning shot, Devra trying to frighten Jack.

But it was also a signal.

Matthew rose up and started forward, the rifle snugged into his shoulder, his cheek pressed against the stock as he peered through the sights.

Then, all hell broke loose.

A scream went up from somewhere off to Natalie's left. A female voice, at least it sounded that way.

Heather?

The sound was cut off almost immediately by more shooting. Muzzle flashes lit up the night and the sulfur smell of burnt gunpowder filled Natalie's nostrils. The chaos was overwhelming.

Matthew turned, searching for the source of the disturbance, and then looked right at her. The muzzle of the rifle began to move.

He's going to shoot me!

Her instincts told her to run, but Hickok's advice echoed in her head. *Run toward a gun.*

A bullet can run faster than you can, so if someone is pointing a gun at you and you think they'll pull the trigger no matter what, rush them.

She held the knife out in front of her like a spear and charged.

There was a flash and the muzzle jumped a few inches. Something plucked at her side. It stung, like a slap, and she wondered if she had gotten snagged on a protruding tree branch. The report followed a millisecond later, so loud it hurt her ears, but she kept going, running straight at Matthew. The muzzle moved again, coming down, shifting sideways as Matthew tried to line up another shot, but she reached him before he could pull the trigger a second time.

The knife hit something hard and twisted out of her hands. An instant later, she collided with him, her weight and momentum bearing him down. He toppled back, like a felled tree, and she landed right on top of him. Something hard struck her solar plexus and she rolled off him, gasping for air, realizing only then that the object which had knocked her wind out was the hilt of her knife. The blade was buried in the center of Matthew's chest.

She stared at him, not daring to believe that he was really dead, then a wave of dizziness came over her, followed almost immediately by an eruption of white hot fire in her side. She clutched the spot, and felt something warm and wet.

Shot.

He shot me.

Crap.

Am I going to die?

There were more shots, too many to count, and Natalie knew their attack had failed. They had lost the element of surprise. The shooting meant at least some of the Starlings were still alive. And some of her teammates, too.

Matthew's rifle lay just a few feet away. She reached for it…tried to reach for it, but a spike of pain through her side kept her pinned to the ground. She tried again. Grazed it with her fingers.

Then the shooting stopped and she didn't know what that meant.

Chapter Forty-Seven - **John**

He drifted in the darkness for a long time, held there by a weariness that seemed to reach down into his very bones. The voices sometimes roused him a little—Sarah, reassuring him that everything was going to be all right and that they didn't have far to go. Paula, telling him he was going to be fine. He dismissed it as his imagination. Paula was miles away.

Then the shaking started, so violent that it sent waves of pain radiating out from the wound in his chest. A cry tore from his lips and he jolted awake.

The rude return to consciousness sent another spear of pain through him, but unlike the persistent shaking, this was something he could control.

"Ow!"

Sarah's face appeared above him. "He's awake."

"John." Paula's voice again. Definitely not his imagination. "You're going to be okay. I'm taking you back to the Academy."

"Taking me…?" He looked past Sarah and realized that he was in the back seat of a moving vehicle. He could just make out the back of Paula's head; she was sitting in the driver's seat. The shaking that had roused him was the tires rolling and bouncing on the uneven terrain of the mountain trail. "How did…?"

He wasn't sure what it was he wanted to know. None of this made any sense. He had been in the shelter with Sarah and Randy, and then….

Philip. The Starlings!

"No! You can't take me back. We have to help Nat and Jack. The Starlings are hunting them."

"Sarah told me all about that. Don't worry. Tim and Madison are on their way to help."

Tim and… Madison?

I am *dreaming*.

It was a dream that would not release him. No matter how carefully Paula tried to negotiate the irregularities of the trail, the Jeep jounced over rocks and dipped into ruts, jostling John and occasionally sending fresh waves of pain through his body. Sleep was impossible, or if he was already asleep, then the deep dreamless void where time would lose all meaning was denied him.

But then, after what seemed like hours, the road became smooth and he felt the Jeep accelerate. A few minutes after that, light began pouring in through the windows, not daylight, but the artificial light of half-a-dozen generator powered pole lamps.

The Jeep stopped and all the doors seemed to open simultaneously.

More voices now—he didn't recognize any of them—firing off questions which Paula answered, and then he was being lifted up, gently, by too many hands to count. As he was brought out into the open air, he was immersed in the commotion. Men and women, some dressed in black suits, others in camouflage fatigues, surrounded him. Some were shouting into handheld radios. Others were touching him, slicing away his clothes with shears, probing his wound and speaking in that strange language known only to medical professionals. They were talking about him, but he had no idea what any of it meant. Behind them, a helicopter was settling down out of the sky, like an eagle coming to roost.

"Paula!" he shouted.

Paula leaned in close. "I'm here, John. Don't worry. You're safe now. They're going to fly you to the hospital and get you patched up."

"They?"

"The Secret Service."

Secret Service? Just like Kevin and Alma. "Starlings," he gasped. "Jack. Nat."

"We know about that. The Secret Service is on their way out there. Everything is going to be all right."

John could hear the lie in her voice. How long had it taken her to drive back from Camp Zero? Hours?

Jack and Natalie might already be dead.

Chapter Forty-Eight - **Tim**

With their NODs pulling back the veil of darkness, Tim and Madison saw Natalie's group from a long ways off, but they couldn't risk alerting them with a shout. He assumed they were still on the run, fleeing from the violence that had occurred at Camp Zero, but if that were the case, why weren't they farther away?

As they closed the distance, he recognized some of the others with Natalie—Heather, the tall girl. His teammates Dan and Luke. But where was Jack? Where were Sarah and John?

Two trails out of Camp Zero, he remembered. Two groups. *One group went west, maybe trying to hike out. The other went east.*

But that had been hours ago. Something about this didn't make any sense.

Then he realized that Natalie and the others weren't running. They were stalking, trying to follow a trail in the darkness.

Hunting the killers, he thought. *But they don't know that Matthew and Ryan have guns.*

Matthew and Ryan might be stalking *them* or lying in ambush.

"We have to catch up to them," he told Madison.

She just nodded.

Before they could cover the distance, he saw Natalie freeze and motion for the others in her group to get down. But for a long time, nothing else happened. Natalie and the others remained where they were, huddled together for several minutes, while Tim and Madison crept forward, closing the gap.

Something moved in the distance past where Natalie's group waited. Another small group—four, no five of them—and while he couldn't make out any faces with certainty, he could easily distinguish one feature that all of them had in common.

"They've got rifles," he breathed.

"Looks like Matthew and Ryan weren't working alone."

That explained how the killers had been able to overwhelm the instructors at Camp Zero, but Tim's instincts told him there was more than just superior numbers at work.

The armed group moved off, seemingly oblivious to the fact that they were being watched, and after thirty seconds or so, Natalie and her small team rose to their feet and started after them.

It was a race now. He and Madison had to catch Natalie and the others before they caught up to the killers and found themselves bringing knives to a gunfight.

They almost made it.

Unaware that they were being pursued the lead group stopped and fanned out, taking up concealed positions in a rough semi-circle. Natalie's group almost ran headlong into them, but stopped just short of giving themselves away, whereupon they huddled together.

"This is it," Tim whispered, shouldering his rifle and looking for a target.

"We'll never make the shot at this distance," Madison warned. "We have to get closer."

Tim guessed they were only about fifty yards away, but if they made a mad dash to cover the remaining distance, it would almost certainly give them away and then there was no telling what might happen.

"Follow my lead," Madison said, and then started forward. She walked with her rifle at the high ready, hunched forward, cheek pressed to the stock, arms tucked in, and took short quick steps, moving only her lower legs at the knees and rolling her foot from heel to toe to minimize the noise. Tim did the same, covering ground fast.

But not fast enough.

A light, painfully bright in the NOD's display, blazed to life in a clearing directly ahead. Tim winced, looking away, but the damage was already done. A large dark spot was scorched into the display. He tore the monocular off his head, grateful that his unaided eye was unaffected, and saw Natalie and her team dispersing, their blades drawn.

They were going on the offensive.

A shot rang out. Tim could see the muzzle flash in the gloom and knew the intended target was somewhere further ahead. For a moment, nothing happened, but then one of Natalie's group made their move and the night erupted in violence.

Some of the gunmen went down, bludgeoned senseless before they got a shot off. But some of them seemed to sense the impending assault, whirling around to face their would-be attackers, firing point blank.

"Down!" Madison shouted, even as stray bullets began zipping past. She dropped to knees and elbows, but kept advancing. Tim got down as well, high-crawling across the scrub prairie to get closer, closer to the people he was trying to save, closer to the people who were trying to kill them.

He saw Natalie charge, cried out involuntarily as a bullet ripped through her, and then saw her slam into the shooter—it was Matthew—tackling him to the ground.

A rifle report sounded right beside him, so loud he flinched. Madison had joined the battle, firing her rifle from a prone position.

Tim brought his weapon up as well, looking down the barrel, sweeping left and right, looking for a target, but saw only the dead and dying. Every single one of them was someone he knew.

Natalie!

He crawled to her, calling out her name as he got close. Her head came up. "Tim?"

"I'm here."

"Jack." Her voice was weak, as if each word took a little more of her life. "Help him."

He looked past her, toward the light, and saw Jack, on his feet, knife drawn, standing protectively in front of someone else. Facing him, pointing a rifle at him, was Devra.

Tim brought his own weapon up, lined the sights up on her back, but before he could fire, Devra advanced on Jack, reversing the weapon in her hands, gripping the heat guard with both hands to swing it like a club. He jerked his finger out of the trigger guard. If he took the shot and missed, he might hit Jack or the person he was protecting.

Jack slashed with his blade at the same instant Devra swung her rifle. The butt of the AR-15 cracked against the knife, knocking it from Jack's hand, and then, almost faster than Tim could follow, she raised her foot up and planted it in Jack's chest, knocking him back. As Jack staggered back, arms windmilling, she brought the rifle to her shoulder and took aim.

"Devra!" Tim shouted. "Don't!"

It was a reflex, and a mistake.

No such thing as fair fight. Hickok's rules rang in his head like an accusation. *Always. Win.*

Devra whirled around, the muzzle swinging toward him. He had already hesitated. She would not.

Shoot to kill.

He fired. So did she.

The rifle bucked in his hands, the report so loud that it felt like a sandbag had been dropped on his eardrums. A tongue of flame leapt from the end of Devra's weapon. Tim saw her flinch and stagger back a step, the barrel of her rifle zigzagging, but then she got control of it and swung it toward him again.

He pressed the butt of the rifle tight against his shoulder and pulled the trigger again. And again. And again, until Devra toppled back and didn't move.

For several long seconds afterward, Tim could only stare at the motionless body.

I killed her.

He didn't know whether to be relieved or horrified.

Then he remembered that she had not been alone. He rose to his knees, bringing the rifle around, scanning for another target, but through the ringing in his ears he could just make out the sound of someone shouting.

"All clear! All clear!"

It was Madison. Waving a hand in front of her face—the signal to cease fire.

All clear.

It was finally over.

Epilogue - **Paula**

There was a knock at the hospital room door, but Paula didn't look up. She had grown so accustomed to the frequent visits from nurses and doctors that she barely even noticed it. This time however, the visitor wasn't a medical specialist.

The door opened a crack and a familiar face appeared in the gap. "May I come in?"

"Mr. Dickson!" Paula straightened, as did everyone else in the room. All six of the Rourke children were there, though only John and Natalie were actually receiving medical care for their injuries, which fortunately, turned out to be relatively minor. They were still receiving pain medication and antibiotics via IV drip, but barring any unforeseen complications, they would be back to normal in a few weeks.

The rest of them were there because they simply refused to leave.

Dickson pushed the door open wide and entered the room, followed by Madison. His arm was in a sling across his chest, but he looked otherwise none the worse for wear. Madison looked very good for someone who had been declared dead just a few days earlier.

"I've got some good news," Dickson said, though the deep creases across his forehead made Paula think he had a lot of bad news, too. "Your parents should be here later this afternoon. The docs say John and Natalie are cleared to travel by medical transport, though they may need to spend a few more days in the hospital in Honolulu."

"How are the others?" Paula asked.

Dickson returned a tight smile. "Ma and Terry are still hanging on." He nodded to Paula. "Thanks to you."

Information had been hard to come by, especially in the immediate aftermath of the attack by the Starlings, but Paula knew that there had been a lot of casualties. Several instructors and a few students had been killed.

Many more had survived with serious injuries and had likewise been air-lifted to different hospitals throughout the state. This measure was partly to avoid overtaxing the resources of any one hospital, but also as a security measure. No one was quite sure who was behind the Starlings and their attempt to kidnap Clayton Reynolds from the Survival Academy, and the possibility of a reprisal against the survivors could not be ignored. None of the Starlings had survived the night, but there was little question that they were part of a powerful entity with a global agenda.

The world had not seen the end of the Starlings.

"And Jeremy?" Paula had learned that Jeremy, the young instructor she had almost given up on at Camp Zero, was Mr. Dickson's son and Madison's older brother.

Dickson's head nodded a little.

"He's still in the ICU," Madison said. "The doctors are doing everything they can. But Paula, he wouldn't have made it this far without you."

It was small comfort.

"When can we come back?" Jack asked, filling the awkward silence. "To finish the course?"

The worry lines deepened. Dickson glanced at Madison before answering. "I'll be straight with you. There's a lot of uncertainty about whether we'll continue operations."

Tim jumped to his feet. "You're closing the Academy?"

"It's not my decision, son. When your father gets here, I'll be tendering my resignation."

There was a collective gasp. "Mr. Dickson, you can't quit," Natalie said, firmly.

"A lot of people died the other night. Members of my staff were killed. Students—children—died. The security of the school was breached. Some of the parents are already talking about lawsuits."

"None of that is your fault."

"It happened on my watch. It's my responsibility."

Paula cleared her throat. "If you're going to insist on taking the blame, then you'd better also take some credit. We were only able to get through that night because of the training we got at the Academy."

Dickson shook his head. "You survived because you didn't give up. All the training in the world is meaningless without inner strength and fortitude. The will to keep going, no matter what. You all have that. That's not something anyone can teach you."

"Mr. Dickson," Tim said. "You aren't to blame for the deaths. That's on the Starlings, no one else. And the training *is* important. We wouldn't have survived without it. Period. I'm going to tell my dad to tear up your resignation. The Academy has to stay open, because the next time something bad happens, it might be even worse."

Dickson chuckled softly. "All right, Tim. I'll think on it."

Madison gave her father a hug. "Dad, we're gonna need some help getting the place back up and running." She turned to the others. "What do you say? We could use a few more student-instructors. If your parents are okay with it, of course."

Paula grinned and nodded enthusiastically. So did everyone else.

Honolulu, Hawaii

"Today's the big day, Billy Boy," crooned the police officer as he settled into the chair near the foot of the hospital bed. "You're getting out of here and moving uptown. Got a nice little cell for you at the FDC. You think the food here is bad, wait till you get a taste of prison slop."

William Alan Davis—who sometimes told people to call him "C.J."—glowered at the police officer but knew better than to shoot off his mouth. Despite the fact that they clearly hated his guts, the hospital staff had at least made sure he stayed in good health during his weeks-long convalescence from a gun-shot wound sustained in the police raid that had put an end to his crime spree. Now that he had been deemed fit for transfer, no one much cared about his health anymore. If he said the wrong thing to the cop, he might very well have an "accident" on his way to the transport van.

Nothing fatal of course. Just a little tenderizing to get him ready for his cellmate at the Federal Detention Center, where he would be held pending the first of many legal proceedings. He might even end up like Lee, paralyzed, dead from the waist down.

He sighed, resignedly. Truth be told, he was looking forward to getting out of the hospital, even if it meant trading in a backless gown for an orange jumpsuit. At least in lock-up, he wouldn't be handcuffed to his bed, with a fat donut-eater watching him 24-7. He had done time before—admittedly as a juvenile offender but a cage was a cage—and he knew how to make the system, and more importantly, his fellow inmates, work for him.

That was his gift. And since there was little doubt that he would spend the rest of his life behind bars, why not make the best off it? "Better to rule in hell" and all that.

So, yeah, he could bite his tongue and put up with a little verbal abuse.

The door opened and the cop was instantly on his feet, on guard. "Yeah?"

A middle-aged man—tall, fit, black hair, graying at the temples, and wearing an immaculate business suit—stepped inside. He had a thick manila file folder under one arm. Davis didn't recognize him, and evidently neither did the police officer. The man looked too smooth to be public defender and too refined to be a detective or someone from the D.A.'s office.

He addressed the policeman. "I'm here to conduct a psychological evaluation of the prisoner. Just a few questions."

The cop's eyes narrowed suspiciously. "You ain't his shrink."

The well-dressed man frowned distastefully. "I am a consulting psychiatrist for the Federal Prison Bureau. This is a routine screening before his transfer. Call it in if you don't believe me."

The policeman appeared to consider this for a moment, but then nodded. "Yeah, all right. Just don't get to close to him."

"Thank you. Would you please give us the room?"

"Uh, uh. No way. Round the clock supervision. Those are the orders."

"You can supervise from behind the window in that door. But I'm afraid rules of confidentiality apply, as does his Constitutional right against self-incrimination." The man then smiled. "You needn't worry, officer. I'm the man who decides whether he goes into gen-pop or solitary."

"Heh. Yeah. Okay. I guess that's all right." The policeman retreated through the door, but kept his face pressed to the glass, ever vigilant.

The psychiatrist settled into the now vacant chair, crossed his legs and opened the folder. "Mr. Davis. My, my. What a fascinating life you've led. Mutilating pets, necrophilia, kidnapping, rape, serial murder. I suppose it was just a matter of time before you ended up here."

Davis, remembering what the man had just told the policeman, said nothing.

"And then you decided to kidnap the children of John Thomas Rourke."

"I didn't know who they were," Davis said, choosing his words carefully.

"Would it have made a difference?" the man asked. He was smiling, but there was something frightening in his eyes.

"Uh... I don't know."

"Hindsight being 20/20, I'm sure you would have been more discreet, but admit it, if you had known who they were, it would have made the experience all the more exhilarating, wouldn't it?"

Davis sensed the trap. Shook his head.

The man continued to smile. "That's what I like about you, William. Once you set your sights on something, you have to have it. It becomes an obsession. That's good. That's something I can work with."

"Work with?"

The psychiatrist leaned back in his chair. "Are you familiar with a story called *The Lady, or the Tiger?*"

Davis nodded. "It's an old story from before the War. A guy falls in love with a princess, but when her father finds out, he gives the guy the choice between marrying someone else, or fighting a tiger. Committing suicide, basically."

The man inclined his head. "Very good. The file also described you as intelligent, charismatic and erudite. I see that it was not mistaken.

"The Lady, or the Tiger... A classic tale of the dilemma. Two choices, neither desirable. Which would you choose? Oh, but I already know. You would choose the Lady. I'm sure you're incapable of true love."

Davis did not reply.

"I'm here to present you with just such a choice, William. Through one door, you face justice..." He smirked as if the word amused him. "For your crimes, most likely in the form of lethal injection. You may be able to postpone that eventuality for a time by cooperating with the authorities, showing them where all the bodies are buried so the families can have closure, but make no mistake, at the end of it, perhaps five or ten years from now, they will put the needle in your arm."

"And the other door?"

"Ah, the other door." He leaned forward. "Go through the other door, and you will get a chance to finish what you started."

Davis blinked at him. *Does he mean...?* His mouth was suddenly very dry.

"You have unfinished business with the children of John Thomas Rourke, don't you?"

"How?" Davis had trouble getting the question out.

"Simple. Choose the tiger."

"What?"

"In my pocket is a fountain pen. In a moment, I am going to lean close to you, just a little closer than I should, and you are going to take my pen and stab it into your neck. The staff will do everything they can to save you, but their efforts will be in vain. You will be pronounced dead no more than ten minutes from now."

"Why would I do that?"

"The ink in my pen contains a substance called tetrodotoxin. It's a powerful nerve agent and paralytic. Once it enters your bloodstream, your body will go into a form of stasis. Your heart and diaphragm will be paralyzed, and to all appearances, you will be dead. Your debts paid, as it were.

"But you will not be dead. Your body will be removed from the morgue—we'll leave a look-alike just in case they decide to conduct an autopsy. The medical examiner won't be paying very close attention. Meanwhile, you will be taken to a private hospital and revived from your death-like state."

Davis licked his lips. "That would really work?"

"Take a chance."

"Why? Why would you do this for me?"

"Does it really matter?" The man smiled again and then stood up. As he did, he flipped his suit coat back just enough to reveal the glistening black pen protruding from his shirt pocket.

"What's to stop me from taking that pen and stabbing it in your neck?" Davis asked.

"Nothing at all. It's your choice, William. The Lady, or the Tiger?"

Davis's heart was racing. "Who the hell are you, mister?"

The man leaned closer, close enough. "When we meet again, you may call me Doctor Starling."

The Survivalist series

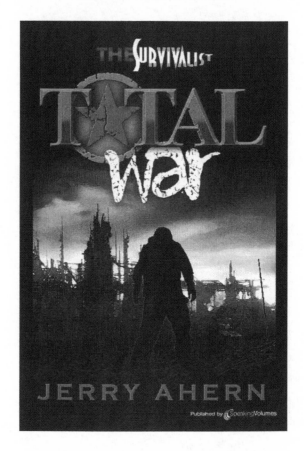

Visit us at <u>www.speakingvolumes.us</u>

The Survivalist series

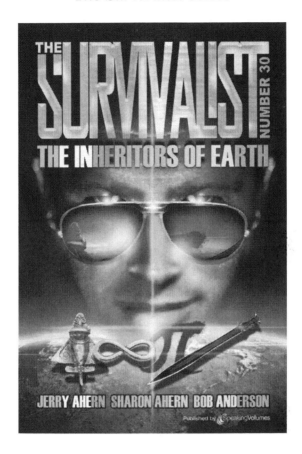

Visit us at www.speakingvolumes.us

The Defender series

Visit us at www.speakingvolumes.us

Surgical Strike series

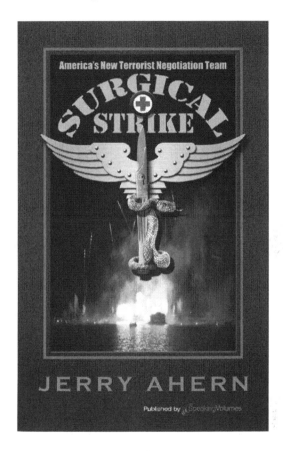

Visit us at www.speakingvolumes.us

The Takers series

Visit us at www.speakingvolumes.us

TAC Leader series

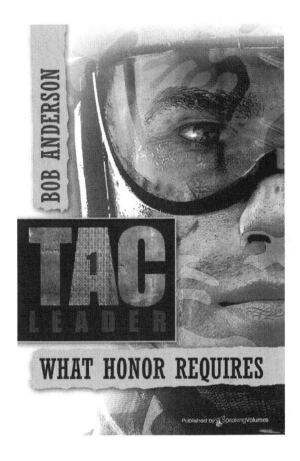

Visit us at www.speakingvolumes.us